Receiving Grace

Regina Maria Freedman

DiMonte Publishing

ISBN paperback: 978-0-578-30112-9

ISBN Ebook: 979-8-9855340-0-9

Cover design and formatting by Cutting-edge-studio.com

Photo image: John Collins, draconianimages

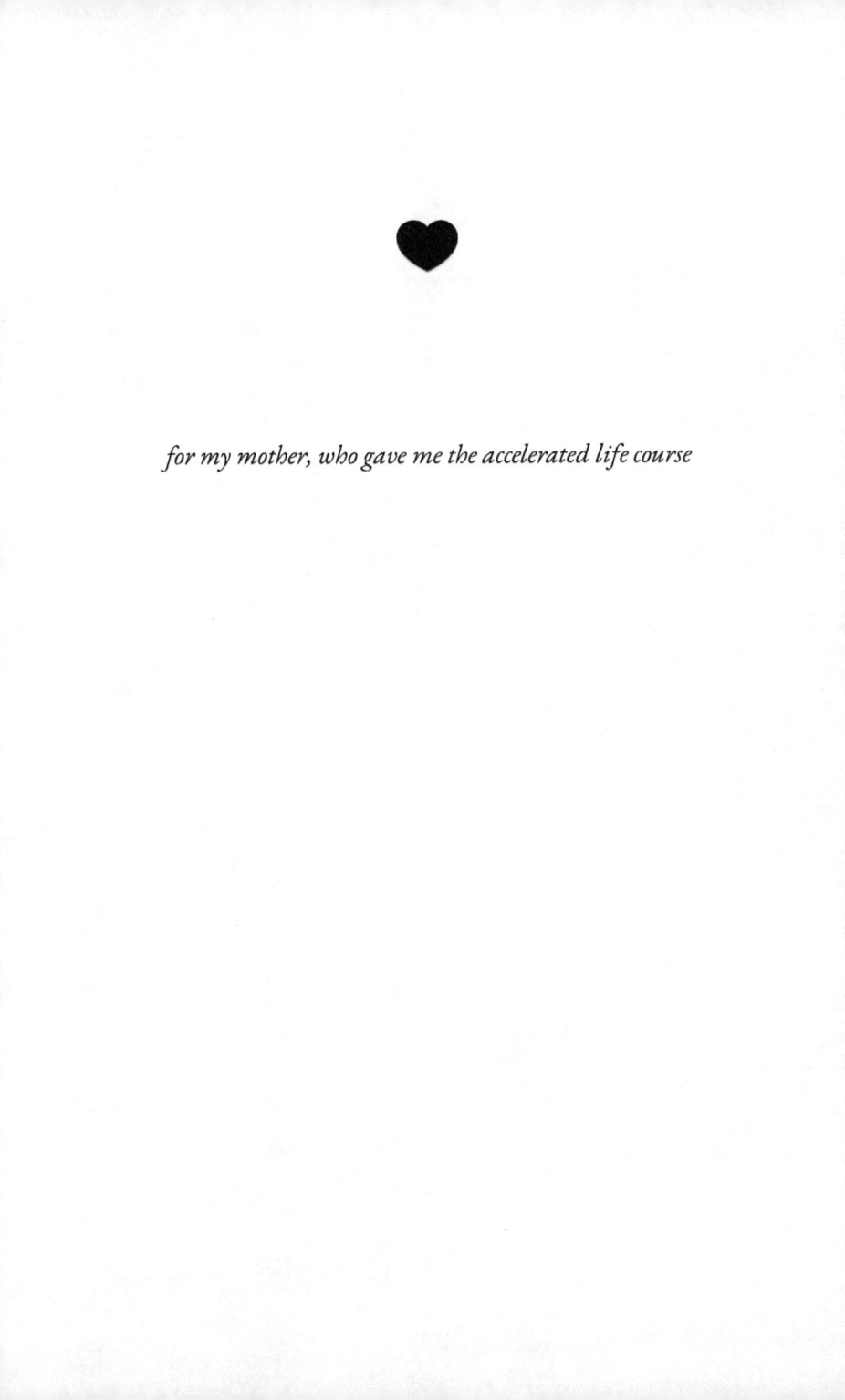

for my mother, who gave me the accelerated life course

♥

"*For I am convinced that neither death, nor life, nor angels, nor principalities, nor present things, nor future things, nor powers, nor height, nor depth, nor any other creature will be able to separate us from the love of God in Christ Jesus our Lord.*"

Romans 8: 38-39

Acknowledgements

THANK YOU TO MY husband, Michael, who is a great listener. He has heard stories of my childhood and adolescence many times throughout our years together, yet he was eager to read several drafts of my novel. Thanks for being kind, funny, and handsome too!

A special thank you to my good friend, Carol Guariglia. Her enthusiasm and support for this writing project was beyond my expectation. Her stellar insight guided me on the development of some of the major themes that are reflected in the story.

I also want to thank, Lisa Collins, my peer coach and mentor, who has encouraged me to keep writing, especially when I hit some road blocks.

Thank you to Roberta Lennon, who was my acting buddy at Temple University and has remained my life-long friend.

Thanks to Corina Douglas of Burning Legacies Publishing Limited. She is an accomplished editor and a talented writer who did a spectacular job of editing through her keen eye for detail and her intuitive nature.

Thank you, Jen Minkman of Dutch Venture Publishing. It was as if she could read my mind and was able to produce a perfect cover design.

Special thanks to Joris, founder of Cutting Edge Studio, a successful author himself, who writes under the pen name, J. Sharpe. He has truly created a great service for authors. He guided me in the right direction every step of the way.

Finally, I like to thank my friends and family who said they would purchase my book, especially if I signed it.

One

W HEN GRACE WAS NINE, she asked, "Who is the devil?"
All through Christmas Mass, even when the choir sang her favorite hymn, "Silent Night," Grace was thinking of that strange board that camouflaged itself as a game. She couldn't wait to receive communion and be on her way home to open the box and play with it.

Grace first saw the Ouija board in September while shopping for school supplies. Once she chose her pencil case, she ventured into the toy section of the store, and there it was sitting innocently next to Monopoly and Parcheesi.

"What do you want that piece of crap for?" Grace's father asked in his suspicious tone.

Certainly, she would not be getting anything other than school supplies, so why bother answering him? Besides, it was a rare occasion for Grace to receive a present other than on her birthday or at Christmas, and that morning, there it was under the Christmas tree waiting to give her a message.

When Mass ended, she pushed through the crowd to find her mom, Kate, in the back of the church. It was her mother who had purchased the Ouija for her.

"I saw you fidgeting in your seat," Kate said as she collected her handbag. "Remember the true meaning of this day, young lady. It's not all about the presents, you know."

"Mom, when I go to high school, won't it be great? I will be able to sit back here with you."

"Don't rush things; that day will come soon enough. Now, let's find Daddy."

Her father, Vince, could be anywhere inside the church or outside on the grounds. He loved talking with the parishioners, and the last thing on his mind was finding his wife and daughter to accompany them on their walk home. He helped with the collections during the nine thirty Mass and stood in the back of the church with the other ushers who collected the envelopes. When it came time for the offering, they split the church into sections.

Her father took the left side where Grace sat with her classmates. He liked performing this ritual every Sunday. It wasn't that he was a religious man, it was the image of a trustworthy member of the community that appealed to him.

As her father approached her pew, Grace looked at him with a new sorrow. He did not notice. She knew that the time had come that she would lose him to his memory of her as a little girl. She was already on the cusp of applying pale lipstick and wearing a training bra—that was not someone her father wanted to know. Vince preferred the child he brought to Mass when Grace was four. The memory washed over her as if it was yesterday.

They had sat all the way in the back of the church that day. She couldn't see much of what was happening on the altar. All she could see were the people in front of her with their big heads. She was finally able to see the priest when he reached the pulpit. He spoke English instead of Latin and Grace was completely mesmerized by the story he told. It was when the priest left the pulpit, that she turned to ask her father a question and noticed that he was gone. All that was left of him was his hat.

Grace thought her father may have seen someone who needed help or maybe he went outside to blow his nose. Her mother always told him to go upstairs when he had to blow his nose because he sounded like Louie Armstrong's trumpet. Church was such a sacred place, and it would be proper for him to leave and not disturb the parishioners.

Grace waited and waited, but there was no sign of her father. People were kneeling now. She started to feel hot and was too frightened to move. She was holding her breath as she stared at her shiny, black patent leather Mary Janes and her white anklet-laced socks. She kept clicking the tops of her shoes together and started rocking back and forth. Suddenly, a straw basket with a long handle was moving past her. She looked up, and there was a frail old man with gray whiskers pushing the basket in front of her. He stretched to reach the people at the end of the pew. Someone placed an envelope in the basket, and another dropped loose change that made a loud jingling noise.

Grace wanted to ask the old man if he knew where her father was, but she couldn't speak. Once the man left, she started to cry.

She was afraid she'd have to sit there until Mass ended and all the people were gone. Maybe a priest or an altar boy would find her and she could stay in the rectory? She would tell them her mother's name and that she lived on Sydenham Street. Grace was learning the numbers of her address, but now that it mattered, she couldn't remember one number.

"Please, baby Jesus, bring my daddy back," she prayed aloud, because there was no way she could go to the bathroom in the rectory.

"Are you all right, honey?"

The voice came from behind her. It was a soft, gentle whisper. Grace could not turn around. Instead, she kept her head down.

"What's the matter?" the woman asked.

Grace pressed her chin further down into her chest. She couldn't speak. She was trying to make herself invisible.

"Who are you here with?"

As the woman was reaching over to touch Grace's shoulder, there appeared Vince.

"How could you leave a child unattended like that?" said the woman.

"I told her I'd be right back," Vince lied.

He turned his back away from the concerned congregate and faced front. That's when he saw that Grace had chewed his favorite gray Fedora. It was wet and crumpled. He studied it for a bit but said nothing. The Mass was soon over, and they were on their way home. Grace skipped and ran, as usual, careful to stop at street corners like she was told. She made Vince laugh; he liked her spirit.

When they reached home, Vince showed Kate his soiled hat. He laughed at how Grace had chewed his cherished Fedora at the nine thirty. Her mother was not amused.

"Where did you go? What possessed you to leave her alone?" asked Kate.

"I went to the vestibule to make sure that the extra baskets for the Little Sisters of the Poor donations were set up," Vince answered.

"You just don't think, Vince. You could have told Grace where you were going—you know she would have stayed in the pew unafraid."

Now, five years later, Vince is collecting the offerings as Grace sits with her class. She couldn't understand why her father, her best audience, began to ignore her. Did he forget those family weddings when they were partners? Where she played the kazoo, and he played the banjo? That had stopped. Did he forget how he used to laugh when she sang "Lipstick on your collar, told a tale on you?" What about when she gave him a "Hollywood kiss," like she saw in the movies? She kissed him on the lips and then slapped him. He got the biggest kick out of that one. Grace saw her father nearing her pew, yet he passed by without any recognition. She adjusted her chapel veil and sensed that he didn't think she was funny anymore.

After Mass, Kate made a scrumptious breakfast. She fried bacon and used the drippings for the eggs and potatoes. As the bacon was frying, Grace hoped that the aroma reached Vince to accelerate his journey home. They hadn't found him on the church grounds earlier, so they left without him.

Vince finally made it home as Kate cracked an egg on the side of the iron skillet.

"Weinrich's must have been very busy," Kate said, knowing this was not why Vince took a long time to come home. He was a *chiacchierone*. He liked to talk to everyone, especially the old Italian ladies in the neighborhood. Who was sick, who died—this was what interested him. Vince was talking in the bakery, he was talking crossing the street, he was talking as he waited for the light, talking to anyone who crossed his path. This frustrated Kate to her wits end but, for Grace, all she cared about was that the bakery didn't run out of cream doughnuts.

Weinrich's bakery was one of the best German bakeries in South Philly. They had perfect cinnamon buns and wonderful jelly doughnuts, but it was the cream doughnuts that were unparalleled by any bakery in all of Philadelphia. The cream was not custard; it was a snowy-white whipped bit of heaven that had enough sweetness in its silky mixture. Vince preferred the jellies so he could make jelly doughnut sandwiches by slicing the jellies in half and putting vanilla ice cream in the middle. They could have dived into the doughnuts at that moment but savoring them for dessert was much better.

As Kate was taking the biscuits out of the oven and Grace sat quietly at the table, Vince was tickling the plates and glasses with the spoons her mother had placed so neatly on their table. Vince started off slowly and got a good beat going. Then he picked up a knife to add dimension, and for the higher pitch notes, he added a fork here and there.

Her father could make music anywhere and with anything. He even had a homemade bass instrument in their basement that he made from a washbasin. He'd attached a broom handle and a clothesline to it and made magic with that thing. Sometimes, Vince helped with the laundry, and while the clothes were running through the washing machine cycles, he played his bass. "Boom, boom, boom," the sound went in time with the washer, and soon there was a concert in the Marco basement.

Grace adored her father's talent for music. The ragtime that came through their ordinary utensils permeated the kitchen. She knew the other kids in the neighborhood didn't have what she had—a real music man. Vince loved the crooners, Connie Francis, Nat King Cole, the Big Bands, and especially Mario Lanza., the Philadelphia opera singer. No one was like Vince. He could sing opera arias, play twelve instruments, and he could whistle the national anthem.

"Vince, why don't you put on some Christmas music?" her mother asked.

Vince reluctantly left the kitchen and went into the dining room that housed their console stereo. He chose the Andy Williams Christmas Album. The music was fitting, but it was disappointing that he had to cease playing his own type of music.

After breakfast, it was time for Vince to open one last gift that remained under the Christmas tree. It was a beautifully wrapped gift from Kate. He picked up the small box and shook it. "I can't tell from the sound of it. What could it be?" he asked.

He unwrapped the box carefully and slowly separated the tissue paper. He took his time trying on his new pair of gloves. They fit him perfectly, and they were so soft too. Then he brought them up to his face and placed them under his perfect Roman nose.

"These gloves stink!" he proclaimed.

"That's the way kid gloves are supposed to be," Kate replied. "They're good gloves, Vince."

"I can't wear these," he said, and he threw them on top of the box under the Christmas tree.

Kate left the living room and walked back into the kitchen. That stern, cold face fell upon her as it often did when Vince deliberately hurt her.

"I don't know why I buy you anything of quality," she yelled from the kitchen. "I should have bought you a cheap pair from John's Bargain Stores."

The mood of the morning changed with one sniff. Grace picked up the gloves from where Vince left them. They didn't smell bad at all. That was the last gift her mother would ever buy him.

"How do you like your Ouija board?" Henry asked Grace as she was putting a black olive on her thumb.

"I don't know yet. I didn't get a chance to play with it today."

"I'm surprised your mother allows you to have such a thing."

"Take those olives off your fingers! For heaven's sake, Grace, food is not to be played with. I've told her that a hundred times," Aunt Amanda said disdainfully as she came into the dining room with a plate of celery and carrots.

"Oh, Amanda, let her be. Stop being such a fuddy-duddy!" Henry said in Grace's defense as he often did.

Kate's sister, Amanda, lived with Grandmom Rosie. Aunt Amanda never married, but she did have Henry in her life as her platonic companion. Henry was perfectly respectful of her, but he couldn't conceal his view that she was a tidy, unadventurous woman who went through life discussing cake and Jonathan Logan dresses. Henry lived a few blocks away from Grandmom Rosie's house, which made it convenient for him to visit often.

It was always a treat to visit Grandmom Rosie, especially on Christmas day. Her house was on Victoria Street, a lovely tree-lined street near Hunting Park in North Philadelphia. It was a row home just like Grace's, but the ceilings were high and the rooms were larger. It felt like thoughts could travel farther in Grandmom Rosie's house.

Grace's parents lived on Victoria Street for years before her father bought the house on Sydenham Street. He paid eight thousand in cash for their house in the newly developed veteran's affordable housing near the airport. Like Vince, many of the World War II veterans bought the tiny row homes so they could get a good start after serving their country.

Grandmom Rosie's house smelled fantastic that day. The roast was in the oven, and the potatoes were boiling, soon to be mashed. It was a tradition to eat dinner first, then enjoy some dessert and conversation before opening the presents under the tree later in the evening. The Christmas gifts weren't as important as the simple pleasures in life like a good cup of coffee, a lively chat, and a nice piece of crumb cake.

Grace took the olives off her fingers by eating them off one by one. Aunt Amanda stormed out of the dining room at the sight of her brazen niece who took every opportunity to get her aunt's Irish up.

"Now that's the way to eat horse's dovers," Henry said amusingly.

"You mean hors d'oeuvres," Grace proudly replied.

Henry was the only person Grace knew who was of neither Irish nor Italian descent. He was of English descent. Henry told her that people like to form groups. They like people who share the same values and customs, but they also like to subdivide within the group and form mini groups. He said that humans are peculiar. They like to belong, and yet, they always seem to find a way to separate. Henry said the best way to beat this position was to be your own person—an individual. Find joy in the similarities and the differences in each person. This was Henry's motto. He believed it gave people a chance to be a member of a group without losing their personal, unique identity. You couldn't be taken over that way.

He warned Grace that people will try to put her in a category—a geographic category, a racial category, a religious category, and a political category. And whatever the category they bestowed upon her, that was the way they would think of her. If someone deviated in any way, it caused confusion, and many would ostracize or criticize or ridicule a person—sometimes all three. Henry had told that she'd need a strong backbone to stay true to herself.

When Henry first traveled to Europe, a customs agent asked him what his nationality was, and Henry answered, "English." The agent looked at Henry's passport and saw that Henry was a citizen of the United States.

"English?" the man said. "But you're an American."

Henry was embarrassed, but at the same time, it opened his eyes. In America, people labeled themselves by the nationality of their family's origin country, even if they were born in America. Meanwhile, to the rest of the world, they were Americans, another category. In Europe, Henry was an American with all the assumptions of what it meant to be an American. They didn't know he was "Henry."

"I can't wait until I can travel all over the world," said Grace. "I will be a citizen of the world."

"You must travel, Grace," Henry said. "You have the natural curiosity."

Grace loved having Henry in her life. He inspired her to be open to many things and think for herself. He called it critical thinking. But the best thing about Henry was how he taught her how to whistle like a sailor.

The roast beef finally made it to the table, and the mashed potatoes were being passed around with the white bread and gravy. Turnips and asparagus instead of succotash marked the special day.

"Isn't the Ouija board considered a false prophet, Kate?" Henry asked as he reached for a dinner roll.

"What do you know about false prophets? You don't even believe in God," Kate replied.

"It is against religion to engage in any form of divination. I think it is in Deuteronomy."

"Anyone for turnips?" Aunt Amanda asked.

"I'll have some. They're my favorite," Grace answered as she marveled at Henry's knowledge of the Bible. He was an atheist, but he made sure he studied the Bible because he said no one could call himself educated unless he read the most influential book on earth.

The roast beef was tender and juicy, but Grace pushed it around on her plate after a few bites. She preferred fish. Henry told her that eating fish would make her smart.

"Have some more bread, Gracie. We have plenty of me brown gravy for you to dip, honeybunch," said Grandmom Rosie.

Grace loved how Grandmom Rosie called her "Gracie" and "honeybunch." She loved how Grandmom Rosie's voice had a lilt and when she said, "me hairpins, me Lone Ranger show." Saying 'me' instead of 'my' was a remnant of her Irish heritage.

Grace's great-grandmother, along with her family, left Ireland and came to America to build a new life. She was twenty years old when she set foot on American soil. Within a couple of years, she met Grace's great-grandfather in North Philadelphia at a church social. He was part of a prominent family that had been living in America since the mid-nineteenth century; they had escaped Ireland's devastating potato famine that killed over one million people. Many nights, Grace's great-grandmother shared stories of the Irish countryside with Grandmom Rosie, and years later, Grandmom Rosie shared these same stories with Grace. Grace was completely captivated by Grandmom Rosie's storytelling. She thought that her grandmom's remnant of an Irish accent kept the thread of the stories alive. Grace hoped that someday she could visit the village where her great-grandmother was born.

"Grace, why aren't you eating your roast beef?" Aunt Amanda asked. She'd noticed that everything on Grace's plate was gone except for the meat.

"I like flounder better," Grace responded.

"For crying out loud, what child likes flounder?"

"A sophisticated one, Amanda," Henry answered.

"Let's clear the table," said Aunt Amanda, slightly embarrassed. "Did you enjoy your dinner, Vince?"

"Delicious, as always," said Vince. "Rosie, no one can make a roast like you."

"I had meself enough practice," Grandmom Rosie said with a twinkle in her eye.

Grace saw Grandmom Rosie wink at Vince. She had a fondness for him.

"I will get the coffee started," said Grandmom Rosie. "You stay there, Kate. Amanda and I can do the rest. We have pumpkin pie, apple pie, and your favorite, Vince, mince pie."

"Before you go, Amanda, can you bring me the Bible, please?" Henry asked politely. It seemed to Grace that Henry was trying to make up for scolding her aunt a few moments before.

The family Bible rested on a small walnut side table, next to the floral-patterned accent chair in the living room.

Aunt Amanda brought him the book.

"I am sure it makes it clear," Henry said, as he took the Bible from Aunt Amanda and opened the front part of the book. "Yes, here it is—Deuteronomy, chapter eighteen, verse ten."

Henry recited the passage from the Bible—*There shall not be found among you any one that maketh his son or his daughter to pass through the fire, or that useth divination, or an observer of times, or an enchanter, or a witch. Or a charmer, or a consulter with familiar spirits, or a wizard, or a necromancer. For all that do these things are an abomination unto the Lord: and because of these abominations the Lord thy God doth drive them out from before thee.*

"Playing with the Ouija board is a tool to develop intuition. I don't see it as true divination or prophecy, and especially not an abomination," explained Kate.

"Is prophecy considered idolatry?" Henry posed.

"False prophecy, of course; but there are many prophets in the Bible who God bestowed upon them with his word. There was Isaiah, Jeremiah, Ezekiel, and Daniel. And then there was Joseph, who had the gift of interpreting dreams. I am sure you remember this since you are such a Bible scholar, but Joseph not only interpreted the Pharaoh's dream, he also acted on it."

"What was the dream, Mommy?" Grace asked.

"There were seven cows coming out of a river who were very fat, and then seven other cows came up after them that were ugly and very thin. Joseph knew that this dream meant there would be seven years of abundance followed by seven years of famine. He suggested to the Pharaoh that they collect some of what they produced in Egypt—"

"One-fifth of what they produced," Henry corrected.

"Yes, one-fifth. Thanks for that detail, Henry. Now, let me get back to what I was saying. Joseph told the Pharaoh to save it in reserve for when the famine came. The Pharaoh listened to Joseph, and it worked. Many people were saved from starvation during the famine years."

"Can you please move me bible, Henry? Here are the pies, I wouldn't want to get pie on the holy book," Grandmom Rosie said, laughing.

While Kate and Henry engaged in their religious discussion as they often did, Vince picked up the *Philadelphia Inquirer* that was sitting on the breakfront and read it as he anticipated his favorite piece of mince pie.

"This is exactly why I don't believe in any of this nonsense," said Henry. "In one place the Bible clearly states that no one should engage in divination or predicting the future in any form, and yet, in other places, God has selectively chosen humans to be able to predict the future. Which is it?"

"The word is 'chosen,' Henry." said Kate.

"How does one know if they are chosen?" he asked.

"I don't have the answer to that, Henry. I only have my faith. My faith to believe that God does things I may not understand, even where they seem contradictory."

"That is always the answer when you can't use logic—you call it 'faith,' ludicrous," said Henry.

"Jesus, Mary, and Joseph! Are you two still at it?" Aunt Amanda interjected as she came back into the dining room with the coffee. "Don't let Henry get your goat, Kate. He's being an intellectual."

"And you know what happens to intellectuals?" Vince said as he put down the paper. "They end up sweeping streets in California!"

"I want to know...what is the purpose of the Ouija?" Henry asked.

"Well, whatever the thing is, I think it's a silly game and that's that," said Aunt Amanda while she poured the coffee. "Let's not get into a heated debate on Christmas."

Kate sat still. She stared a hole through Henry, who seemed happy with himself that, once again, when the debate came down to it, faith was Kate's answer. Now that the debate was over, they switched their concentration on the pies. This was something they all could enjoy.

Grace couldn't help but think that Henry had a point; atheists often did. It was a diversion for a devout Catholic like her mother to encourage her to play with the Ouija board. Kate followed the doctrine of the Catholic religion. She went to Mass every day. Grace wondered why her mother made an exception for the Ouija?

"Let's open our presents now. Henry, please go down to the basement and add more coal. It's getting a wee bit chilly in here," Grandmom Rosie suggested.

"Certainly, Rosie. Grace, do you want to come with me?"

"Certainly, Henry," Grace responded with glee.

Grace loved coal. It was dirty and messy, especially when it turned to ash, and there was something about the ritual of putting coals in the furnace that was thrilling. It was much better than wood, Henry said, since it produced less creosote in the chimney and it needed less storage space than wood.

When Grandmom Rosie got a delivery of coal, which came in fifty-pound bags, Henry came by and emptied the bags into a heap in a corner of the basement. This way Aunt Amanda and Grandmom Rosie had easy access to the coals to keep the house warm. Henry also made sure the ash bin was emptied when the coal had turned to ash, as he was in charge of removing it as well.

Henry let Grace scoop up coals and throw them on to the red-hot coals that had been burning in the furnace from earlier that day. Mornings at Grandmom Rosie's house were cold since the coals had turned to ash during the night. The trick was to put a good amount of coal in the furnace just before heading to bed. Most of the night was warm but there was no sleeping late in the winter for Aunt Amanda and Grandmom Rosie because, no matter how many blankets they had on their beds, it wouldn't matter if the furnace was cold.

The houses in South Philly had gas heating, and some had oil heat. Grace understood that things progressed in the world, but she also had a solid respect for the ways of the past. Kate said that Grace was an old soul and that she had a hearty constitution against illness since she had built an immunity to the toxic fumes of the passing cars and trucks on the Walt Whitman Expressway adjacent to their dead-end street. Breathing in the ash dust in Grandmom Rosie's basement and living near oil refineries added to the toxic air that Grace inhaled, but Kate often said that a little bit of dirt wouldn't hurt.

When Henry and Grace finished with the furnace in the basement, they returned to the living room upstairs to find everyone was ready to open their gifts. Although there was some debate about prophecy and consulting the Ouija, Grace knew it wouldn't interfere with her Christmas spirit. Kate and Henry often had heated discussions at the dinner table, especially religious ones. There was no way anything would overshadow the thrill of opening the huge silver box with the red ribbon that sat under the tree with Grace's name on it.

Two

T HE FOLLOWING DAY, GRACE was eager to play with her Ouija. School was closed, and the kids on the block could play with their new toys. Each year during the week between Christmas and New Year's Day, the neighbors visited each other's homes to wish good cheer and share Christmas goodies. It was a delight to see the decorations and sip eggnog.

There were two kinds of eggnog, one for the adults and one for the kids. Grace managed to taste the grown-up eggnog once. It had brandy in it, and that was nothing new for her, as Grandmom Rosie gave her a sip of apricot brandy now and then to ward off colds. Every neighbor had a real Christmas tree except for the Marcos. It probably made sense to Vince that a silver artificial tree would save the cost of buying a real tree every year, even though the fun of shopping for a real tree was gone and the wonderful scent of pine disappeared. Kate disliked it, but she tired of arguing over it with Vince and gave in to his wishes. She did that once in a while, not letting on that she was the true head of the family.

The adults didn't like the fake tree. Maybe they thought aluminum was for the siding on a house but not for a Christmas tree. It was different for the kids; they liked the way it sparkled and the way it rotated as it changed colors. The reflector that came with the tree sat on the floor, turning its filters of green, red, gold, and blue. It was like the whole tree was made of tinsel, and the kids loved that.

It was a tradition to return the gifts in their original places under the trees so that the children could display them properly for the neighbors to see. When it was Grace's turn to show her Christmas presents, most of the attention went to her Barbie house. Even the adults were impressed with Barbie's abode. No one seemed interested in the Ouija board. She tried to evoke excitement by telling the neighbors that it was a unique board that could answer questions and predict the future. There wasn't a tiny flicker of light in any of the eyes staring back at her.

When the neighbors were leaving, Grace drew the two girls who lived next door over to her. She proposed that if they stayed to play Ouija, she would let them borrow the Barbie house for the rest of the week. They liked that idea.

Once everyone was gone, the girls settled in the middle of the living room floor, near the aluminum tree and the reflector. The atmosphere was set by the changing colors on the revolving tree, the lights around the big mirror over the couch, and the glow of the outdoor lights coming through the bay window. It was dusk, and Kate was in the kitchen preparing dinner.

Grace took the board out of its box. She told the girls that they had to be careful because it was a magic board. She read over the simple instructions and told them to put their fingertips lightly on the pointer. Grace placed her fingertips on the device as well and asked the board if it was going to rain. The pointer was moving to the word "no." This wasn't fun because the girls were pushing the pointer. Grace thought it would be better if they could ask a question without putting their fingers on it at all.

The girls sat there waiting quietly until Grace formed a new question.

She asked the board, "Who is the devil?"

The girls were confused when Grace asked this question, but when she instructed them not to put their fingers on the pointer, they did as they were told. Neither of them said a word as they sat there for a long time waiting for something to happen. As they waited patiently for the impossible, Grace thought that this was probably not a good game for the girls. It was perfect for her since she was nine, but they were younger than Grace. She felt that she was more mature in her understanding of such things.

To their surprise, the pointer began to move on its own. Grace was thrilled, unlike her little neighbors who looked petrified. The pointer was moving slowly but it was moving. The pointer landed on the letter "B." Next, it pointed to an "A." It began to move faster as it pointed to the next letter, "R." With each letter it was moving faster and faster. They couldn't keep up with the speed as it frantically, purposefully pointed to the letters.

Grace was trying to keep a record in her head of what the letters were spelling. She started to notice that there was a pattern—it was repeating, always bringing itself back to the letter "B," the first letter of the chain. There appeared fifteen or more letters before returning to the letter "B." It seemed like it was spelling a name.

Grace ran into the kitchen to get a pen and a piece of paper from the junk drawer next to the stove.

"What do you need paper for?" Kate asked as she flipped over a Mrs. Paul's fish stick.

"I want to write an answer down. We're playing with the Ouija."

Grace ran back to the board and eagerly watched the pointer to see if it would move when she asked the question again. "Who is the devil?" But the pointer had stopped moving. The girls waited, but nothing happened. Grace knew this board probably had rules, just like other rules such as gravity and motion. She had one chance and she blew it.

Disappointed, Grace asked a new question. "Will I win the religion prize in the future?"

The pointer started to move on its own again, and the girls saw it was moving to a big "YES." But then it shifted direction. It went to the "B" again, then the "A," then over to the "R." Grace realized it was repeating the same pattern, and she jotted down the letters on the paper.

B, A, R, T, H, O, L, O, M, E, W, T, H, A, R, R, O, D. Bartholomew Tharrod. That was the answer. Grace had never heard of this name. It was different from Freddy Bartholomew, the child actor. It wasn't a congressman or a name she'd read in a book. She looked over to the girls. They were staring at the board, hypnotized. The younger one started to cry. They didn't like this game. Grace packed up the board, and in silence, the girls left to go home. They forgot to take their bribe, the Barbie house.

Grace felt guilty—not for something she did, but for something that she was about to do. She was going to hide what she did with the Ouija from her mother, and this would be the first time she would hold something back from Kate.

Grace went into the kitchen and sat in her seat at the table as Kate continued to prepare dinner.

"So, what did the Ouija reveal to you girls?" Kate asked.

"Nothing really."

"What did you ask it?"

"If it was going to rain."

"Well, is it?"

"I don't know. It answered 'no' but that was fake. I could see that the girls were pushing the pointer, so I stopped playing with it."

"Really? Then why did you run in here and get that pencil and paper out of the drawer?"

"Well, it was sorta trying to spell something. I think."

"Did it spell anything?"

As Grace was about to make up something, Kate said, "You can't hide anything from me, so you may as well tell me now before I find out anyway."

"It gave us a name," Grace answered. "The pointer was moving on its own, and it was going fast."

"It was moving on its own?" said Kate. "What were the three of you doing?"

"We watched. The pointer moved on its own."

"I see." She paused for a second and then continued, "Well, I guess it should move on its own if you're good at it. What did you ask?"

"I asked if I was going to win the religion prize."

"Are you?"

"I guess so. It was moving to 'yes,' but then it stopped and went in another direction, answering my second question."

Her mother raised a brow. "You're confusing me. You first asked if it was going to rain, then the third question was if you would receive the religion prize? So, what was the second question?"

Hesitantly, knowing there was no way she could hide anything from her mother, Grace said in a soft whisper, "I asked it 'who is the devil?' It looked like it was spelling out something, but it happened so fast that I struggled to keep up with the letters, and that's when I ran in here to get the paper and a pencil. When I returned, it stopped, so I asked it another question about the religion prize. That's when it started over again, I was able to write down the letters. It answered with a name."

"What's the name?"

"Bartholomew Tharrod."

"T. Harrod, I would think," said Kate.

Kate's hazel eyes widened. Grace felt that they were peering through her soul. She looked back into her mother's intense eyes and Grace could feel a warped sense of time at that moment. A vague sense of foreboding penetrated the moment.

"You must never say that name again, you hear me? Never!" Kate demanded.

Suddenly, the front door opened. Vince was home.

Grace watched her mother as she finished placing the fish sticks on the serving dish and then turned back to cook the fries. Her father started to play the spoons. Everything was as normal as it could be, but Grace knew something unexplainable had transpired that day.

She stared at the back of her mother's neck and mused how she loved the strands of ash-brown hair that fell upon it. Kate always wore her hair up in a bun. Grace loved her mother's hairstyle, just as she loved her mother's apron and her housedress, her high heels, and the way she laughed. She loved her mother's scent, even her steely gaze. But most of all, Grace loved how they could communicate without words.

The Ouija was put away on a shelf in the basement. It was safer to play with the stupid Barbie house instead.

After playing with the Ouija earlier that day, Grace and Kate played the "guess what I am thinking" game. They were in the front bedroom, where they'd slept ever since Grace was born. Vince was relegated to the back bedroom, where he slept in his single bed. For some reason, Vince had his own room. The other kids on the block had fathers who slept with their mothers in the same bed. It was quite a shock to Grace when she discovered that she was the only one in the neighborhood that shared a bedroom with her mother, as she'd thought all fathers slept in the back bedrooms of their homes.

Grace jumped into her single bed that was nestled in a corner of the bedroom, and Kate curled up in the double bed that was in the center of the room.

"Okay, you go first. Close your eyes," Kate said, "and please, don't take all night."

Grace looked around the room carefully. They had to choose an object in the room, hold it in their minds, and then say what they thought was the selected object. Sometimes she chose the wooden crucifix that hung above her mother's bed; other times she chose a subtle thing like the pattern on the gray and white linoleum floor. Often, Grace chose the huge Emerson air conditioner that was positioned in the middle window, or the aluminum blinds, the old oak rocker, the electric alarm clock, or even a specific article of clothing that was hanging in the closet behind the sliding wooden doors that Vince had made.

Most of the clothes in the closet were Grace's. Her mother only had a few housedresses—a Sunday dress and another she wore on special occasions. Kate also had one winter coat and one spring coat, two pairs of high heels, a pair of sandals, and a pair of slippers. She never wore flats, and no one ever saw her in slacks.

Grace decided to concentrate on the night-light that was clipped on to the headboard of her bed. It was made of material that looked like paper, but it was sturdy and had vines painted on it.

"I'm ready, Mommy. What do you see?"

"Your night-light."

"Wow, that was fast."

"Not if you count how long it took you to decide."

"Now it's your turn, Mommy."

Grace waited before she could see an object in her mind so she could check to see if her mother was breathing. Whenever Kate was resting or sleeping, Grace looked to see if her mother was breathing. She did this almost every night, and she'd wake in the middle of the night to see if Kate's chest was moving. When her mother moved or made a sound, only then was Grace able to go back to sleep. Grace loved her mother so much that she had to make sure that nothing bad would happen to her. She couldn't imagine life without her.

Kate coughed, so Grace was able to continue to play the game now that she could see her mother was okay. It was a strange obsession—checking to see if her mother was alive on a daily basis. Even the neighbors knew about it. It happened during the day as well. Countless times, Grace went to the corner store to ask the store clerk if he had seen her mother. Inevitably, the clerk told her that he had. He would reassure her that Kate was fine and that maybe she went to another store, or she was doing some other errand. Over the years, the people on Sydenham Street knew about Grace's over-protective obsession, and eventually the people on the block thought that Kate's daughter was a touch peculiar.

Grace cleared all thoughts from her mind. She relaxed and concentrated on her own breath, letting an object slowly take form. Usually, as soon as something became clear, Grace would blurt out what she knew was the object. She particularly liked when Kate thought of a costume jewelry piece. Kate had a large, red jewelry box that sat atop her blonde wood bureau. In it were her pearls, some necklaces, and pins. Pins were popular in Kate's day. Women wore them on their hats, dresses and their coats. The younger mothers in the neighborhood relinquished this adornment, and the dress of the day was more casual. It was 1962, and there was a shift happening in all things, fashion included.

Yet Kate was not one to adopt the current trends. She liked to keep with tradition and was the only one on Sydenham Street who had scapulars in her jewelry box. It was a custom for the very religious to wear the Sacred Heart of Jesus or the Blessed Mother on their underwear to protect the faithful from illness or other dangers. The scapulars were made of cloth and looked like S&H green stamps.

Grace sensed that she was leaving the room in the present time. She heard someone walking down the hallway, coming nearer and nearer to the bedroom. With each footstep, Grace became more frightened. She was alone in the room; her mother wasn't there anymore. Grace pulled the covers up to her chin and stared at the doorway. In an instant, a powerful scent encompassed the room, and a bright glow emanated around the doorway. She felt a splash of water hit her forehead, just like when a priest blessed the congregation on holy days. Then she heard a voice.

"It's the font," a man said in Grace's ear.

There was a small holy water font on the inside wall of the bedroom doorway that Grandmom Rosie gave to Kate and Vince when they moved into their new home. There were holy water fonts in all three bedrooms in Grandmom Rosie's house, and the tradition extended to Grace's family home on Sydenham Street as well. Grandmom Rosie liked to dip her finger into the font and bless her loved ones to protect them from harm.

The room suddenly came back to the present, and Grace realized her mother was still in her bed. She blurted out, "It's the font!"

"That's exactly what I was thinking," Kate replied.

"But I didn't see the font like I see the other things, Mommy. I saw a glowing light near the font. The room smelled of something I can't explain. It was a strong scent, and then I heard a man's voice—a voice I've never heard before. He said, 'It's the font.' I'm afraid, Mommy. Who was that man?"

"There's nothing to be afraid of," Kate said, trying to console Grace.

"But who was the man I heard in my ear?" Grace persisted.

"Maybe it was some random voice you picked up. We have an antenna in our heads. Most of us don't use it. Think of it as a radio. You have a tiny radio in your brain and when you are adjusted to certain frequencies, you can pick up all kinds of things. That's probably how we can play our game. We are focusing on the same channel. That's good. It means you are a receiver."

They ended the game and were nestled under the covers ready for a nice, long sleep, but before Grace shut her eyes, she touched her forehead and felt the remnant of the holy water.

Three

♥

G RACE HEARD THE THEME of *The Late Show* playing on the television downstairs. A Marlon Brando movie was scheduled for that night. She decided to go to sleep instead of watching the actor who mumbled and everyone thought was great. She could use the sleep, anyway, since she had been up late most of the week watching some of her favorite movies.

Grace had watched a series of movies about priests. Monday night had Spencer Tracy in *Boys Town*. Tuesday night, *Angels with Dirty Faces* was featured with Pat O'Brien. Bing Crosby was in one, too, and on Wednesday night, he played the younger priest who comes to the church where Barry Fitzgerald is the pastor in *Going My Way*. None of these roles were anything like the priests at her parish—certainly not Pastor Tillian. He had no sense of humor like the priests in the movies. When Grace was in the confessional for the first time, Father Tillian was behind the window in that small, mysterious cage. She was slightly nervous, because she often saw adults exit the confessional a few inches shorter than when they entered. They never looked relieved. It was all very serious. Now it was her turn to join the ranks of the guilty. She couldn't think of any sins to confess, but then she thought of something her mother had taught her.

"Please bless me, Father, for I have sinned. I stole a banana and ate the skin!" confessed Grace.

Father Tillian immediately exited the confessional box and opened the door where Grace was kneeling. He pulled her out of the confessional by her hair and scolded her in front of all the people waiting to confess their sins. He said to have someone commit a sin in the confessional box was unforgivable, and Grace was the worst sinner of all. He gave her a whole rosary for penance.

"I only told you that as a joke. I didn't mean for you to actually say it in the confessional," Kate said when Grace returned home. "Even so, don't let Father Tillian make you think you sinned. You will know it in your heart when you do something wrong. It's not like it's a commandment— 'thou shalt not joke.'"

Kate learned the saying from Father Brice who used to tell her all things wise and witty. Father Brice was a Catholic priest and her mother's best friend. Grace loved hearing the story of Father Brice and what happened to him. Father Brice visited Grandmom Rosie's house back when all three sisters, Amanda, Mary, and Kate lived there together with their mother, Rosie. Grandmom Rosie in her youth was an Irish beauty with black hair, dark hazel eyes, and lovely pearly-white skin. She came from a wealthy family but soon found herself having a difficult time when she fell in love with a poor artist, and married beneath her station. Grandmom Rosie was left a widow at the age of thirty-six, and she had to fend for herself and her three daughters.

Those times were hard, but a bright light came into their lives through their wonderful friend, Father Brice. Grandmom Rosie appreciated Father's presence at her dinner table, and her daughters adored him. He was the only male figure in their lives after their father died. The sisters seemed like ordinary parishioners, but there was something about them that attracted Father to come to dinner at their house at least twice a week.

He first joined them at their table when Kate was fourteen years old. Right from the start, he took a particular interest in Kate. It did cross Grace's mind that Father Brice could have been secretly in love with her mother but that seemed too ordinary. No, this relationship was about two highly spiritual people who found each other among the common and the mundane. Kate was his match, and he knew he could confide in her about his secret.

Father Brice had been coming around to break bread at Grandmom Rosie's house for three years when they lost Mary. Kate would have lost her mind at the time if it wasn't for Father Brice. Her sister, Mary, was only twenty when she died in childbirth. At seventeen, Kate lost her favorite sister.

A year after Mary's death, Father noticed a striking young man donning the church steps of their parish, St. Stephen's. The man was a compelling figure with jet-black hair, sharp dark eyes, and perfectly arched eyebrows. He was impeccable in appearance, thin and astonishingly handsome, and his clothes were stylish. Sometimes, Father saw this haunting figure coming down the steps, and other times he saw him walking up the steps, but he never saw him in the church or anywhere else in the parish.

All during that fall when he came to call on Kate, Amanda and Grandmom Rosie, Father seemed agitated. Kate did her best to make their special guest feel comfortable, but she could see that he seemed to be bottling something up. Kate had never seen Father look this way. He had to deal with the sick and the dying, and he helped people in severe spiritual crises, but none of it reached him. Father Brice was always able to bounce back from his deep feelings for his parishioners and appreciate life.

However, it wasn't until one night when he was having a cup of tea with Kate, together in the living room, that he told her about this extraordinary man he had encountered on the church steps. He said that he had heard that the devil comes in many forms and that he can often make himself beautiful. However, the only thing the devil could not disguise was his feet, as they were always ugly or deformed in some way. That morning, Father Brice had seen the beautiful man again, and for the first time, he was able to pull his eyes away from the man's outstanding face. He had looked down and noticed the stranger was wearing the ugliest shoes he'd ever seen. The shoes looked like they held something unnatural within them.

After that night, Father Brice disappeared. He was not at church giving homilies, and he stopped coming by Grandmom Rosie's house. The pain of losing his company was unbearable for Kate, as there was no one else who came close to sharing their fiery exchange of ideas. They had talked about the big questions, the possibilities of life and death, the afterlife, the seen and the unseen, and Kate loved him.

Six months after their last conversation, Father appeared on her doorstep. When Kate opened the door, she was shocked to find an old man standing before her. His face had deep lines, and his great head of black hair was completely white. The last time Kate saw Father, he'd only had one white curl that fell upon his forehead. It was a distinguishing feature she loved. Not anymore, and his smooth, perfect face had been replaced with a gray, sickly pallor. Kate was heartbroken at the sight of him.

Father Brice had performed an exorcism. Only certain priests appointed by the Vatican were able to do this. Her mother said that Father was able to do this spiritual ritual because he was a receiver—an extreme empath. Receivers can align themselves to the forces that exist beyond the five senses. Thus, the only priests able to perform exorcisms had to be receivers, but they were in danger if they didn't know how to protect themselves.

During that visit, Father revealed to Kate that a young girl in the parish had been struck down by an entity that lived within her, and he'd had to exorcise it. Father Brice had performed these dangerous exorcisms several times, and he soon realized that this time he wasn't dealing with a lesser demon but something more.

Father suspected that the man he saw on the steps of the church was the entity that had possessed his young parishioner. Father knew it in his bones that the figure was of the devil. He felt that it was a presence of a higher order, possibly an archdemon.

Father told Kate that just as there are levels of God's heavenly beings, there are also levels of the devil's evil. In Christianity, the heavenly beings had three levels. The first level includes the Angels, the Archangels, and the Principalities, all of whom are the workers. The second level is comprised of the governing angels—the Powers, Virtues, and Dominions. The third level contains the Thrones, the Cherubim, and the Seraphim, all of whom are the closest to God.

Father delved into the findings of many priests and scholars who were experts in the subject of the fallen angel, Lucifer. According to ancient beliefs, there are demons that cause men to sin, and there are other demons who cause calamities, disease, famine, mental disease, and emotional disorders. These demons are all individual aspects of the evil one, Satan. Lucifer was known as the most beloved angel who rebelled against God. After the war in heaven, which Lucifer lost, he was cast out of heaven. Then he became known as Satan who rules over the fallen world. There are many depictions of the devil. Medieval scholars ascribed the seven deadly sins to a hierarchy of seven archdemons—Lucifer being pride, Mammon being avarice, Asmodeus being lechery, Satan being anger, Beelzebub being gluttony, Leviathan being envy, and Belphegor being sloth.

Father knew he was faced with the biggest challenge of his life. He needed all his strength, all his wisdom, and all his faith to discern which one of the archdemons was possessing the young girl. Even though he understood that Satan was Lucifer and there existed a concept of seven archdemons, he considered that an archdemon was a unique facet of a singular creature. He made seven attempts to expel the evil entity that confronted him by performing the exorcism prayer with each of the seven names in his point of convergence. Father was unsuccessful in all seven attempts. The only thing he knew was the earthly name of the demon, as the young girl repeated it over and over. He told Kate the earthly name of the demon to warn her in case this name appeared before her in some manner.

Father had lost the battle. The girl died, and the devil's disciple escaped into the invisible poetics of space. Poor Father Brice. He was a broken man. Kate never saw Father Brice again after that day he appeared at her doorstep. He died a year later in a home for retired priests.

Even though Grace was surrounded with all the familiar objects in the front bedroom, she was unusually frightened. She stopped thinking about the story of Father Brice and the devil to eliminate her fear and thought of other things—nice things.

Visions of Brigantine Island swirled in her head. Grace loved the island that was north of Atlantic City, New Jersey. It was named after a brigantine ship that had been ship-wrecked on the beach in the seventeenth century. In her mind, Grace could see the sand dunes with the winding narrow path of bleached pebbles, and she followed it until she could see the expanse of the pristine beach laid out before her. She remembered her red bucket and shovel and could see herself digging into the hot sand until she reached China.

Grace tried her best to remember those wonderful days on Brigantine Island, but she couldn't help herself from thinking about the storm. The Marcos vacationed there every year for two weeks in August with Grandmom Rosie, Aunt Amanda, and Henry. It had been a bright, sunny day at the south end on the 7th Street Beach when a warm breeze had turned into a whirlwind. Grace should have known something was off since there were no greenhead flies that day. The flies typically pestered the beachgoers in August, but that day, there were none at all. It was a perfect day with blue skies, warm water, and surprisingly, no jellyfish.

"If you dig deep enough, you will dig all the way to China," Henry said, as he and Grace dug a hole in the sand.

"Really? How long will it take?"

"Look at the sky out there, seems like a storm is approaching," said Kate as she sat under the umbrella sheltering her delicate pale skin.

Vince was in the water navigating the waves. Grandmom Rosie and Aunt Amanda had opted not to go to the beach that day and were in the house preparing dinner.

"Seems far off. Maybe later tonight it will hit land," Henry said.

As the day progressed, the wind grew stronger. At first, the wind was a welcome guest on the humid beach. But then it felt like it overstayed its welcome, and everyone on the beach wanted the wind to move out. Soon, the clouds appeared, and the sky above them became black. The sand was whisking about, and the people on Brigantine Beach absconded in droves.

Henry taught Grace about the flight versus fight biological reactions that were genetically passed down since the caveman days, and she saw it with her own eyes that day on the beach. She could see the flight response manifest itself in everyone there, except for her father. He was going to fight instead.

Her mother and Henry gathered the beach paraphernalia together, then Henry took Grace by the hand to lead her off the beach. Vince, however, cared more for saving the beach umbrella than getting to safety. It had been ripped out of the secure hole her father had dug earlier that afternoon. They saw him running down the beach trying to catch the tumbling thing as it outmaneuvered him. As the rest of the people darted off the beach, Vince was the only one running on the beach alongside the water. Grace broke away from Henry's hand and ran after her father.

"Daddy, come back!" she cried out.

Vince ignored Grace's plea and kept chasing after the umbrella.

"Please, Daddy, come back!" Grace screamed.

The winds were growing fiercely, and there was one gust that blew Grace up in the air. She fell face down into the sand. Henry ran to her and scooped her up into his arms. He carried her past the dunes. Grace could see her father getting smaller and smaller as he disappeared down the beach.

They made it back to the house. Grandmom Rosie and Aunt Amanda sighed with relief when they saw them coming through the door.

"Good heavens, we were worried. Where's Vince?" Grandmom Rosie asked.

"He's still on the beach," Kate replied. "He is trying to save our umbrella."

"Is Daddy going to die out there?" Grace asked. She started to sob.

"Henry, why don't you get in your car and see if you can find him?" Grandmom Rosie proposed.

"I don't understand Vince, why would he risk his life to save a beach umbrella?" Henry asked. But he grabbed his car keys anyway.

"There's nothing to worry about. He's pretty strong," Grandmom Rosie said in Vince's defense, as she often did.

"You honestly think it was a good idea that he left Grace crying on the beach?" Kate asked. "This isn't the first time, you know. He left her alone in church once, and what about the time he lost her when they went shopping for the transistor radio?"

"She did find her way back to the car on her own, though," Grandmom Rosie stated.

"Oh, for heaven's sake, Mom, the point that I am trying to make is that he is an unthoughtful—no, let me rephrase that—he is an unfeeling person who doesn't have much of a nurturing bone in his body," said Kate.

At that moment, the door blew open, and there was Vince, soaked through. Henry was right behind him, still with his car keys in hand.

Grace ran to her father and threw her arms around him. "Please, Daddy, don't you ever run away like that again."

"Why would you ignore Grace's screams to save an umbrella? There is something fundamentally wrong with you, Vince," Kate said furiously.

"Now, Kate, calm down. He is here and all is well," said Aunt Amanda.

"Not so. It's getting pretty rough out there," said Henry. "We better get off the island."

"It's just a rainstorm," Vince said. "It will blow over. The funny thing is the wind changed direction, and the umbrella actually started chasing me. I got here in no time." Vince sounded quite amused. At that moment, the power suddenly went off.

"Turn on the transistor," Henry instructed.

The voice coming through the battery-operated Emerson 888 had validated Henry's hunch that this was more than a rainstorm—the newscaster was warning the islanders to evacuate. Grandmom Rosie turned off the oven and placed the half-cooked chicken and potatoes in a paper bag and threw them in the garbage pail outside the back door.

"Sorry, but me chicken had to go." Grandmom laughed. She then gathered the perishables in the refrigerator, intending to bring them home.

They gathered their belongings quickly and piled in Vince's Dodge and Henry's Buick. When they were pulling out of their parking spots, Grace looked out the rear window of the car. Through the torrential downpour, she saw the tattered beach umbrella that Vince had tried to save. Its spokes jotted out of the torn canvas. Deep within her she knew this was a foreshadowing. As they pulled away, Grace felt a chill throughout her body, and the mangled umbrella faded from view.

Little did they know that the summer storm was a precursor of the big one that came the following spring. The storm was named the Ash Wednesday Storm since it was ushered in on the first day of Lent. It was a rare occurrence since the storm was actually two storms combined into one. One came up the coast from Florida, and the other from Mississippi, and they converged, making it one of the most horrific storms to ever hit the barrier island and most of the eastern coast. Many lives were lost. The grand piano that was housed in the Brigantine Hotel was found on the town of Longport's beach, which was thirty-one miles away. The Brigantine

Pier disappeared into the angry sea. Grace and Henry loved that pier. On early mornings, they rode their bikes there and watched people fishing. Sometimes they spotted dolphins swimming by. Often, they shared an order of pancakes, even though they would be going back to the house for a full breakfast.

Grace had a favorite motorized kiddie horse she liked to ride on the pier. It cost a nickel a ride. Now the horse was somewhere in that vast Atlantic Ocean. Even though it was only a motorized horse, Grace was afraid it would be alone in the darkness of the water. She hoped that by some miracle the dolphins would adopt the horse and it would have friends to get through a lonely place. Henry and Grace didn't need any more nickels to put into the metal box by the kiddie ride, not only because the pier was gone but something would change in their lives. From then on, they would never return to Brigantine.

The memory of those recent island storms had passed and she managed to feel safe again there in the front bedroom, as she had her mother to protect her. That is all Grace ever needed in this world. She would forget that she was a receiver like Kate had said. Being a receiver could bring trouble. It did for Father Brice.

Four

♥

NEW YEAR'S DAY ARRIVED. It was the most festive day in Philadelphia because of the Mummer's Parade where the mummers paraded up Broad Street. Vince had been in the parade for years but had retired a few years back. He used to be in one of the string bands and had played the glockenspiel, known as the bells. Banjos and bells gave the string bands the distinctive sound of the mummers. To Grace, music was a rejoice of life. She loved how music brought people together.

Grace wanted to be a mummer, but no females were allowed to perform. Henry knew the history of the parade. He said that it started with Scandinavian immigrants who wore lavish costumes and engaged in mockery, masking, and frolicking to bring in the new year. The first documented celebration occurred in 1778. From 1790 to 1800, when Philadelphia was the capital of the country, President Washington often celebrated the New Year with groups of people who would masquerade and go door-to-door telling jokes and reciting poems. It grew into an official parade in 1901.

The parade was sectioned into four divisions—comic, fancy, fancy brigade, and string band. The comics were the first to strut up Broad Street. They traditionally acted out skits based on national political and social themes. Grace avoided the comics since they could get a little rough and touchy. Lots of girls walked around

Broad Street with heavy makeup on their faces from being kissed by the drunken comics. Each year, most of the mummers in the comic division started drinking on New Year's Eve and continued throughout New Year's Day.

Next to strut up Broad Street was the fancy division. The men in this division wore large, ornate costumes as they performed using floats and props. Immediately after the fancy division performed, the fancy brigade division took a place in the parade. They were similar to the fancy division, but they performed intricate dances and drills with elaborate props and recorded music. Grace's favorite division was the string band, who not only wore elaborate costumes but drilled while playing musical instruments. They featured banjos, saxophones, accordions, double basses, drums, glockenspiels, and violins.

The competition within the divisions was fierce, and there were substantial cash prizes. It took a whole year to plan for the parade. Each division had a social club, and the men would rehearse while their wives made extravagant costumes of sequins and feathers. The captains of the brigades had the most outstanding costumes. Their headdresses were exaggerated representations of Native American headdresses and were coupled with designs that reflected an annual theme. As a result, Broad Street was a sea of plumage on New Year's Day.

Grace and her family watched the parade outside the funeral parlor that her cousin owned. Even though her father had retired from the mummers, the Marco family still had an obligation to watch the parade every year. Most years New Year's Day was freezing, and during the parade, it was great to be able to take breaks and go inside to a warm place with lots of good food.

Grace watched some of the fancies and then decided to go into the funeral parlor to warm up. She approached her mother, who was sitting with some of Grace's aunts on the Marco side of the family. Her mother looked miserable. She never liked the parade.

"Can I have some anisette later, Mommy?" Grace asked as she removed her coat, hat and gloves.

"That would be a nice treat after coming in from the cold, but first, eat some of the food. It is delicious as always."

"The roast pork is better this year," Vince said, pulling up a chair next to Kate. He wedged himself between her and the aunts.

The aunts adored Vince; he was a handsome man. Vince also felt more comfortable around them than being with the other men, even his brothers. Grace thought it odd that her father was a great charmer with women when he didn't have an ounce of that charm for his wife.

"I prefer the roast beef to the pork," said Kate. "How long will we stay? I would really like to get home earlier this year."

"Oh, don't leave too early, Kate. We hardly see you," said Aunt Dolores.

"She thinks there's stiffs in the basement," Vince said, laughing.

The other women laughed too.

Vince called over his cousin, Ricky, the funeral parlor director. "Do you have any cold ones down there in the basement?" asked Vince.

"I'd rather not say."

"That means there is," said Aunt Dolores.

"Well, let's put it this way, statistically there are more deaths around the holidays than any other time of the year. And with that said, I will leave it to your imagination. Now, *Mangia!*"

Grace couldn't care less if there were dead people in the basement. Instead, she concentrated on the Italian spread on the main floor. Pepperoni, provolone, salami, prosciutto, soppressata, capicola, olives, macaroni salad with shrimp, Italian rolls, sausage and peppers, and roast pork were all on the menu. The pastry table was a beautiful display of Grandmom Marco's homemade cream puffs, rum baba, sfogliatella, and pizzelles. Grace loved the pizzelles. They were thin cookies that were made in a pizelle waffle iron and looked like stars. There were homemade liqueurs on the table that were also made by Grandmom Marco. At Christmas time, Grandmom Marco bought alcohol at a dollar per gallon. She blended some of the alcohol with cherries and some with anise. Kate and Grace loved the anisette.

Grandmom Marco wasn't a person that people liked as much as they loved her food, and Grandpop Marco was a quiet little man. Grace didn't know him at all. Whenever he was around he stayed to himself. He didn't speak English well. Grandmom Marco disapproved of Kate since she was from an Irish background. She once told Grace that she should be grateful that Vince married her mother because he was so desirable in the neighborhood. She said that a homely-looking woman like Kate had a beautiful child because of his good looks. Meanwhile, other people told her mother that she looked like Deborah Kerr, the pretty actress.

One Easter when they visited Grandmom and Grandpop Marco, Grace was offered candy from an assorted chocolate box. When she tried to take a second piece, her Grandmom slapped her hand and said, "These are for your cousins."

That was it. No more did they need to visit Grandmom Marco on Easter. They did see her on New Year's Day and other family occasions, however. Kate said that it was a good thing that Grandmom Marco could cook, because if she didn't have that, no one would visit her. Grandmom Marco didn't have an authentic bone in her body. She was a professional mourner, and others paid her to cry at wakes for dead people she didn't know.

Unlike Grandmom Marco, Grace's uncles were a welcoming bunch. Vince and his brothers had a band. They played at family occasions. Vince was the lead singer and he would perform his repertoire of songs at the funeral parlor on New Year's Day. He made sure to sing "Pennies from Heaven," his all-time favorite. Then he and the band played mummers' music that featured "Golden Slippers," "Happy Days Are Here Again," and "When You're Smiling."

Every year some of the mafia stopped by the parlor on New Year's Day. They loved the spread of Italian food, but they also wanted to make sure that Vince's cousin paid up for the protection they provided in the neighborhood—even though there wasn't anything to protect against, except the Mafia itself. The mob guys' families came from Sicily, whereas most of the people in the Marcos's neighborhood came from families in Naples. The Sicilians had very dark hair and black eyes and many of the Napolitano had blue or green eyes.

Grace noticed one of the men standing by the doorway to the basement. He didn't partake in the festivities. He didn't eat or drink anything. She couldn't take her eyes off him; there was something mysterious and compelling about him. He had piercing black eyes, and his dark hair was perfectly combed into place. His facial features were chiseled as if Michelangelo had sculpted them. He wore a starched, white shirt and a tailored suit that framed his thin body. But there was one imperfection about his appearance that disturbed Grace—his shoes were big and wide, and they were ugly. As soon as she noticed this particular feature, she turned away.

There was something unnatural about this mysterious guest. Grace conjured up enough courage to look at him again, but he was gone. Father Brice had described a man such as this on the steps of the church. Grace forced this suspicion out of her head. It was ridiculous. This guy was a mob guy, a Sicilian. Just because he wore weird shoes didn't mean anything. He may have been in an accident—a mafia-type accident.

The Marcos hated the Mafia. They felt that it depicted Italians in a bad light. There were so many hard-working Italians in the city who were not involved with the mob, yet they carried that stigma. Grace's Uncle Tony really hated the mob the most. He made sure not to deal with them. Therefore, it was a big deal in the Marco house when Uncle Tony made the front page of the *Philadelphia Inquirer* one year.

All of Grace's uncles, including her father, helped in the funeral parlor business. They were pallbearers if a family was short of guys to carry the casket. They drove the cars and even picked up the bodies. Uncle Tony ended up on the front page of the newspaper because he drove the hearse with a well-known mobster inside. A reporter took a photo of Grace's uncle standing next to the gravesite where the mobster was buried. The whole city saw it, and they thought Uncle Tony was part of the mob. Vince thought it was one of the funniest things that happened to his brother.

The Marcos had many stories to tell about the funeral parlor. Grace's favorite story was the one where her father had to pick up a body at the old widow's house. Vince arrived at the home where the family had been grieving for two days at the private viewing of the deceased man. The entrance to the home opened to a steep staircase. The old widow was standing at the top of the stairs, and she kept telling Vince to be careful. "Please be careful with my Dominic."

Vince brought the stretcher up to the second floor, and he entered the parlor. He put the body on the stretcher and, as he returned to the top of the stairs, he lost control of the stretcher. The stiff body soared down the staircase and onto the pavement in front of the house. The widow kept saying, "My poor Dominic, my poor Dominic." Grace's favorite part of the story was when Vince would say, "I don't know why she was so worried, he was dead as a doorknob."

For a place that held much sorrow, the funeral parlor had more in common with the mummer's parade than most people realized. The closest thing to this type of parade was the funeral march in New Orleans. The people strutted in a distinctive way with their umbrellas as they celebrated the dead.

Grace hoped the parties continued and that the mummers strut would go on forever.

Five

G RACE IMMERSED HERSELF IN her schoolwork since it was a great distraction from the emotions of others. Everyone around her was worried about Grandmom Rosie. The breast cancer had been taking its time, but lately it had quickly advanced. Even though Grace loved Grandmom Rosie with all her heart and didn't want to see her suffer, she was more concerned that Kate would not recover if Grandmom Rosie died.

However, it didn't matter what Grace wanted, the day she feared soon arrived. She came home from school and saw her mother ironing school blouses. Kate ironed Grace's blouses on Sunday mornings, never on weekdays. This was a Thursday. She noticed that her mother was moving her lips, but nothing was coming out—she must have been saying a silent rosary.

"What's wrong, Mommy?"

Kate stopped moving her lips and put the iron in its resting position and took a deep breath. "It's Grandmom. She made a turn for the worst and is in St. Mary's Hospital. I am waiting for Daddy to come home so we can drive up there."

"Can I go with you?"

"Yes, but they won't let you see her. You are underage."

"That's okay," Grace said, not wanting to be a problem in any way. "I'll sit in the waiting room."

Vince came home as early as he could, and they arrived at the hospital shortly after.

Grace did have to stay in the waiting area. St. Mary's was a Catholic hospital, and they had nursing nuns that wore shorter head pieces then the Blessed Sacrament order at her school. These nuns wore dresses with aprons, and they had a crucifix hanging on the side of their aprons.

Grace watched them in awe. These women were religious, and they could take care of sick people too. They were like angels, not like the nasty nuns at school.

An hour had passed when one of the nursing nuns brought Grace to Grandmom Rosie's room despite the rules. Grandmom Rosie was sleeping. She had several tubes attached to her. Grace wondered if Grandmom Rosie could hear them in the room. Henry and Aunt Amanda were standing on either side at the foot of the bed while Kate sat on a chair next to the bed. Her mother was holding Grandmom Rosie's hand, and Vince was on the other side of the room looking out the window. Grace could see he was crying. She felt compelled to say something to Grandmom Rosie, but as she was about to say something, a nursing nun came into the room and said they should all leave as visiting hours were over. Kate did not want to leave, but she managed to let go of Grandmom Rosie's hand. She leaned in and kissed Grandmom Rosie on her forehead, and then she blessed herself with the sign of the cross before leaving the room. Everyone followed.

But as they were walking down the hallway, Grace turned and ran back into Grandmom Rosie's room. She couldn't leave without saying something.

She walked to the side of the bed. "Goodbye, Grandmom. You were the best Grandmom in the world. I will always remember how you made me bacon sandwiches and threw holy water on me when I was about to go to sleep, and I remember when you told me about the time you knocked off that cop's hat and stomped on it because he was hitting your brother with a night stick. I loved how you called me 'honeybunch.' No one else will ever call me that. I promise I will make Mommy laugh. She will miss you so much."

Henry stood at the doorway as Grace said her last words to Grandmom Rosie. "It is good that you said goodbye, Grace. Stay as you are."

They left the hospital quietly.

It was the middle of the night when they received the call that Grandmom Rosie had passed.

Grace was worried. She knew how much her mother adored Grandmom Rosie. She knew that her mother would have been perfectly happy to live with Grandmom Rosie instead of getting married; it was Grandmom Rosie that encouraged Kate to marry. She didn't want her daughter to be a spinster like Aunt Amanda, and besides, Kate loved children. She reminded Kate that Vince was a good candidate for marriage since he was able to put a roof over her head and he didn't gamble or drink. In the end, Kate finally accepted Vince's marriage proposal after years passed at the insurance company where they met. Vince was patient. He knew that Kate wanted a family, and he also knew that she did not love him, but as her mother told Grace, her father said that he had enough love for both of them. Yet Grace knew her father probably hoped that his wife would come around to love him in time.

It was disturbing to see Grandmom Rosie in the coffin. Grace had never seen a dead person. She couldn't stop thinking that this was once a feisty Irish woman who worked for many years in a factory to raise her three daughters. A woman who had dancing eyes and a lilt in her voice. She was a wise force. Now she had become a shriveled old lady with a chalky complexion, stiff and lifeless.

People came by and said consoling things to her mother and Aunt Amanda. They also said nice things to her father and Henry. Grace was ignored since she was too young. The room had the stale scent of funeral flowers. Kate looked like a statue, almost as dead as Grandmom Rosie. Aunt Amanda was wiping her nose all the time. It was Vince who lost his composure. After the priest finished saying the rosary, Vince stood by the coffin and cried. He'd just lost his best ally.

Grandmom Rosie saw something in Vince that Kate could never see. She was able to look past his outward, stubborn behavior. She knew he loved her daughter, and that was important to Grandmom Rosie. She wanted Kate safe, provided with the basics of life, including children. True, Vince did stupid things, like how he bought the house on Sydenham Street without Kate's consent. He took her to South Philly, showed her the row home and asked her if she liked it. She said yes, but she didn't want to live in South Philadelphia. He then told her that was too bad because he had already bought it. Kate had wanted to stay in North Philadelphia to be near Grandmom Rosie, but Vince didn't care about that and made the decision for them. This was the beginning of Kate's resentment toward Vince.

However, unlike her mother, Grandmom Rosie always treated Vince with kindness, and she understood him. So, while Vince sobbed uncontrollably, Kate sat there, stoic and straight. He then threw himself on Grandmom Rosie's body and tried to hug her. Henry had to pull him away from the casket and brought Vince outside for some fresh air.

Grace gazed at the crucifix that used to be in Grandmom Rosie's bedroom and now was in her casket. She contemplated that there was probably a shadow on the wall in Grandmom Rosie's bedroom where the crucifix had hung. That bedroom was huge. It had an extra sitting area across from the bed with a writing desk. Grandmom Rosie liked to write notes on that desk using her particular stationery and the pen that she dipped into an inkwell. Grace liked writing with that pen even though it was messy. The metal-tipped pens with ink cartridges were much better, although it was annoying to change the cartridges. But Grace loved the sensible ballpoint pens best. Grandmom Rosie, however, was loyal to the dipping pen; no ballpoint pen for her.

New inventions seemed more about convenience than quality to Grandmom Rosie. She said that with new things, beauty and craftsmanship often slipped away. Grace had frequently sat with Grandmom Rosie in that room, savoring the attention lavished upon her. Now, as Grace stared at the lifeless corpse in front of her, she did the next best thing to revive the spirit of Grandmom Rosie—she evoked a memory.

Grandmom Rosie was sitting at the writing desk in her bedroom and Grace was seated on the edge of bed.

"Tell me more, Grandmom," she begged. "What was the factory like?"

"It was hot, that is what I can say. Me own stockins' stuck to me legs. Funny, since I was workin' in a hosiery factory."

"You're too funny, Grandmom."

"Those days were long, and the work was hard. I had to make a livin' since your Grandpop died. He left the world when he was a mere thirty-six years old. I was the same age when he departed, God rest his soul."

"Mommy told me he had something wrong with his heart."

"Well, ya see, he was an artist, ya know. He was a glass blower. He made a beautiful vase for me parents. He delivered it one day, and as soon as I laid me eyes on him, I was stricken. And before ya knew it, we were in love. Oh, me parents were in an uproar. You see, he was adopted. They didn't like not knowin' where he came from or what he was, ya know his nationality. We ran away and got married. That was it. We had nothin'. We were livin' in a shack on Second Street up near St. Michael's parish. Then the Tanner family, who were bricklayers, gave him a chance. He worked on the buildins' layin' brick by brick until a big *mahoff*—you know, a big shot—came along and brought your Grandpop into a business partnership. It seemed sneaky to me; I didn't like the smell of it. The business went sour, and they blamed the losin' thing on ya Grandpop. He was never the same. His heart failed him. But if you ask me, he died of lost pride."

"That was a long time ago, Grandmom. So, it was you and Aunt Amanda, Aunt Mary, and Mommy left?"

"Yes, that was it. I had me love of me life, I didn't want to marry ever again. No one could take the place of ya Grandpop. We lived in a one-room flat with a coal stove for many years. The Tanners gave me some money, but it wasn't enough to save up for a better place to live. Finally, me parents gave me this house. It belonged to your Great Aunt Marguerite. They were very rich, me family, but I was an outcast because I married down."

"When you moved, was Aunt Mary with you?"

"Yes. Our dear, sweet Mary, God rest her soul, was happy in the new house. Happy until she met that good for nothin' policeman. Oh, he was a looker, and he had a rovin' eye, if you know what I mean."

"What was he looking for?"

Grandmom Rosie laughed at Grace's innocence. She had forgotten that Grace was only eight years old at the time.

"Rovin' means he was lookin' around at other girls."

"Like Don Juan?"

"Exactly, but in a cop's uniform. Your Aunt Mary was smitten with him, and they soon married. I couldn't see her much. She was livin' with him and his mother. She died in the hospital during childbirth, where she lost her baby too."

"Mommy told me the story."

"It was the second time that me heart broke in pieces. But I had to go on. I had ya mom and Aunt Amanda to think about. The years went by, and Aunt Amanda worked up the ladder at the telephone company. Your aunt was happy with her highfalutin position and had no interest in marriage or children. There are some ladies who are like that, ya know, Gracie."

"Maybe it had something to do with Aunt Mary. Maybe Aunt Amanda was afraid to have babies because of what happened to Aunt Mary," said Grace.

"Could be. You are a smart whippersnapper, honeybunch."

"Aunt Amanda made her choice. Even though she didn't marry Henry and there were no blessins' from that marriage that could have been, Aunt Amanda was able to pay the bills here, and I was able to stop workin' at the factory. When ya mom was gettin' older and showin' no signs of marriage, I started to get worried, ya know. Oh, Kate loved children, and I didn't want her to miss out on bein' a mother. When your father pursued her for all them years, I thought to meself, she better take him up on his offer to marry. She was no youngster, ya know. Your mother finally gave in. They lived with your Aunt Amanda and me until your father bought the house on Sydenham Street. He was so excited about it. When ya mom didn't want to live there, I saw such a sorrow take over ya dad. The poor fella, he never knew how to please ya mom. I told him many times to take her out once in a while. Buy her Russell Stover assorted candy instead of Whitman's candy—she loved Russell Stover. He wouldn't listen. Every Valentine's Day, it was the same thing—he'd buy her the "Whitman's Sampler" because he liked the way they had the types of chocolates in a diagram and that the candy company originated in Philadelphia. These were the little things, but what seems small can matter, Gracie. There was a story of a woman who loved her beautiful tree in front of her house. The city needed to destroy it—one more bad storm and kaput! Somehow the woman saved the tree over the years from the city's warnins' but this time they were determined to take it down for good. She begged them not to. She told them she would die if they removed the tree. Everyone thought she was crazy. It was such a small thing, ya know. The tree was cut down and the woman died the next day. So, you see, Gracie, even the wrong box of chocolates could have real meaning to ya Mom, not that she would die or anythin', but somethins' have special meanins' even if they don't seem important in everyday life. Your mother just couldn't take that your Dad wasn't listenin' to her. There were other things between 'em too but me gut told me not to meddle. I had done enough by pushin' ya mom to marry. I am happy I did it, though, or ya wouldn't be here, my little honeybunch."

Grandmom Rosie stood up from her chair and walked over to Grace and patted her on the head.

Grace had been lost in her memory until Henry patted her on her head. She came back to the reality of the present and watched her mother. Grace wondered if she would be enough to keep her mother in this life. Kate had lost her favorite sister, Mary, and she had lost Father Brice. This would be the third death to touch her. Grace knew there was a time when one can see a person's light go out—a resignation to not continue on this earth. Grace knew that people could die of broken hearts, sometimes suddenly, and at other times a little bit each day over many years.

The thought of not being able to draw her mother back from grief cut through Grace's heart and mind. She knew it was going to be tough to make Kate happy again, but Grace was determined to find a way to keep her mother focused on the here and now.

Grandmom Rosie's death swiftly changed the course of life at the Marco home. Kate needed more quiet time for prayer and reflection. There were no more telepathy games and late-night talks. Aunt Amanda busied herself with selling Grandmom Rosie's house and finding an apartment. Vince retreated more into himself and spoke less and less to Kate. It was Henry that Grace could depend on more than anyone else. He was teaching her French words, and he shared stories about his travels around the country when he was a salesman for the long-distance communications company where he met Aunt Amanda. She was adapting to the new melancholy in the house when Henry proposed an idea that could lift their spirits. President Kennedy was scheduled to visit Philadelphia, and Henry thought it would be good for them to watch the President's motorcade as it passed by on Broad Street.

It was a mild day in October, only a month since Grandmom Rosie had died, when they gathered on Broad Street to see the President's motorcade. Vince couldn't get time off from work, but Grace suspected he didn't want to go anyway. He wasn't interested in the Kennedys. He said they were snobby New Englanders who had too much attention for their accents. Her mother, however, adored the Kennedys.

Grace was glad to see her mother happy about something. There was hope that Kate would recover, and life could return to the way it was. It would take some time with lots of small steps.

The elation of the crowd when President Kennedy passed by in his motorcar was phenomenal. The crowd was cheering loudly, and some bystanders were crying. The motorcade stopped in front of them, and Grace couldn't refrain from staring at the President's tremendous head of hair. It was wavy with a beautiful shade of red strands running through it. No wonder why he took off his top hat at his inauguration. There had been a big debate about that in the news. Henry said he thought it was fitting for the age. Aunt Amanda said it was rude. Kate, on the other hand, said the President's hair was his best feature. Grace was happy she could see his wonderful hair, and when he reached down to pat her on her head, she felt like she was floating above herself.

A month later, the President was dead. Grace came home from school, and once again, there was her mother with that sullen look on her face while she was ironing anything she could get her hands on. Henry and Aunt Amanda came by that night, and they were glued to the television. Vince was moved even though he didn't vote for the President. There were lots of opinions about the tragic assassination. Vince was convinced it was a mafia thing. Henry blamed it on the CIA, because he had the opinion that the CIA ran the country. Grace suspected Vice President Johnson; she thought he had the most to gain. Kate felt it was God's will. Aunt Amanda didn't know what to think. One thing they each had in common was that they knew things were changing in the world. America lost its innocence. It was the end of an administration that they called "Camelot." Maybe it had something to do with the earth's axis, maybe it shifted.

Kate used to say that what happened on a large scale in the world affected the personal lives of people on a smaller scale. Then if you studied what was happening in your personal life, you could see a parallel in the outside world. It worked both ways. And so, it was that President Kennedy and Grandmom Rosie died that fall of 1963. Two deaths, one of the world outside and the other of a smaller world, Grace's world; they both made her life different. There was a growing distrust in the way things were becoming in America. Music, art, and fashion were exploding with a sense of revolution. And in Grace's world, Aunt Amanda put the house on Victoria Street up for sale. Brigantine was a place of the past, and something was changing on Sydenham Street too.

Six

I T WAS THE SUMMER of 1964. Grace, Kate, and Aunt Amanda rode the train from 30th Street Station, Philadelphia to Penn Station in Manhattan where they transferred to the local train that brought them to the borough of Queens. Here, they would enjoy the New York World's Fair. It cost a total of five dollars for them to enter the fair. Admission was two dollars for adults and one dollar for kids under twelve. It was spectacular to see the Unisphere, the huge globe of the earth, coming into view as they neared the station. There were so many things to see.

Henry had prioritized what they should see on the trip, since they were only spending one day at the fair. It was a mystery why Henry didn't accompany them that day, and Grace surmised that it had something to do with not upstaging her father. She had noticed there was an escalating tension between Henry and Vince.

The first stop was the IBM Pavilion, where they were able to fill out a card with a random date. They put the card into the computer slot, and then on a screen above, a current event appeared that correlated with that specific date. Henry said that it would not seem like much, but this was the most important part of the fair. He said computers would change the world; they would get smaller and smaller. He said that, someday, people would communicate through the computer. He said that all information would go through a network and he believed that the computer would be of great benefit to the world and of great detriment at the same time.

Next on the list was the Ford Pavilion, where they were able to ride in fancy convertibles circulating on a conveyor system in the Magic Skyway. They also made sure they took notice of the New York State Pavilion, which was designed by the architect, Philip Johnson. There was a lot of walking to get to the pavilions, and they spent a lot of time waiting in lines. None of that bothered Grace. She was in total awe of everything, even the people that were walking to and from the exhibits. Grace felt proud of the country for all its inventions and how people could just have plain old fun. Even though America had gone through some sad things, it really was a happy place.

Grace was glad she dressed up for this day of adventure. She liked the blue dress that her mother had bought her, and she liked her hair tied up in a bun, a blue and white flowered ribbon surrounding it. Her white-laced gloves, her new white shoes, and her white patent leather purse finished off her sophisticated look.

There were many times during the day that Kate and Aunt Amanda needed to stop and sit because their feet hurt. They both wore high heels. While they rested, Grace visited the souvenir shops nearby. Her mother and Aunt Amanda positioned themselves on benches outside the stores to make sure Grace was safe, but they were too tired to go inside with her. Grace had her own spending money in her purse that she had saved since her last birthday back in December. Henry gave her some too. She was thrilled with the items in the store. Grace chose wisely. She bought key chains, coasters, replicas of the Unisphere, and pens since she could fit these items in one bag, and it wouldn't be too heavy for the trip home. Each time Grace left a souvenir store she liked to sit on the bench with her mother and Aunt Amanda to show them what she had purchased. They both were excited to see what she had chosen.

"Let's see what you bought this time," said Aunt Amanda.

As Grace pulled out what she had purchased, Aunt Amanda noticed that Grace had multiples of the same items. "Oh, Grace, I see what you are doing. How nice of you to think about bringing gifts home. That was very thoughtful."

It was the first time Grace could remember that Aunt Amanda said something nice about her.

It was getting late, but they still had one last pavilion to see. 'It's a Small World' exhibit was saved for last. Grace, Kate, and Aunt Amanda stepped into the small boat and sat back as they were transported along the indoor canal. The song played with children's voices singing "It's a Small World After All," and it played throughout the journey. It was a delightful testament to all the children of the world. The animatronic dolls were depicted in their cultural garbs as they sang to the guests traveling through the waterway.

Grace was hypnotized by the exhibit, but slowly, as they moved along, a feeling of foreboding fell upon her, a presentiment. She knew that her mother made an effort to visit the fair so they could share this memory of a special day. Yet Kate had been despondent since Grandmom Rosie's passing; she couldn't give much of herself to Grace and was closed off. Grace understood, but she hoped that, in time, the sorrow would lift and her mother would bounce back, and they would continue in the way they were before Grandmom Rosie's death. Somehow, in the little boat surrounded by the small children of the world, Grace knew that her mother would not fully recover from her grief.

They had a glorious day at the fair, and now it was time to return home. Grace determinedly left her sorrow in the pavilion. Instead, she thought about what she would tell everyone about her experience at the great New York World's Fair.

A few days after they returned home from the fair, Aunt Amanda was shocked when she found out Grace had set up a souvenir store on the Marco's front porch. When Grace bought the souvenirs at the fair, she'd had the intention of selling them to the kids on the block. She marked them up to double her money. Aunt Amanda was appalled that Grace would take advantage of their day at the fair. Kate, on the other hand, was amused. She thought it was enterprising as long as the buyers wanted the souvenirs and the price was fair. This was quite different than what Grace had done in the past.

When Grace was five years old, she found books in their basement. She decided that something useful needed to be done with the books instead of letting them sit there on the shelves. In the living room of the Marco home there was a radiator with a cover that created a shelf under the window. It was summertime, and the window had a sliding screen that Grace thought would make a good means of passing books through.

She stacked some of the books from the basement on the radiator cover in preparation for her free library and then made a big announcement to the kids on the block that she was opening a library for them. The kids were excited. None of them were able to read to the level of these books, but they showed up anyway. Grace gave them two days to read the books, and after that, she charged them a dime a day if they were late returning them. A few days later, Kate noticed that the kids who came to the window were crying because they couldn't read the books. In one way, Kate thought Grace was creative, but she didn't like the bit of exploitation that Grace exhibited with her unfair practices; it wasn't fair business. So, she sat Grace down and instructed her to immediately shut down the not-so-free library. However, the souvenir shop on the porch was a different thing. It was fair enterprise, and Kate allowed it.

Grace liked to produce things even if it wasn't for a profit. In second grade, she was impressed with her two classmates who took dance lessons. The girls showed Grace a routine they were practicing for an upcoming dance recital. Grace wanted to share the girls' talent with the class. One day she asked Sister Ignatius if they could take time to see the girls' dance routine. Sister Ignatius liked the idea, and she set a time for the dancers. Grace was so excited to put on the show. She was the producer and the director. She cleared an area in the front of the room and instructed the girls to go out to the hallway so they could make an entrance. She then followed them to the hallway. It was time for the show to go on but, suddenly, the girls seemed frozen. They were frightened. Grace reassured them that they were great dancers and that they knew their routine well. But they still wouldn't budge.

She then pointed out that if they couldn't do this for the class, how would they be able to dance in a recital? Still, they remained frozen in place. Then Grace scolded them. She said they were cowards, and they were letting the kids down. Then, since shaming them didn't work, she tried reassuring them again. Finally, Grace opened the door, entered the classroom, and danced the routine herself. She remembered a few steps, but mostly she made up the dance by jumping, leaping into the air, and twirling. The class loved it and gave her a great round of applause. Sister Ignatius phoned Kate to let her know that Grace was an enterprising child. Kate was grateful to hear this compliment and hoped that Grace wouldn't flunk self-control as she did in first grade. No such luck, Sister flunked her anyway.

After Grandmom Rosie's death, Grace noticed that the world was changing dramatically. The discussions around the table on Saturday nights when Aunt Amanda and Henry visited were heated. Henry predicted that America was moving more toward a socialist country with Johnson's plan for the "Great Society." Kate heralded the signing of the Civil Rights Act of 1964, even though the streets in Philadelphia had violent race riots. Vince, and even Aunt Amanda, agreed that segregation in public facilities and discrimination should be illegal. Henry agreed on that point as well. Where Henry differed was the signing of the food stamp bill. He believed that this would be the beginning of a new dependency on government. He felt it would grow and make many people unable to attain the American dream on their own.

Grace was completely fascinated with the difference in opinions at their dining room table. Henry said that the waves of change were upon them, and that they could kiss the liberty the Founding Fathers gave them goodbye. It would take many decades to feel the effects, but he was convinced that sometime in the next century, America would fall to the whim of bad leaders and the warped minds of professors who were teaching in the universities. He believed this had happened over and over again throughout history—a group of people wanted to dominate what others think.

The world was in an uproar. The first soldier stepped foot on a Vietnam battlefield. Young men were burning their draft cards. There were civil rights marches that developed in the nation, with the most famous one in Selma, Alabama known as "Bloody Sunday." Thirty-five people died in the Watts race riot that lasted six days in Los Angeles. One hundred thousand anti-war protesters assembled in eighty cities. The word "hippie" came out of San Francisco, the "peace and love" movement started, and *American Bandstand* moved from Philly to Los Angeles.

American Bandstand started in Philly and this daily music show became famous when Dick Clark took it over—the original host was arrested for driving under the influence. All of Philly were glued to their TV sets to watch the musical acts on the live show. In 1960 the show morphed into a dance craze when Chubby Checker appeared with his version of a Midnighter's R&B song. The Midnighters were scheduled to perform on Bandstand but when they failed to appear, Dick Clark brought Chubby into the studio and within a half an hour, "The Twist" was born. Grace loved to watch the local celebrity dancers and when she learned to dance the "Twist," she did it everywhere—in the house, on the street, family weddings, and in the schoolyard. All the dancers were just friends and neighbors in Philly that were known as the "Bandstand regulars" and they had a local following of fans. Grace dreamed of becoming one of those dancers when she was older but that never happened; *American Bandstand* moved from Philly to Los Angeles in 1964.

That year when Bandstand moved to California, debates within the family, on the news, in the schools, and other public places began to divide people. Sometimes, kids can see things more clearly than adults. She sensed that some hidden, powerful group had eliminated President Kennedy or they wouldn't have been able to take over. He'd been in the way of something, she thought—what that was would probably remain a mystery.

Meanwhile, in Grace's smaller world, she noticed change as well. Why weren't the girls on the block not wanting to play "Mingle Mum" anymore? It was such a fun game. A bunch of girls and boys stood in a circle while a designated player gave the command "Mingle," and they walked around in a circle, mingling about. Then the designated player gave the command "Mum," and everyone had to freeze in place. Anyone who was caught moving was hit by the other kids—no real hard punches. It was silly and made the kids laugh. There was always someone who threw a real punch, and that ended the game.

The girls stopped playing that game. They feigned being hurt too quickly, and they blinked their eyes and whined like babies. If that wasn't sickening enough, they also stopped playing with their Barbies. They still liked playing with dolls, but whenever any of the boys came around, they threw the Barbies in a bag.

Puberty was like a contagion. It was infecting the girls mostly; the boys had a lot of catching up to do. One hot summer day, Kate was hanging Grace's tee shirts on the line in their backyard when a bunch of boys came down the alley. They ridiculed Grace because she still wore tee shirts instead of bras like the other girls in the neighborhood. When Kate went inside, Grace told the boys that her mother was doing laundry for their neighbor, Shirley, who lived next door. It was a way to make extra money, and the tee shirts belonged to Shirley's girls.

Eventually, Kate became aware of the rumor that she had to take in laundry to make ends meet. She was furious and scolded Grace like never before. But it wasn't the rumor that bothered Kate as much as it was that Grace had to cover up something about herself in order to be accepted by her peers. This didn't sit well with Kate. She taught Grace to be her own person, even if it meant she would be ridiculed or excluded from the crowd. Grace had to tell the boys that they were her tee shirts and if they didn't like it, lump it.

Grace knew that the boys didn't really care if she wore tee shirts. She still liked to play games with them. She also liked sitting with them in the schoolroom and being their buddy. The class was separated. The boys sat in the seats up front, and the girls were in the back. She sat up front with the boys in the first seat by the window. This suited Grace fine, because many of the girls were acting sneaky and whispering a lot. The boys were simple and honest.

Grace sat in the front seat by the window throughout her eight years in elementary school. It started in first grade when Sister Marie Bernadette saw that Grace was left-handed. Sister said she would disrupt another classmate since the rows were separated by a set of two desks and Grace would need to be on the left side. But why did she need to sit in the first row all the way by the window? The nuns loathed people who were left-handed. They thought that left-handed people were part of the devil. Sister explained to the children that Grace was left-handed and, therefore, not only different from them, but she was part of the devil. She also said if they were born right-handed or left-handed, that is what they would write with for the rest of their lives.

Grace started practicing writing with her right hand. When she practiced the circles and the big letters, she used her right hand at the same time as her left hand. Every night she made shapes with both hands. Her right hand felt weak, but she didn't let that stop her. Grace kept practicing until her right hand finally felt as comfortable as her left.

On the last day of the school term, Grace was taking an exam that would determine if she passed on to the second grade. This test was different from all the other tests she had during the year. It was on unusual paper, and it had a strong smell of ink. Sister Marie Bernadette told the kids to wait until the ink dried before they started. Grace waved the paper so it could dry faster. The test was pretty simple, consisting of alphabet letters, some numbers, and naming things.

When Grace nearly reached the end of the test, she thought it was the perfect time to show Sister Marie Bernadette how she could use both hands to write. She watched until she caught Sister's eye, then she switched the pencil to her other hand. She did this a few times to make sure Sister noticed. Sister did notice and immediately rushed over to Grace's desk with her big, black rosary beads bouncing in the air. Grace could smell Sister's Jean Nate toilet water as she neared her desk. It smelled like the blue ink on the exam paper.

"What are you doing, young lady?" asked Sister Marie Bernadette.

"I am finishing the test, Sister. I started with my left hand, but then I switched to my right hand. I like to go back and forth."

"You are a belligerent girl! You are doing this on purpose to deliberately discredit me."

"No, Sister, I only wanted to see if I could learn to write with my right hand. You said that we could only write with one hand."

"Get up," Sister said as she pulled Grace out of her seat by her school blouse collar. "Now go outside in the hallway and stay there!"

Grace did as she was told and, while she was standing in the hallway, she could still see in her mind's eye the rage in Sister's eyes, and she could still smell the mix of fresh ink and Jean Nate. Fortunately, Grace knew she only had one question left on the test. It didn't matter, she knew she passed it with flying colors.

When Grace arrived home that day, Kate was standing at the front door.

"I received a phone call from Sister Marie Bernadette, young lady," Kate said in a stern voice. "She said you deliberately made a fool out of her in front of the whole classroom."

"I didn't do anything wrong, Mommy. I was taking the test, and I switched hands to show her that I learned how to write with each of them and that I didn't have to be left-handed anymore. She was angry and sent me to the hallway."

"Did you talk back to her?"

"No, Mommy, I thought she would be happy I wasn't part of the devil anymore."

"What?" Kate asked. "Where did you get that idea?"

"From Sister. She told the class that I was part of the devil because all people who are left-handed are, and that we would never write with our right hands because whatever we were born with was what we use all our lives."

"That is unacceptable!" Kate exclaimed. "I am going to call the convent and give her a piece of my mind!"

Kate phoned the convent, and when Sister Marie Bernadette answered the call, she was met with what must have sounded like a defense lawyer's opening statement. "Sister, with all due respect to the habit, I am astonished that you did not applaud Grace for her effort. Instead, you punished her. She worked diligently every night practicing her letters with both hands. It is shameful to tell a child she is part of the devil because she is left-handed. I don't have a sheep for a daughter and that's that!"

Kate hung up the phone before Sister could reply.

"Mommy, why did you say something about sheep?"

"I just meant that you did something on your own and you didn't follow what Sister believed. If you hadn't tried to write with your right hand, then you would be like a sheep who just follows."

It was great to have Kate in her corner. Yet, Grace knew that her mother would not defend her if she did something wrong. That was what Grace loved about Kate—she was fair. From then on, Grace vowed to follow her own ideas. She would refuse to do anything that made her popular or liked by others if she did not think it right for herself.

Things didn't change much with the nuns. Even though she was never late or missed school much, and she didn't disrupt the class, Grace continually flunked self-control throughout elementary school. The nuns saw something in her they didn't like. It may have been the same thing Aunt Amanda didn't like about her. In the end, she decided to keep writing with her left hand in school. Not only did it guarantee her the best seat in the class room, but she could sit with the boys and peer out the window when she wanted.

It was great to sit with the boys in class, but it was even better to sit on her porch and play records with them during the summer. Grace had a portable record player that looked like a small piece of luggage. It played 45 rpm single records. One year, Henry, Aunt Amanda, and Grandmom Rosie chipped in to buy Grace her own record player as a Christmas gift. Kate showed Grace how to plug the portable player into the electrical socket inside the house, then pull the wire through a slight opening in the front screen door.

Most of the neighbors had the same door. They could change the glass for a screen during the warmer weather. The inside door was a different story. Vince had designed and built the inner door so the Marcos had something unique. Henry was so impressed with Vince's carpentry that he suggested to Vince that he should make custom doors for the neighbors. Henry believed that this enterprise would grow into a successful small business. He offered to rent a workshop space for Vince and invest in the initial expenses as well. Henry said they would split the profits. However, in the true nature of her father's resentment of Henry, Vince declined the opportunity.

Grace had many records that were part of the top 100 hits of 1964. Those hot summer days were filled with playing the Beatles, including "I Want to Hold Your Hand" and "She Loves You." Another favorite was "We'll Sing in the Sunshine" by Gale Garnett, and the Supremes song, "Where Did Our Love Go?" Then there was always Grace's favorite, "Under the Boardwalk" by the Drifters.

The mood was upbeat, but there was one song that Grace liked that the boys weren't crazy about. It was "The House of the Rising Sun" by the Animals. She didn't understand the song but she felt an attraction toward the sense of mystery in the song, and the tone of the vocals. Grace liked instrumental music more than songs with lyrics. She had a fondness for orchestral music, both the Classical and Romantic compositions, but she refrained from playing that type of music since the kids preferred pop tunes.

Even though Grace had a sophisticated appreciation for all types of music, she still did not have a love for playing the violin. Instead, she preferred the piano. When she was five years old, Henry bought her a toy piano. She was able to play songs by listening to a song and recreating the melody on the piano keys with her right hand. Grace wasn't able to play the left-handed notes at that time, and she didn't have sheet music either as she played by ear. Grace was eager to learn to read music and play full piano compositions, but Vince didn't give in to what he referred to as a "child's wish." In other words, he didn't want to get stuck with a piano when the novelty wore off. Her father was happy that the music department at school loaned out violins, so the violin is what Grace would play.

Grace practiced the violin but not enough to play well. She didn't like how the strings hurt her fingertips and she had to play scales over and over without playing a song. Most of the time, her violin sounded like an alley cat in heat.

The boys really liked the song "Bread and Butter" by the Newbeats. Grace could never forget the lyrics—*I like Bread and Butter, I like Toast and Jam; that's what my baby feeds me, I'm her loving man. She 'don't' cook mashed potatoes, she 'don't' cook T-bone steaks; don't feed me peanut butter, she knows that I can't take.*

The boys really learned to harmonize with the Beach Boys song, "Barbara Ann." All over South Philly, young men harmonized on street corners. Music was everywhere.

It was a nice break when Kate came out of the house with glasses of water and sometimes homemade lemonade. The boys came by the Marco's house for three summers. They mixed in with the kids on the block. Grace loved climbing the street poles, riding her bike, and roller skating with her ball bearing skates. The kids put the skates on their shoes. There was a leather strap that they buckled at their ankles. The skates came with a skate key, which tightened or loosened the skates. Grace also loved to play stick ball. The kids bought pink pimple balls at the corner store, and they cut them in half and eventually stick ball became half-ball.

It was exciting when the men on the block did roof work. On those days, all the balls that landed on the rooftops were thrown down to the street, and the kids had a whole replenished stash for their stick ball games. Usually at the end of the summer, some of the kids threw their worn-out sneakers on the utility lines. They stayed there for many seasons. Grace never threw her sneakers on the line. When she needed a new pair, Vince cut up her old pair and saved the shoelaces as well. He conserved what other people would consider trash. He was a great sewer. He repaired Grace's stuffed animals by sewing materials he had saved. There was a huge Singer sewing machine in the basement where Vince did his work, and he also had a portable sewing machine for buttons and a quick hem. He provided many services for the kids on the block. He did haircuts and pulled loose teeth by putting a string around a kid's tooth and placing the other end of the string on a doorknob. He pulled the door shut, and in a second, the tooth flew out of the kid's mouth.

One summer when the kids were having a water balloon fight, some of the parents joined in. Kate was cleaning the front bedroom, and she stuck her head out the window when one of the kids threw a balloon at her. She laughed so hard that the kids really enjoyed it. She came down and brought a bucket of water with her. She threw the water from the bucket on a bunch of kids and that had started a whole water fight with other parents joining in on the fun.

The kids loved her mother. This was one thing Kate and Vince had in common more than anything else—they both really loved children. Her father was a major attraction at the bank. He was the security guard at PSFS on Broad and McKean Streets, and he stood by the doorway welcoming customers. He was well-known as the man who spoke many Italian dialects and helped the immigrants with their banking questions. But he was most popular with the children who visited the bank with their parents; Vince always had lollipops for them. Grace often thought that if her parents had more children, they would have been much happier.

Seven

♥

"DON'T STAY AROUND HERE all the time," Kate said while she and Grace were watching *The Late Show* on TV. "You should be out having fun. Take advantage of your youth, Grace. Time passes quickly. This year will fly by, and you will be in high school soon. It's not so hot when you get older, life has many obligations and people get ornery."

"I'm fine with things just as they are, Mom. I have the boys in school and the kids on the block in the summers."

"Soon that will end. After you graduate from eighth grade, you won't see the boys as much. They will go to Bishop Neumann, and you will be in the girls' school. The neighbors' kids won't be as interested in playing games anymore, so I think it is a good idea to find new friends. You should always have many resources; don't become too dependent on any one person or any one group. The more you have in your sphere of friends and acquaintances, the better off you will be. You will have work friends and, perhaps, college buddies in the future. It would be nice to have a fun girlfriend at your age."

Grace remembered a girl in her class who had invited her to parties. Janice lived a block away, and she was nicer than the other girls in the neighborhood. She knew that Janice liked to spend her Saturday afternoons at Murphy's on Oregon Avenue. Some of her classmates liked hanging out there at the lunch counter. Grace planned to go on a Saturday. She could pretend to be there buying something and accidently bump into Janice.

Her plan worked. Soon, they frequented Murphy's together on Saturdays. They had pie and ice cream at the counter. Janice had heard that Steven Baccaro hung out there with some of his buddies. Grace soon realized that was the real reason Janice spent her Saturdays there. Janice was a skinny girl who never finished her pie. She was only there on the look-out for Steven, not dessert.

It was several weeks before Steven showed up. He was with a few boys, and they sat at the counter to order sodas and fries. Janice cast her rod quickly, and soon enough, Steven was hooked.

Grace was not interested in these immature boys who made a lot of noise. They were different from the boys she knew. It was boring to sit at the counter next to Janice, who often had her back to Grace since she was busy flirting with Steven.

One afternoon, a boy sat next to Grace at the counter. He ordered a triple-decker baked ham and cheese sandwich with a chocolate milkshake. Grace turned to see who was seated next to her, and she recognized him—he was the new boy in her class. She had never spoken to him before, and she felt sorry for him when the kids made fun of him. He was grossly overweight. She could see why, he certainly enjoyed food. She decided to speak to him.

"Isn't your name Angelo?" Grace asked politely.

"Yes, and you are Grace. I didn't want to disturb you here with your friends," Angelo responded.

"Friends?" Grace laughed. "I don't know those boys, and I don't want to."

Grace leaned into Angelo, and in a whisper, said, "And this one next to me is Janice. She doesn't even know I am here. She's so enamored with Steven, her new conquest, I kinda don't exist."

They both laughed.

"I know how that feels—to be ignored. Story of my life," Angelo said candidly.

Grace sensed immediately that Angelo was more sophisticated than boys his age and he may have cultivated other interests and talents. This boy could be just what Grace needed. Sure, her mother wanted that she'd find a girlfriend, but that wasn't in the cards for Grace. Janice couldn't cut it.

"Do you think your friend, Janice, is going to finish her pie?" Angelo asked.

"No, she never does. Not once in all the Saturdays we have been here has she ever finished it. She orders it so she can sit at the counter with Steven. Let's sneak it away from her."

They were both giggling as Grace moved the pie onto her own plate, then transferred it onto Angelo's.

"I like you, Grace, you have guts."

Grace had never seen anyone eat with such gusto. She had a feeling that food was Angelo's first love, maybe his only love, and that was comforting. She wouldn't have to fend him off. Grace was not in the market for a boyfriend; a buddy would do fine.

It was a delightful spring day when the boys gathered on Grace's porch to play records. Since their eighth-grade graduation was on the horizon, they wanted to get a jump on the fun before their lives changed. Angelo looked happy. The boys had accepted him since Grace had taken him under her wing. Angelo came around often, and he and Grace sat on the steps and talked for hours. Kate peered out the window when they were together. She watched them with some trepidation.

"You know, Grace," Kate said one day, "Angelo is okay, but what happened to Janice?"

"She dumped me. She is too busy with her boyfriend, Steven."

"Isn't she too young for that?" Kate asked.

"She's a year older than me. You forget, Mom, I was five in first grade."

"I think you spend too much time with Angelo. It is kind to have compassion for the underdogs, but I don't want you to make a habit of it. He has no friends at all, and that worries me. There is something about this boy I don't trust. You may want to think about it. There is a reason why people who have no friends, have no friends. Sooner or later, you will find out why, and you will get hurt."

"Angelo is a good person. The kids make fun of him because he is so fat," Grace responded.

"Yes, that I understand, but I see something else in Angelo. The other boys were trying to include him in things. I saw that the other day. He turned them down, and he was actually quite rude about it. Anyone who has been bullied would jump at the chance to be accepted by the crowd. Be careful with him. He could turn against you."

Graduation was a few weeks away when Janice came back into the picture. Janice thought it would be fun to have a double date; Janice with Steven and Grace with Angelo.

Grace agreed to meet but not as a double date since she and Angelo were just friends. They planned to play Monopoly and make popcorn at Angelo's house. Grace rode her bike to Angelo's neighborhood. He lived in Packer Park, which was on the other side of the Walt Whitman expressway. A tunnel connected Grace's neighborhood to a better part of South Philly. Grace knew the tunnel well; she had been riding her bike through it for years. There were names and sayings written on the walls. Once she rode through the tunnel, there was Packer Park that had hilly driveways at the back of large homes. The homes had lawns with trimmed hedges. There were flowers nestled in window boxes and in the ground bordering the front doorways. On Grace's side of the tunnel, the homes were like the size of matchbooks, and the only green in her part of the world peeked through the cracks of the unending concrete. Angelo's house had the most outstanding landscaping of all the homes in Packer Park. Not surprising since his parents owned a popular florist shop. Angelo knew a lot about flowers and trees. Grace thought he could become a botanist. He was bright, certainly college material.

She pulled up to his house and found the three of them sitting on the steps. Angelo suggested that Grace put her bicycle in his garage.

It was an organized garage with lots of garden tools. Suddenly, as the three of them were walking through the garage and before they reached the kitchen door, Angelo threw Grace's bicycle on the ground and pushed her against the wall. Grace was stunned. She thought that this must be a prank. He then thrust his body on to her. A gardening tool fell off the shelf above her head. Grace stared down at it. Angelo picked it up. It was a three-pronged forged fork. The tips were sharp. She couldn't say anything. Angelo put the fork up to Grace's neck and held it there.

"Come on, strip for us! We know you want to," said Angelo. He pulled Grace's top down, and her small girlish breasts were exposed. She wasn't wearing a bra that day since she was still underdeveloped.

There was no room for embarrassment or shame for Grace. This was violence. In the corner of her eye, she saw Janice bolting away on her bicycle. Grace had to do something. She heard Henry in her ears—"fight or flight?" Grace felt a hot, boiling liquid run through her veins. Her whole being was on fire. With all the strength she could draw upon, Grace chose to fight her assailant.

She pushed Angelo as hard as she could. His obesity hindered him, and he reeled back. "You can't scare me, you jerk!" she yelled.

Angelo fell to the floor of the garage. Steven walked over to him and tried to help him up.

Grace quickly retrieved her bike. "You think I have guts? Well, you were right. You will pay for this," Grace said as she walked her bike out of the garage.

She hopped on her bike and began to ride away. She could see Janice pedaling fast in the distance ahead. Grace rode through Packer Park with her heart beating fast. She almost cried, but she was determined to keep her resilience. Somehow, she would get back at them.

Grace was not going to tell her mother what had happened to her. She would tell no one about this incident and would act as if life was normal.

However, the incident did not stay silent. Grace's name was plastered all over the tunnel in the underpass. Written there was *Grace Marco strips for boys. Grace Marco blows boys.*

It wasn't long before word reached Kate. She walked with Grace to the tunnel to see for herself what was painted on the walls. Her mother was incensed. She questioned Grace about what was plastered on the tunnel wall. Grace said that the girls in class were spreading rumors about her. Grace was not going to reveal to her mother that it was Janice who was spreading the rumors. She didn't want to risk that Kate would find out about the physical assault, but she knew she had to do something about it. Grace couldn't let her mother defend her this time. She didn't want it to fuel into a major incident with parents involved. She had to face this problem herself.

"You know what's strange? You haven't talked about Angelo in a while," her mother said. "I think he may have something to do with these rumors."

"I know, Mom, it could be. He wanted to be my boyfriend, and when I told him I wasn't interested, he became angry and didn't talk to me. It still doesn't mean he is the one who wrote those things on the tunnel wall. Lots of girls don't like me at school. They don't like that the boys hang around our house in the summers. I sit with the boys at school too. It really could be any one of the girls at school," said Grace.

They left the tunnel and went home. Dinner was quiet. Grace knew that her mother wouldn't say a word to her father. Grace had to think about what to do. Finally, an idea surfaced. A few days later, Grace knocked on Janice's door. She could see a light go out when she peered through the window. She knocked again, but there was no answer. She went by Janice's house several times that week, but Janice wasn't there. Grace was not going to give up.

At last, she caught Janice coming out of her house. Janice tried to scurry away from Grace, but Grace stopped her.

"Why did you write those things about me?" she demanded.

"Because you're a cock tease, and all the girls know it. You think you are better than us. You think you are important because the boys like you."

"You know what? You're jealous because Steven wanted to see me strip too," Grace said. "That's why you ran out. You're the one that is easy. They don't need to force you to do anything. They're not interested in you! You see this?" Grace took out a can of spray paint. "I am going to have some fun with this. Now go back in your house and hide, you coward!"

Grace had rummaged through Vince's shelves in their basement and found a can of spray paint. She knew instantly what she would do. It would be a small act of vindication. She walked to the tunnel. She took out the can of paint and sprayed, *Janice blows Angelo in Wanamaker's window.* Then she sprayed over what was written about herself in the tunnel.

There was some satisfaction for Grace that she had confronted the culprit. Yet, she felt guilty that she was keeping a secret from her mother. But Grace thought this whole awful incident could blow up into something major if Kate was involved. She didn't want to let her mother see how she was betrayed. Kate was right—there was something wrong with Angelo. Grace wanted to put this behind her. Someday, she may be able to get back at Angelo and Janice, but that would have to wait.

The harassment didn't end. The girls in school wrote vulgar poems about her. They also excluded her from activities and ridiculed her in the school yard. The worst of it was when Grace did not receive the religion prize. For eight years, she had the highest mark in religion, and it made sense that she was going to receive it. This was an honor the school bestowed to the student who had the highest average in religion over the course of eight years. Sister Angelica gave the prize to the girl who had the second highest grade instead.

It looked like the Ouija was right. She had asked if she was going to win the religion prize years ago, and the pointer was going toward the "yes" when it suddenly stopped. Now she knew why. It really was hers, but it was intercepted by slander.

Kate was seething with anger when she found out that Grace wasn't receiving the religion prize. Nothing could stop her from confronting Sister Angelica. She took Grace by the hand and the two of them marched over to the convent. Sister Angelica answered the door. Her complexion went pale when she saw Kate at the door. Sister looked like someone who was staring down the barrel of a shotgun.

"How could you steal what was rightfully Grace's? Was it because of those horrible rumors?" Kate asked.

"Mrs. Marco, Grace has exhibited bad behavior over the years. It was evident that the boys liked her a little too much. I had pressure from parents."

"Pressure? Who do you answer to? A rumor mill, gossipmongers, or God?" Kate screamed at her. "You don't deserve to wear that habit! Let's go, Grace. Let's get out of here."

When they returned from the convent, Kate told Grace that she shouldn't obsess about trying to fix her reputation. She said that a reputation was like a bag of feathers. If one stood on top of a building and took that bag of feathers and opened it, they would all be swept up in the wind. They would fall far and wide, and there was no chance of ever being able to retrieve all those feathers. That is what a reputation is—it is like a bag of feathers falling where they will with no getting them back.

Graduation came, and they announced another girl's name to receive the religion prize. Sister Angelica wasn't there to see her decision play out. She had a fatal heart attack a week after Kate had confronted her. Sometimes words can cause these things to happen, "they have wings," as Kate would say. Grace knew her mother had a certain talent, but she would never really know if Sister died because of it.

It was a good thing that Kate sat with Grace on school nights to go over her homework or she may have slipped in her grades.

She learned more from her mother than the nuns at school. Grace's attendance was outstanding, and she received honors each year, but her conduct was still judged by the nuns as insubordinate. Grace asked a lot of questions and The Blessed Sacrament order of nuns either did not want to answer questions, or they were unable to answer them. They were like politicians of the Catholic religion.

It may have been a consolation for the loss of her religion prize that Henry gave Grace a wonderful gift for her eighth-grade graduation—he surprised the Marco's with a trip to Atlantic City and planned a week at the Claridge Hotel. He included Vince, but Vince couldn't take that week off from work. Grace suspected that her father made up that excuse because, again, it was an offer from Henry. Why adults held grudges that depleted their own joy, was a mystery.

What a great summer! Grace experienced the shore in a whole new way. The Claridge was an entirely new style of vacationing. The hotel reminded Grace of the Crystal Tea Room back home in John Wanamaker's department store. The Crystal Tea Room was elegant and had an old-world quality about it. There were many Saturdays that she and her mother shopped at Wanamaker's, and they often had lunch there too. The white linen tablecloths and the chandeliers left a lasting impression on Grace. The Claridge Hotel had that similar style.

Aunt Amanda, Henry, and her mother looked like perfect characters in an Edith Wharton novel as did the other guests as well. The hotel had a grand solarium with a roof deck. That is where they took in the sun while they overlooked the beach down below. They could spend a few hours on the beach in the mornings, and then they could enjoy the roof-deck in the afternoons.

It was a civilized experience. Lunch was served in the solarium by waiters wearing white gloves. Grace ordered the tea sandwiches. There was something about the way the watercress peeked out of the triangles that Grace adored. Her iced tea was served in a tall, thin glass with a sprig of mint on top. As they sat having lunch in the solarium, Henry reminisced about the Grand Hotels he had visited, and he promised to give Grace a book illustrating the beautiful architecture of the Grand Hotels of the world. Grace thought of her father and how he despised anything that seemed above the ordinary life of a regular neighborhood. To Vince, it meant that people thought they were better than others when they liked a certain style. Henry had read that "civilization keeps authenticity at bay," and that must be what Vince didn't like about a highly civilized society—it was fake to him. She couldn't help but think if her father could see them eating a delicate lunch in the shady, circular room in the solarium of the Hotel Claridge, he would vomit.

Life was getting better, and it seemed as if a good time would be coming after Grandmom Rosie's death. Maybe if they kept doing new and interesting things, life would heal itself.

Henry and Grace rented bicycles to ride the full length of the Atlantic City boardwalk. Sunny sea mornings that held the scent of clams and mussels always made them hungry, and they stopped to have a bite. These were good days—starting off with a bike ride, then visiting the beach before returning to the hotel, dressing for the solarium, having a civilized lunch, reading a book, and dreaming. These simple things created an air of hope within Grace, and she wondered if somehow that hope had reached her mother. Grace wanted more than anything else that Kate would find happiness, even though Grandmom Rosie was gone.

Some afternoons, they skipped the white glove hotel lunch and ate at Taylor Pork Roll, a cozy place on the boardwalk that served pork roll sandwiches and birch beer. Other days, they strolled over to the Million Dollar Pier for pizza and *zeppoli*. In the evenings, they dressed for dinner and the boardwalk. Grace wore her white-laced gloves and her new summer dresses that her mother bought her at Wanamaker's. They alternated between Hackney's for great fish dinners and the Gem restaurant that had the best cheesecake in the world—that's what it said on their window. Even though she loved the cheesecake, Grace only took a few bites of Henry's because she was excited to have a custard on the boardwalk instead.

Kohr Brothers's soft custard was a special treat. Henry told Grace that the Kohr brothers invented the soft custard. They were from York, PA, and they made fresh ice cream that was delivered door-to-door by a horse-drawn carriage back in 1917. One of the brothers wanted to expand the business, but they had trouble with the large gasoline machine that powered the ice cream. They experimented with the recipe and had to add eggs so the ice cream wouldn't melt too fast. They were delighted with the silky, creamy custard. Their uncle told them to sell these new frozen desserts at the seashore. They first sold their custard at Coney Island in 1919, and since then, the custard was being sold all over the East Coast shore spots.

As they strolled on the boardwalk one night, they were coming out of the Planter's Peanut store when Kate's heel caught in the small crack between the wooden boards.

"Stop, I'm stuck," Kate said.

"I told you to wear your heel guards," said Aunt Amanda.

"I thought I had them in my pocketbook, but it is in my other one. I changed bags."

Henry tried to get Kate's heel out of the crack, but it was wedged in there tight. "Take your shoe off and let me take it out. It is really wedged in here."

Henry tried harder, and finally Kate's shoe came out of the opening in the board.

"Let's take a rolling chair and we can go to Irene's. You can get boardwalk guards there," said Henry.

Irene's souvenir store had plenty of merchandise. It still featured the wooden Dutch shoes that Henry had bought her and the plastic

Eight

K ATE WAVED GOODBYE TO Grace from the window. This was
something she did every school day. On this particular day, at
the end of October, something was wrong. She felt a sharp pain run
through her, but she kept waving in spite of the unbearable pain.

Kate did not want Grace to see that a terrible thing happened in
that instant. Grace was in her first year of high school, and Kate
didn't want to ruin these important years for Grace. She knew this
day would come but she hoped it would be sometime in the future.
She desperately wanted to see Grace enjoying her teenage years and
playing in the orchestra. Maria Goretti High School for girls had an
excellent music department. She wanted to see Grace go to her prom
and then graduate. She also knew that Grace would need her to help
fulfill her dreams of going to college.

After Grace turned the corner, Kate immediately went next door
to tell Shirley about the pain she was having. Shirley, Kate's trusted
confidant and only friend on the block, said that the pain didn't
seem right and that she needed to see a doctor.

Kate sat silently as Shirley scolded her about not going to the
doctor thirteen years before when she started showing signs of
something abnormal with her breasts. Immediately after giving
birth to Grace, a dark substance had stained Kate's bras, and she'd
found her breasts were seeping a thick fluid. She had a follow-up

appointment with her doctor, a routine examination that all women had after childbirth, but once Kate saw the blackness oozing out of her breasts, she canceled her appointment. The only person who knew of this was Shirley, and she was adamant that Kate make another appointment. But Kate was frightened. She opted not to go. Soon after that a lump appeared on her left breast, and she removed it with a black gooey ointment that came in a tube. Black salve was in the Marco's medicine cabinet ever since Grace could remember. It was for warts and moles, but some people thought it could reduce tumors. Kate followed her instinct. She had to raise Grace and give her daughter the most time she could.

Kate gave Grace the accelerated life course. She wanted to teach Grace as much as she could about life just in case her health failed. She was afraid that her time on earth would be short. Kate had two choices—go back to the doctor and have them open her up and hope she wouldn't be dead soon after or ignore it and maybe she could extend her life. Kate believed that once they opened her up, the cancer would spread, so she decided to take the chance of keeping silent.

Thirteen years had passed without a trace of cancer. But now she promised Shirley that this time she would see a doctor.

It was an ordinary fall night in the beginning of November. Grace was sitting on the couch doing homework when her mother returned from the corner grocery store. Kate put the paper bag down on the side table next to the chair by the front door. She took a breath and then matter-of-factly stated, "I went to the doctor's today, and he told me I have cancer. I have breast cancer, an advanced stage. I will need an operation, a double mastectomy. They think I have two years since the cancer probably spread. I don't want you to cry, and I am going to make dinner now."

Kate picked up the bag of groceries and brought it into the kitchen. She placed the bag on the kitchen table and then took off her coat and hat, which she hung in the cellar stairway. Grace watched her stoic mother as she did these things.

Grace couldn't help but think it finally came true—all those nights of watching her mother to see if she was breathing was not some weird obsession. Now, Grace knew that it was real. She felt a tear roll down her face, and her heart was beating loudly in her ears. She felt flushed and stared down at her shoes, just like she had when she was left alone in the church pew when she was four. She was trying hard not to cry. She wanted to run into the kitchen and hug her mother as tight as she could. She would tell her how much she loved her and that she was the best person in the world. Grace wanted to tell her to please stay here on earth so they could be together.

She stayed on the couch instead. Her mother deserved better than a slobbering, selfish daughter. So, Grace wiped her tears and continued to do her homework.

Dinner was quiet. Vince didn't play with the utensils. He did not tell any stories, and he didn't mimic the people he met at his bank job that day. He knew about the cancer.

Kate had a double mastectomy immediately after her diagnosis. She was admitted to Jefferson Hospital where a great cancer surgeon performed the procedure. It was a slow recovery, an arduous one. Grace prayed for her mother at Mass, and she added a nine-week novena as well. She dedicated the novena to her mother's health. She prayed harder than she ever had in her life. She said a daily rosary, and she also prayed to St. Jude, the patron saint of the impossible.

The radiation was killing the cancer, but it caused Kate immeasurable suffering. Grace went with her mother for the radiation treatments for weeks. The scheduled treatments were late in the afternoon so she wouldn't miss school. On those nights after the daily treatments, the nausea hit Kate with a vengeance. Grace would never forget the sound of her mother heaving from the hall bathroom. It was a violent sound, like something emanating from a tortured animal. There was nothing Grace could do but pray that this would soon end. Finally, the day came when Kate had her last radiation treatment, and she began to become herself again.

A few months later, Grace's prayers were answered. Her mother's cheeks regained color, and her hair became thicker. Her appetite was restored, and she had cravings for cherrystone clams. Kate often said that the cure for cancer was in the sea. On Friday nights, Vince worked late, and he stopped by Anthony's on Broad Street for fried oysters. He also brought home mussels from South Philly Bar & Grill on Mercy Street. He brought a big pot with him when he went to the bar for mussels. The staff filled the pot with the best Atlantic wild mussels steaming in a white garlic, red peppery sauce.

Grace adored Friday nights for this feast of fish and a bit of beer. A few sips of Ballantine beer made a good companion to the hot mussel juice and oysters. Her mother beamed with a new sense of appreciation for her favorite foods, and she enjoyed a state of renewed health. They were back to watching late-night movies, and life was the way Grace wanted it again. It was God's will.

Kate's next check-up proved that the cancer had vanished and the dangerous period was over. Grace had her mother and that was the most important thing in the world. She believed she would have her for many years to come.

Kate and Grace did everything together—they shopped the new fashions, they listened to rock and psychedelic music, and they started visiting museums. They were both fully aware that there was a great sorrow in the nation due to many assassinations since President Kennedy. Malcolm X in 1965, then Martin Luther King Jr. and Robert Kennedy both in 1968 were assassinated in a short period of time and the memory of this violence continued to shock the world. Kate did her best to instill in Grace, hope, no matter what was happening in the world and that she should always put her trust in the Lord. She encouraged Grace to eliminate distractions and to concentrate on what was in front of her. And that was what Grace was determined to do. During this time, Grace played in the spring high school musicals. She was in the second violin section and made new acquaintances in the orchestra. The girls were nerds. They had high grades and were good musicians. The other girls in the school were rough around the edges. They cursed a lot and they had boyfriends on their minds. There was some comradery to be found with the nerdy-type girls—at least they had music in common.

However, Grace missed the boys she knew in grade school. They were at Bishop Neumann High School. But Grace was too busy with her schoolwork and the orchestra to care about having close friends. She almost lost her mother, so all she needed was time with Kate.

Two years had passed— it was now the summer of 1969. Grace and her mother liked browsing at Sam Goody's record store. They couldn't wait for the *Soft Parade* album to arrive. That summer a man walked on the moon and the Doors album was released. They were on a journey together and there would be joy along the way.

A snowflake fell upon the windowpane of the hospital room when Kate took her last breath.

Vince was in the hallway while Grace sat in the chair across from her mother's hospital bed. There was a small breathing bag over Kate's nose and mouth. Grace had watched it puff out and draw in for three days. Then, when her mother's last breath drew in, nothing came out. Grace saw what she always feared—her mother stopped breathing. Kate was now still.

Grace walked to the window and watched the snow fall. Kate had said years ago that the day she died it would snow. And it was true—a blizzard paralyzed the city. As Grace looked out at the white-drenched vista, she realized she would face the world alone.

In the weeks that led up to her mother's passing, things deteriorated at a fast pace. Kate lost her last remnant of strength. As she was unable to use the stairs, they had a portable commode set aside the couch. One night, Kate couldn't position herself on to the commode and soiled herself. Grace woke up in the middle of the night to hear Vince yelling at Kate. He was furious that she had ruined the furniture. He told her that she belonged in a nursing home. Grace heard those awful words come out of his mouth, but she did not make a sound or come to her mother's rescue. Instead, she crouched down near the banister petrified of the rage in her father's voice.

A few days before her mother was taken away, Grace was practicing "Somewhere Over the Rainbow" on her violin upstairs in their front bedroom. Kate was lying downstairs on the couch suffering from that ravenous, ugly killer. The cancer that started in her breasts had returned and now metastasized throughout her body. The doctors were correct—Kate had only two years to live since her initial diagnosis.

Grace realized that the song she was playing was indeed her own story. She knew that she would spend the rest of her life trying to find her mother on the other side of the invisible string that connected them. She played with her heart for the first time as tears fell upon the bridge of her violin. Grace had a renewed respect for the instrument now that she was able to finally play it with passion. When the piece was over, Grace went downstairs. She put a smile on her face; she didn't want her mother to see that she had been crying.

Kate, with her weakened voice, said, "That sounded great, Grace. It was beautiful, keep it up."

"I love you, Mommy," Grace said as she leaned down to kiss Kate's cheek.

"Sit here with me for a bit."

Grace sat at the edge of the couch. She tucked her legs under herself and faced her dying mother.

"If anything happens to me, promise me that you will go to school and not wallow in self-pity, Grace. It is time for me to go; I can't tolerate the pain anymore."

"I know, Mommy. I did like you said—I prayed that God would take your suffering away. I know that means I won't see you anymore, but I don't want you to suffer. I will keep your love here with me, and you can take my love with you."

Kate sat silently as she took in the words that Grace had said about love. Then she broke the silence. "I know you will be strong enough to do good things. You will also find love. Don't get too bogged down with people who you cannot trust, Grace. Be careful. I know you are too smart to get involved in drugs but make sure you have fun."

"Will I make it, Mommy?"

Kate laughed. "You will have trouble on the way, but you will land on your feet. I can see you having many interests and trying new things. Don't let anyone influence you. Listen to your own intuition and do what God wants you to do. Don't forget God."

"How will I know what God wants me to do?"

"When you sit in a quiet place and you let all the clutter of your thoughts leave, you must be still. Then listen to your breath and ask the Holy Spirit to come upon you. You may have an answer then or it may take time, but eventually, you will know what to do. There will be signs. God sends us signs, most of them are subtle ones, but we need to be able to recognize them and then to make a choice. Remember, as I've told you many times before—don't follow the crowd. It is all true."

Grace knew what her mother meant. Kate believed in God wholeheartedly and that He sent his son to save his children. That is what she meant by "true." Grace would be left to her own devices in a cruel world. She knew her mother wanted to protect her, but Kate had to go. She had to pass on to a place without pain.

Later that night, Aunt Amanda, Henry, and Vince had coffee with dessert in the dining room. They tried to keep the conversation light, but they all could see they were losing Kate. Grace stayed by her mother in the living room. The silver Christmas tree was turning as the reflector lights changed colors. They had kept the artificial tree from years ago; Vince got his money's worth. There were presents under the tree, not as many as in years past, but Kate made sure that the tradition continued despite her illness.

"We are getting ready to go," said Aunt Amanda as she cleared the table.

"I can hear the wind. You should get going, you two," Kate suggested.

Aunt Amanda and Henry put on their coats and hats. Vince went upstairs. Grace could see that her aunt and Henry were slowly taking their time leaving. Like a closing scene in a movie on *The Late Show*, Aunt Amanda went over and kissed her sister on the forehead. Whatever differences they had between them faded away in that moment. Henry stood by his biggest debater, who was lying there so frail and silently suffering. This was the woman that he admired more than any other woman. He knew this was his final goodbye.

"Goodnight, Kate. We'll see you Christmas Eve," Henry said. Then he turned to exit the house.

The next morning, blood poured from Kate's back where blisters had formed. Shirley came by early. She took off Kate's nightgown and cleaned her ravaged body. As Grace watched the compassionate care that Shirley gave to Kate, she noticed the scapular of the Sacred Heart pinned to her mother's underwear. At that moment, Shirley removed the blood-soaked undergarment. Grace had never seen her mother naked before. Privacy was an important part of growing up in the Marco family. There was modesty about one's body. Grandmom Rosie taught Grace that prudence about one's body was a Cardinal Virtue. Grace was surprised to see red hair on the private part of her mother's body. Kate was a brunette with red highlights; to see such a burst of red was unexpected. Grace thought it was fitting that she saw the place from where she came just as it was going away.

The blood from her mother's back continued to pour out profusely. Vince grabbed more towels and gave them to Shirley. She placed them on the sores that had burst open. Grace cried as she sat there watching the blood seeping out of her mother. It was all over the couch and spreading on to the floor. It was then that she reached for her mother's underwear. She unpinned the scapular and secured it in her hand. Her tears came pouring out at the same time. Grace had promised herself not to cry, but she couldn't hold it in any longer.

She heard the ambulance siren approaching in the distance. It became deafening as it rode up the dead-end street and parked outside. Grace looked out the window and saw the neighbors were gathering around her house. She wouldn't tolerate anyone looking at her mother as she left their home on a stretcher. She realized she needed to do something to thwart the curious onlookers. Grace stood up from the chair next to the couch and walked to the door, where she waited for the men to bring in the stretcher. Then she went out of the house and on to the porch, staring out at the gathered crowd.

"Didn't you ever see a sick person before?" Grace exclaimed. "Please go away. Please, my mother wouldn't want you to see her like this."

She went back into the house—the medics were wrapping Kate in a blanket. They carefully put her mother on the stretcher. When they came back out onto the porch with Kate securely placed on the stretcher, Grace saw that the neighbors were gone. Grace rode in the ambulance with her mother while Vince followed in the good old Dodge. She saw one tear fall from the corner of her mother's eye. Even though they made a pact not to shed any tears, they both cried that day, both aware that their journey on this earth together was ending.

Following Kate's death, Vince and Grace left the hospital and returned home. Grace knew the house would never be the same. It smelled of sorrow and sickness. Vince phoned Aunt Amanda and gave her the news that Kate died at three sixteen that afternoon. To the world, it was an ordinary Monday, a school day, a workday. For Grace, it was the day that changed her life. Now back on Sydenham Street, she and her father would try to exist with each other.

Shirley knocked on the door and invited them for dinner, but they declined. Vince changed his clothes and went to the church hall.

Grace went upstairs to the front bedroom. She opened the closet to look at her mother's belongings. She removed one high heel shoe. It was a taupe-colored ankle strap. Grace hugged the shoe close to her heart. The thought of living with Vince without her mother plagued her mind.

The wake was set for Friday night and the funeral on Saturday. The family funeral parlor where they celebrated the Mummers Parade was holding her mother's body in the basement. They had to wait until Friday since Christmas was that Thursday. Aunt Amanda and Henry came to Sydenham Street on Christmas Eve. There was still plenty of snow on the ground from the blizzard that lasted Monday through Tuesday and there was more snow coming in the forecast. Despite the snow, Henry and Aunt Amanda managed to make it to the house by taking public transportation. The main streets were cleared and the buses and trains were running at a slower pace, but at least they were running. Grace was so happy to see them both. It would have been excruciating to spend Christmas Eve home alone with her father.

There were only a few gifts under the tree. They had agreed that one gift for each other was sufficient this year. Vince gave Grace cash. Grace bought her father a carton of Kent cigarettes. She gave Aunt Amanda a pretty apron and Henry a small reading lamp, as he always complained that Aunt Amanda didn't have a good lamp at her apartment. She pictured him sitting in Grandmom Rosie's oak rocking chair by the light of his new lamp and reading a compelling novel. Aunt Amanda gave Grace a pair of leather gloves. Vince, Henry and Aunt Amanda didn't exchange gifts, so there was only one gift left to open. Grace picked up the heavy box that was sitting under the tree. It was from Henry. She opened the box, removed the tissue paper, and saw there were the three volumes of Marcel Proust's *Remembrance of Things Past*.

"This is perfect, Henry. Thank you so much."

He smiled. "I thought you would enjoy it. Proust can describe a flower for six pages. The translation from French to English is decent."

"Grace, here is something else for you. It's from Mommy," said Aunt Amanda, and she handed Grace what looked to be a jewelry box. "She gave me money and told me to get you a Christmas present. She specifically told me what to get you."

Grace was stunned as she opened the box, for there inside was a silver watch. It was a dainty timepiece with a silver band that clasped shut. In one way, it was wonderful to receive something so precious from her mother, and in another way, Grace was left with the dilemma of not being able to thank her or kiss her.

After they exchanged gifts, they moved into the dining room for the traditional cold cuts, pickles, and beer they ate on Christmas Eve. Kate's potato salad and cookies were missing. Aunt Amanda brought pastries and they had their coffee. They decided not to have Christmas dinner together since they were in mourning and needed to prepare themselves for the wake and funeral service.

Grace managed to go to Christmas Mass. She tried to celebrate the birth of Christ, but she was too heartbroken. Every time Grace glanced at her cherished new watch she saw the seconds moving toward the future. Each second was another one further away from her mother.

The last somber Christmas was back in '63 when Grandmom Rosie had passed in September of that year. Kate was grieving but she'd still managed to keep all the traditions of the holiday. This Christmas was different, the family was falling apart. Kate was the glue that kept them together. They were drifting apart. Grace needed to make sure that Henry would be there no matter what was in store for their future.

Grace rested on Christmas. She wrapped herself in a soft blanket as she curled up on the couch and listened to Christmas music while watching the aluminum tree rotate. Vince spent the day at the church hall.

The next day came too fast. It had snowed again during the night. The small group of people at Kate's wake approached Grace with sympathy. This was in direct contrast to Grandmom Rosie's wake where she was ignored. She was older now, and that gave her the privilege of receiving sorrowful statements and soft embraces. Meanwhile, Grace resented every person there—she resented that they were breathing.

Mass the next morning had few attendees since a blizzard was upon them. The wind had really kicked up, and it was dangerous driving to the cemetery. It was as her mother had predicted—the snow was relentless. Only Grace, Vince, Henry, Aunt Amanda, Shirley, and the priest made it to her mother's gravesite. It was difficult navigating the grounds with the snow blinding them. They stood at the site for a short time before putting their roses on the casket and watching it go into the ground. The howling wind marked the importance of the day. Kate would have loved it.

Nine

T HE NEIGHBORS LOOKED AT Grace as if she had a contagious disease. She was already an outcast in the neighborhood, but she was even more of a stigma now that her mother had died. She was at the mercy of silent stares and whispers. At least she still had Henry. Grace thought that "God does provide," as Grandmom Rosie used to say.

Both Vince, the entertainer, and Henry, the intellectual, finally had something in common—the loss of the woman they loved. Grace realized that Henry truly was in love with her mother. There had been too much passion in his debates with her. Henry had dismissed Aunt Amanda whenever she said something silly and superficial, which was most of the time, but he came alive when he and Kate discussed things political and religious, both topics that were considered taboo in social discourse. They really went at it.

Now that Grace was watching the girls in her neighborhood taunt the boys, and now that the boys were responding, she understood that this was a sexual game being played. It made sense that the only way Henry could touch her mother—a married woman—was to argue with her. It seemed like a fire that had to be contained, and she wondered if that fire was extinguished now that her mother had left the earth.

Henry and Aunt Amanda soon stopped coming to the house every Saturday night. Henry had trouble being in the house where Kate had lived and where they had shared years of conversations and coffee. Those Saturday nights had been transformed into a European café like the ones he had visited in Paris on his travels. Henry said that coffee was the cause of the Enlightenment Age. Many intellectuals and inventors made great progress because they drank caffeine. The coffee houses in Europe were stimulating, fostering new ideas with bright energy, all because of a coffee bean. Without Kate, the Marco coffee café was closed. Henry had to live with the embers of his loss.

Vince dealt with the loss of Kate by spending more of his time at the church hall. He started going there when Kate was first diagnosed with cancer. This was probably his escape of accepting that Kate had the big "C," but it could also be compensation for the loss of his vaudeville career.

Vince had needed to give up a career in the entertainment industry because he had to help take care of his brothers and sister during the Depression. He loved vaudeville and traveled the circuit. But when it was time to sign with a talent agent, the Depression hit, and he was forced to work. The church hall was a place that gave him the opportunity to entertain people again. He was an emcee, and he played the piano during church events. He had a flair when he called out the letters and numbers at the weekly bingo game. Even though these activities made up for his missed opportunity as an entertainer and it continued to help with his loss of Kate, it meant that he had less and less time for Grace.

The church hall had a huge refrigerator filled with food and beer. There was always someone around to share dinner with Vince. They had steaks and great desserts, as many women in the congregation baked pies and there were always leftovers in the refrigerator. Her father also had access to cable television at the hall.

The Marco's neighborhood was one of the first areas to have cable in Philadelphia. As there was a monthly charge for it, there was no way Vince would pay for cable television when he had access to it for free at the church hall. Grace knew not to dream of cable when they still had an old black and white TV at home. She had to adjust the antenna to get a clear picture. Vince had attached aluminum foil on the "rabbit ears" for better reception. Fortunately, Grace's favorite movies were in black and white, so she could wait for cable.

She'd been watching an old classic film one night and while she took a bathroom break during a commercial, she found her father sitting in his bedroom. The only light that existed was a dim one coming from the alley in the back of the house. He looked as if he was in a private torture chamber rather than seated on the edge of his bed. He was staring at a photograph of Kate on the wall. She existed for him in the shadows. Grace knew that her father never understood the woman he married. He had been enamored of her, but that spark inside her that he had adored was what he'd tried to diminish over and over. Maybe he thought if he could have extinguished Kate's spark, there would have been room for her to love him.

On Sundays, Vince and Grace visited Aunt Amanda for dinner in her new apartment. Without Kate and Grandmom Rosie, it was hollow—lacking spirit. No amount of mashed turnips with brown butter could alleviate the grief they felt.

At least Henry tried to mitigate Grace's sorrow by awakening that intellectual curiosity he saw in her. He gave her a list of books to read, and he promised to discuss the themes of the books with her. This helped them both begin to heal their wounds from the loss of Kate.

"There are one hundred books listed here to start," said Henry as he presented Grace with the list after dinner. "These are just some of the classics. Of course, there will be non-fiction books you will read for your studies, and there will always be new best sellers. You can become an expert in your field of study, and you may even write books, but before you do any of that, this is a good place to begin your scholarly pursuits. Many books repeat themes, and they are poorly written. Don't concern yourself with how many books you read, but more importantly, how many quality books you read. It is what values you have learned from reading books that count and, of course, the knowledge of other places and other worlds."

"That's true, Henry. And then there is style. Isn't it the way a story is presented and the writing style that makes people want to hear the same things over and over?"

"Exactly, some say you only need to read the Bible, as all the themes reside there. But it could be boring to only have one account of life without the shadings of many authors. A good author paints a picture for the reader, and you can mentally travel."

Grace looked through the list, and she chose *To Kill a Mockingbird* as the first book to read. She then decided *Pride and Prejudice* was next in line. She had already read *The Great Gatsby*, but *East of Eden* looked like a good candidate to follow. Henry suggested that she read *Tale of Two Cities* and *Les Miserables*.

Grace visited the local library and borrowed the books on Henry's list. She wrote short reports on each of them. Henry read them over and discussed them with Grace on Sunday's when she and Vince visited Aunt Amanda. It appeared as if Aunt Amanda and Vince were irritated when Henry and Grace discussed the reports. Neither of them were interested in literature. But what existed more than disinterest was a tension that was building between them. The only relationship that was fluid was Henry and Grace's. Otherwise, without Kate, it became uncomfortable to be all together.

It was a mystery to Grace how Henry could be compassionate and supportive of her yet, he lacked belief in God. How did he develop his moral character? Maybe he had found a type of moral discipline in classic literature? She was certain he gave credit to the authors, but he couldn't give credit to God.

Grace didn't care that Henry was an atheist, and she certainly wasn't going to waste her time talking about it. He was now the most important person in her life. All she wanted was to have a buddy who knew about the world and could teach her things that she needed to know so she could become a scholar.

Those Sundays at Aunt Amanda's continued without the luster that once had been at Grandmom Rosie's, but Grace was able to find solace focusing on her violin and bathing in the delight of classic literature. She was able to complete the rest of her junior year with excellent grades despite her loss. This was the promise she made to her mother—keep up the grades and do well.

A year had passed since Kate's death. December twenty-second marked the day, and now that it had arrived, Grace knew that even though she made it through the year, she was dreading another Christmas without her mother. It wasn't only because she had sustained a personal loss, either. She noticed a dimming of light in the world around her and wondered when someone's light goes out, could it change the world they left?

For some reason, the men on Sydenham Street stopped decorating the street with the strings of light that made their block glisten during the holiday season. Perhaps it was not a coincidence they stopped this tradition the year after Kate died? She thought that the neighbors could be in sync, and when a death came upon them, they changed inside their hearts too.

It was a tradition for the men to gather together on a Saturday near December fifteenth and spend the day stringing the multi-colored lights along the sides of the brick houses and across the street as well. There was always a huge white star in the middle of the streetlights. The women brought eggnog and cookies to the men while the kids played together. It was particularly disheartening that this Christmas tradition disappeared since Sydenham Street brought joy not only to the neighbors who lived on the block but to others as well.

Many people visited Sydenham Street to see Mr. Cianfrani's exceptional oil painting that appeared each Christmas to honor the nativity. There were other neighborhood streets that strung lights but none of them had a true artist on their block. Mr. Cianfrani was a talented painter who came to America from Italy, and he painted the most beautiful oil painting of Jesus in the manger. It depicted the nativity in its traditional form with the wise men and animals, all of whom were watching the babe while a twinkling star of Bethlehem shone above them. There was a rare beauty expressed in the painting and a reverence that made the onlookers gaze at it with awe. The painting was placed at the end of the dead-end street on the stone wall that was part of the Walt Whitman Expressway. It was huge, and it had a proper spotlight. This captured the true meaning of Christmas.

Antonio Cianfrani was the only father on the block that had his own business. He converted a part of his corner property into a greeting card store. It had cards, gifts, wrapping paper, and some of his artwork was displayed there as well. Grace was fascinated with the store. She pictured Mr. Cianfrani coming to America with nothing but his love for art. He couldn't speak English, and he knew it would be difficult to find employment, but he was able to work on the railroad. He learned English as best he could, enough to be able to give directions to the men laying down the tracks.

The tracks were laid for freight trains that traveled short distances between industrial buildings near the Navy Yard. He saved enough money to buy a corner home that had ample space to convert into a shop. He dreamed of having his own gallery one day, filled with his oil paintings. But he knew that was a long shot, so he looked around to see what was missing in the neighborhood. He decided a card store was a service that the neighbors could use and the store could also double as his art gallery. Most of the neighbors bought their cards and small gifts there but his artwork stayed on the walls. That was to be expected since, Grace rarely saw artwork on the walls of her neighbors' houses. They had pictures of their families and some decorative pieces of seascapes or mountain peaks that they purchased at the five and dime stores. Henry, however, appreciated

Mr. Cianfrani's artwork, and he purchased a small painting of a Tuscan landscape as a gift to the Marco family one Christmas. Vince placed the painting on a wall in the upstairs hallway when it should have been displayed in the living room for all to see. There had been contentious discussions between Kate and Vince about the placement of Henry's gift but it eventually found its permanent home in the hallway upstairs.

Grace greatly adored Mr. Cianfrani's nativity scene, so it was disturbing to see the blank stone wall at the end of her block that first Christmas when the men stopped decorating. Grace never knew the reason why the men suddenly stopped the tradition. She wondered since her father was the leader of the team, and he was a man in mourning, maybe the rest of the men relinquished the tradition. But Grace knew it was more than these small reasons for the changes in the neighborhood. She had a sense that traditions were changing, not only on her street but in the country and the world, both big and small.

The neighbors still decorated their own homes, but the community spirit was gone. Grace still had the spirit to keep the tradition of putting up the Christmas tree, even if it was the artificial silver one that her mother loathed. Grace just needed some twinkle in her life.

Ten

M R. O'HARA SHOWED UP in Grace's life just when she was open to new perspectives and people. Sitting in her Algebra class would have been the last place for intrigue, however, her substitute teacher delivered plenty of it.

Once the announcement was made that their original Algebra teacher was not coming back to school due to an illness, the class assumed that the substitute would be another nun or maybe a lay teacher, a woman, of course. The day Mr. O'Hara walked into the room, the girls were in shock. Never had there been a male teacher on the premises. The only men the girls came in contact with were the janitors, the cafeteria help, and the priests who visited occasionally; these men were far outnumbered as the school housed three thousand girls.

Grace couldn't understand how this man landed in her classroom but she easily accepted his presence in this all girl lack luster environment. She was set to learn variables, solve quadratics, and understand inequalities under his guidance.

It all began when their new male teacher confessed that he didn't know anything about Algebra, but he would try to do his best by following the book with them. His class consisted of a short period of time focusing on Algebraic formulas and then he went straight into topics which included the lost continent of Atlantis and the lesser known continent, Lemuria that was lurking below the Indian Ocean. The Lemurians supposedly had four arms and they were huge hermaphrodites. Grace thought this was interesting since Mr. O'Hara was the tallest man she had ever seen. Could he have time-travelled here from this lost society? Or was he just a basketball player?

The girls were bored with his lectures except for Grace and another student, Jennifer. They instantly hooked into Mr. O'Hara's knowledge of lost continents, Edgar Cayce, and The Rosicrucian order. It had been the writings of Edgar Cayce that Mr. O'Hara discovered the possibility of the continent, Atlantis. But it was Cayce's reputation of predicting future events that fascinated Mr. O'Hara. Edgar Cayce was known as the "sleeping prophet" since he would fall asleep during a trance state. He answered questions pertaining to past-life, dreams, and the after-life. Meanwhile, Cayce believed that his subconscious mind was connected to other minds without the dimension of time. Mr. O'Hara particularly liked that Mr. Cayce was a devout Christian and a Sunday school teacher and his preoccupation with channeling, troubled practitioners of his faith and they branded him a "demon." Could Mr. O'Hara see himself as another Edgar Cayce? Here he was, teaching in a Catholic High School to a group of naïve girls and his curriculum was, certainly, a departure from "x equals y."

Soon Grace started dreaming of Mr. O'Hara every night. Each time she had seen him, he looked as if he existed in another time. She had observed him in her dreams like a voyeur, as she never interacted with him. It wasn't until one day in the cafeteria that Grace discovered that Jennifer, her classmate, was also dreaming of Mr. O'Hara. Jennifer had sat next to Grace since there was an empty seat available. She just made it to the lunch period and luckily there was one place open for her to eat her lunch. Jennifer noticed that Grace had these elaborate doodles on the cover of her notebook.

"Wow, those drawings are familiar to me. They look like symbols I see in my dreams."

"Really? These are things I see in my dreams," said Grace.

"You know, I have been having some pretty weird dreams lately," Jennifer confessed.

"Me, too," Grace responded. "I am also dreaming of the same person every night."

"That's happening to me too. I hope you don't mind me asking, but is it Mr. O'Hara?" Jennifer asked, cautiously.

"Oh, my God, yes!" exclaimed Grace.

"I dream of him every night," said Jennifer. "But we don't talk to each other. He doesn't see me. I just watch him."

"Exactly! What's going on? Do you think he's putting himself in our dreams?"

"Probably, he is into all that stuff, you know, the collective mind thing," said Jennifer.

"I wonder if any of the other girls are having these dreams?"

"Are you kidding? The girls in our class have no interest in what he discusses. It is only you and me, I am sure of it."

"What do you think we should do?"

"I am not sure, Grace, let's think about it."

This unexpected diversion could have the makings of a major distraction for both of the girls. They were two of the best students in their grade level and they needed to stay on track. But how? Who could they tell? They didn't want to get Mr. O'Hara in trouble. She thought of discussing this with Henry but he was still mourning her mother and she didn't want to disturb him. He would have some cognitive explanation for this anyway and Grace knew that this was not something that could be put into Henry's logical basket of cause and effect. Even though it was somewhat scary that she and Jennifer continually had dreams of this peculiar man, she was happy to see that a bond was beginning to form between them—they were becoming sisters of their own order.

Jennifer and Grace compared the details of their dreams and astonishingly they were both having the exact dreams. It took a while but they eventually decided to approach Mr. O'Hara and reveal what was happening and demand an answer. It took many conversations before Grace and Jennifer had enough courage to come forth and show their strength. When they finally revealed what was happening, Mr. O'Hara was not surprised. He said that they were receivers and highly sensitive empaths.

Both Grace and Jennifer started to draw the image of a cross that held a rose in the center of it. They brought their drawings into class and Mr. O'Hara was amazed that the cross was the symbol of the Calgary cross which was associated with the original symbol of the Rosicrucians. He suggested that they read about the Rosicrucian order and even consider joining the modern Esoteric Christian Rosicrucian group. He said it would only mean learning the mysteries of which Christ spoke in Matthew 13:11 and Luke 8:10 and to prepare themselves in the spirit of unselfish service to mankind. They would learn awareness of the inner worlds and the subtle bodies. This could have been above Grace's level of understanding but she had a natural ability to understand the esoteric. Maybe all those debates between Henry and her mother prepared her for this revelation. Jennifer wasn't as keen on joining the Rosicrucian Fellowship as Grace was.

"Grace, I went to the library over the weekend and I did some research on the Rosicrucians. It was pretty dense and there were references to freemasonry. It all seems good and it promotes altruism but I don't think we should get involved with this."

Grace sensed that Jennifer was holding back some information. "What is it? Did you find something about the order that could be, I don't know... sinister?"

"No, it was the image of a man that disturbed me. He looks exactly like Mr. O'Hara. The man was born in 1378 and that year is known as the birth of the "Christian Father." The research mentions that it is a legend that this man who was a German doctor and mystic, was able to spread the knowledge he had learned in the Middle East and gathered a small circle of friends to form the Rosicrucian Order. Look, I photocopied the illustration of "Frater C.R.C.""

Grace studied the drawing and was shocked that the image looked exactly like Mr. O'Hara as Jennifer had said. It was a drawing of a man seated at a desk where he was writing in a large book with a feather pen. The book was leaning on a skull and he had an hourglass to the right of him. There was a glowing pyramid candle in the background and the cross that Jennifer and Grace had been dreaming of was sitting on a shelf high above the room.

"This is extraordinary. Let's keep this to ourselves. I don't think we need to let Mr. O'Hara know about this. What do you think?" asked Grace.

"I agree," responded Jennifer. "Let's concentrate on other things, if we can."

Other things had been comprised of playing music with Jennifer and her sisters. Jennifer was able to borrow her parent's car to bring Grace to and from her home on Second Street. Grace thought she had stepped into the world of "Little Women" when she met Jennifer's sisters and mother. Their father was a sweet, quiet man who lit up around his daughters. Grace could see the love between Jennifer's parents; the house was a refuge for Grace. They were a close family and loved to play their instruments together. Grace brought her violin with her when she visited and it was the first time she played with an ensemble. Jennifer played the piano and one of her sisters played the viola, and the other played the cello. This was a wonderful departure from practicing her violin alone on the school's staircase landing. Who needed the Rosicrucians when she had been invited to this home with these lovely ladies? They made music together for weeks and the closeness Grace felt for Jennifer and her sisters grew with the passing of this peaceful, sweet time.

Mr. O'Hara took a back seat and the dreams of him had faded away until Grace began to dream of numbers. Each time her dream consisted of three numbers. She had wanted to bet the "street number" but she didn't know who was taking the numbers in her neighborhood anymore. She often heard about playing the numbers but it was a rule that minors shouldn't play them. There were three numbers that were associated with the horse races. A number would drop early in the day and the remaining two would drop later in the afternoon. People could play the numbers straight or boxed. Straight rendered more winnings. Without having any connection to a "numbers writer," Grace decided to let Mr. O'Hara know that she was dreaming of these numbers. Whenever she had a strong set of three digits in her head from a dream she remembered, she revealed them to Mr. O'Hara and bingo, he hit, straight, not boxed. He never shared a portion of his winnings with Grace. He said that there was a strong possibility that this kind of betting and sharing money with a student would bring trouble for them with the school authorities. Grace knew better; she knew he just didn't want to share his winnings. He would have been in trouble just for having these conversations with her anyway. But that didn't bother her much; it was more important that she was able to dream of the numbers then it was for her to make money. Jennifer didn't approve of Grace giving Mr. O'Hara these tips from her dreams. She didn't trust this man.

It was getting to the end of the school year and graduation was approaching when Mr. O'Hara introduced the class to his wife, Elyse. She had stopped by the school since she had been shopping on Passyunk Avenue and would be driving him home. She was a pleasant woman with a beautiful French accent. Grace and Jennifer were brought up to the front of the class and asked to remain there while the other students left the classroom. Elyse immediately welcomed them with her charm and insisted that they come to their home. Grace thought this was unusual and not proper that a teacher would have his students in his home. Elyse had said that her husband had spoken of them often and that they were amenable to his teachings. He felt that each of them had special abilities and if they could gather together, they may be able to do important work.

The girls were flattered even though they thought it peculiar that their teacher would bring them into his home. What was this really about? Grace's curiosity led her to accept the invitation. With some negotiating with Jennifer, she was able to convince her that this could be a great experience for both of them.

Jennifer managed to borrow her parents' car the night that she and Grace drove to Mr. O'Hara's house. He and Elyse lived in Media, a popular suburb of Pennsylvania that was known for its affordable living and good schools. The house was a three-story single home on a tree-lined street. It was a dark house filled with dark wood floors and antique furniture. Incense was burning and a pot of tea sat on the coffee table. They sat in the living room and had tea with lemon in the flowered painted tea cups that Elyse had served them.

"This will sooth you and clear any anxiety you are carrying with you," said Elyse in her graceful way.

"You have a lovely home," Jennifer said, politely.

"Thank you. It has served us well," Elyse replied.

At that moment, Mr. O'Hara appeared. He was dressed in a long robe and a pair of leather sandals. Grace could see that Jennifer looked like she was going to run out of the house when she saw that he was wearing the Rose Cross that they both had dreamed of. He was wearing it around his neck.

"I am glad you two made it. We are going to 'channel' tonight," Mr. O'Hara said, enthusiastically.

"Now, Jim, I don't know if that will work. Maybe we can try raising the table first," Elyse suggested.

"She's a bit afraid of my channeling, so let's start off with something small and see if we can raise the table."

"I don't understand, Mr. O'Hara, what has this to do with the Rosicrucian order?" asked Jennifer.

"These are exercises that help tap into a higher level of being. We invited you here because the two of you have the capacity to enhance the exercises."

"See, Jim and I have been practicing many of the ancient ways of the Rosicrucians. When he was offered the position at your high school, we knew that there was a reason for it. We want to form a group, much like the one our Christian Father had formed many centuries ago. We hope to form a group of disciples in order to maneuver in this world doing good works and helping others."

"Let's begin. Now finish your tea and come with me into the dining room," said Mr. O'Hara.

They entered the dining room and positioned themselves around a mahogany round table. There was a candle in the center that Elyse lit. They sat quietly with their hands placed on the table with their palms down. The only sound that broke the silence came from the mantle clock above the fireplace. The Westminster chimes reminded Grace of Grandmom Rosie's clock she had on her mantle in the house on Victoria Street. Once the clock stopped, the candle began to flicker. The table slowly started to rock from side to side. Grace looked at Jennifer; she looked like she was going to faint. Then the table slowly began to rise. Elyse took the candle off the table and held it. They removed their hands from the table as it rose a foot above the floor, hovered there, and then it crashed back down; it made an angry sound. When the event seemed to be over, each of them could see that Mr. O'Hara was in a trance. Grace remembered that Jennifer's research revealed that when the Christian Father was in his trancelike state, people would ask him questions.

"Are you the Christian Father?" asked Grace.

"*Ja,*" replied, Mr. O'Hara who was probably channeling the founder of the Rosicrucian order.

"What is it you want us to do?" asked Elyse.

"*Gruppe gründen,*" answered the spirit.

"What does that mean?" asked Grace.

"It is German for 'form a group,' I believe. My German may be a little rusty. My father was German, and my mother who is still alive is French and my French is much better," Elyse responded.

"What do you want us to do?" asked Grace.

"*Blockiere den bösen Geist.*"

"Block the bad spirit," said Elyse.

Mr. O' Hara stopped speaking. He sat in a trancelike state with his eyes fixed and his lips tight. Then, he opened his mouth wide and a deep, guttural cry filled the room. It sounded like it was coming from the depths of hell. Jennifer was shaken and ran out of the room. Grace sat still. She closed her eyes and prayed to the Blessed Mother to protect them. She envisioned Mary with her foot on the head of the serpent. The harsh sound had stopped and Mr. O'Hara was back. The spirit left.

"What happened?" he asked.

"It seemed like you channeled the spirit of the Christian Father and he had a message for us to form a group and to block a bad spirit," explained Elyse.

"And then a presence was here, a horrible sound came from you. I prayed to the Virgin Mary and it stopped," said Grace.

Mr. O'Hara looked about the room as if he just woke from a deep slumber.

"Where's Jennifer?" he asked.

"I'll go find her," said Elyse.

"I don't think this is a good idea, Mr. O'Hara. You should stay away from this channeling thing," Grace said as Elyse left the room.

"I did get close this time. You see, I want to find the spirit of the Christian Father. I thought if I could gather together a group of empaths, it would help me find him. But it was a mistake. Something else interrupted the channeling. I think it is because of you, your presence ignited something dark. I want you to leave my home," demanded Mr. O'Hara.

Grace was speechless. He had turned on her in a split second. She left Mr. O'Hara at the round table and she proceeded to the front porch where Elyse and Jennifer were sitting on a swing.

"Come on, Jennifer. Time to go. Thank you, Elyse, for an interesting evening."

That was it. The event was over. Jennifer and Grace left the house and drove home. After that night, Grace wasn't invited to Jennifer's anymore. No more playing instruments with the family of sisters. Jennifer had wanted nothing to do with Grace and Mr. O'Hara wanted nothing to do with the girls.

Right back where she had started, thought Grace—people disappeared. She was beginning to think that it wasn't in the cards for her to have a friend. The one constant in her world was Henry.

Spring arrived and it was the day of the Baccalaureate Mass for the girls graduating high school. The Mass was celebrated at the Cathedral Basilica of Saints Peter and Paul, the mother church of the Archdiocese of Philadelphia. It was a special Mass for the girls and their mothers.

Grace was the only one who didn't have a mother, but it was an outstanding day despite not being able to share it with Kate. She was asked to play a solo violin piece at the Mass. This was something that Grace never dreamed could transpire since she was such a poor violinist. She did manage to move up to the violin first section, fourth chair, but she still did not think that a solo was in her ability level. Moving the bow across the strings, Grace let the notes fill the Cathedral, rising up to a place where her mother could hear them. If she never played the violin again, it didn't matter—she now possessed the honor of playing this solo piece at this memorable event.

When the ceremony ended, Grace exited the Cathedral to find Henry and Aunt Amanda. While looking for them, one of the students approached her.

"Your solo was very touching. I love "Ave Maria,"" said a dark-haired girl who wore the school uniform with a red ribbon sash across it.

Grace recognized the girl as one of the student council representatives at her high school. "Thanks," she replied. "I've been practicing a lot."

"I remember seeing you in the school yard back when we were in elementary school. You always had the newest fashions, you wore the first mini skirt and I remember the day you were being made fun of—you had on a mod black and white vinyl raincoat with a vinyl jockey hat and that fancy umbrella. You even had gloves that were black with white vinyl stripes."

Grace laughed. "I couldn't wait until it rained to wear that outfit."

"I'm Diana, you know you look like Angelique from *Dark Shadows*."

"Really? I love Angelique, and that's my favorite TV show."

At that moment, Henry rushed to Grace, and Diana walked away. Grace didn't have a chance to say anything more to the girl, but she waved goodbye to her.

"What a beautiful ceremony that was, Grace," Henry uttered. "What made it more meaningful was your personal tribute to your mother."

"Yes, I finally hit the notes right," Grace said trying to interject some levity.

They planned to have lunch at the Melrose diner where they were meeting Vince who worked nearby. They walked to the car and drove back to the heart of South Philly.

"Park over there, Henry. It will be better," Grace directed him as he looked for a space outside the diner.

Vince stood outside the entrance. He wasn't able to take the day off from work but he could join them for a lunch celebration.

"The Mass was beautiful, Vince. I wish you could have been there," said Aunt Amanda.

"Grace played with such passion, you would have been proud," Henry added.

"She did practice a lot," Vince said as he opened the door to the diner. "We have to get in before it gets too crowded."

The Melrose diner had circular booths that strangers shared. Each side of a booth sat three people comfortably. Sometimes four people squished together on a side. People lined up in the aisle next to the tables and stared a hole through the people occupying the tables. People were discouraged to linger at their tables once they finished their meals. The Melrose was a diversion for her father since he liked to have lunch at the five and dime store counter a few doors down from the bank where he worked. He ate *pie a la mode* for lunch every day. Grace bet Henry a nickel that Vince would order creamed chipped beef on toast and lemon meringue pie for dessert. Henry agreed that chipped beef would be Vince's choice as well, but the dessert would be the buttercream cake, the most famous dessert at the Melrose. Grace won; the meringue it was.

It was the first time they went to a restaurant without Kate. It was awkward. Grace tried to keep the conversation going. She hoped that Henry would take over with some historical reference to the diner itself or what Passyunk Avenue was like when he was young. Instead, it was Aunt Amanda who dominated the conversation at the table. She chattered on and on about cakes and icings and how Lintons had better pound cake, but it was true that the Melrose had the better buttercream. Then she compared Horn and Hardart's pies to the Melrose and declared Horn and Hardart the winner.

As Aunt Amanda went through a list of bakeries and how they compared to the dessert menu at the diner, Grace couldn't help but drift back to the thought of how she was going to get through the daily things in life. She looked at the people around her. They were going about their day as they usually did. They didn't know that her mother had died. How could life go on as if nothing happened when the best person in her world was no longer on earth? Grace gazed out the window and watched the cars stopping and starting with the lights turning yellow, red, and green. Everyone was adhering to the order of things. How boring and mechanical it all seemed. Grace realized her extraordinary day had ended when she played the last note of the "Ave Maria." They say that you can hear the universe, that the sound waves create songs in space, and Grace wished that her mother had heard her song.

Graduation was approaching in a month, held soon after the Mass at the Cathedral. Subsequently, there was a lot of talk about college or jobs. But only half of the girls in Grace's graduating class would be looking for jobs, as some of the girls would be getting engaged immediately after graduation. Grace's guess was that a small percentage would pursue college. Henry offered to pay her college tuition, but Vince refused. Her father's philosophy was that girls waste space in college.

Jobs didn't interest Grace. The only consolation she had was that Henry was there for her after graduation, and he would serve as her own private mentor— an intellectual she would have all to herself. He would help her find a decent job that suited her while she continued to study under his tutelage.

That summer, Grace was losing interest in attending Mass. The priests were uninspiring. She wasn't as strong in her faith as her mother was. She couldn't understand how Kate believed in a religion that failed her. Grace knew that her mother must have prayed for things in her life, yet she had lived with a man she did not love; she suffered the loss of her mother, her sister, and Father Brice; and then she had to tolerate excruciating pain from terminal cancer, all while she went to daily Mass. Meanwhile, Henry lived a calm life of reading and rational thinking. He had no bad habits, and he was smart with his money. The fact that he had no faith in God didn't ruin any part of his life. Grace could choose a scholarly path and forget the religious one if she wanted to. With Henry's guidance, she may even become a college professor.

Eleven

"**W**E'RE MOVING TO SUN City, Arizona," Aunt Amanda said as she served the pot roast.

Grace, Vince, and Henry were seated at the table for their traditional Sunday dinner. Shock went through Grace's body like a fiery arrow. "Arizona?" she asked.

"Yes, we have been thinking about moving for a while, but we didn't want to say anything until it was definite," Henry said.

Henry was not for shame or guilt, two unnecessary emotions that seemed a waste of time to him. He believed in stating the facts with no harm intended.

"It is a nice retirement town, and we will have our own house. We need to leave Philadelphia. The city has an element in it that we don't appreciate, and we want to live the last part of our lives in a safe, sunny place," said Aunt Amanda.

An incident had happened outside the house Henry shared with his sister. Two youths attacked him on a cold night that past February. They knocked him down and took off with his wallet. It really shook Henry. Henry and Aunt Amanda didn't discuss it much, so Grace had no idea that this was the impetus for their plans to move to Arizona. It all seemed a bit sneaky to Grace. She thought if her mother was alive, Kate would have disapproved of them moving across the country.

Grace knew that her aunt didn't care about Grace being left with Vince. Aunt Amanda was a survivor, and she only cared about keeping her life smooth and even. She lacked the depth and character Kate had possessed, and Sun City was a perfect, sanitized place she craved. The thing that hurt Grace was how her best buddy, Henry, chose to leave her.

Questions swirled around in Grace's head. What about their reading club? How was he going to teach her to play chess? Why did he need to move across the country to a desert land without the ocean nearby and no humidity? Why let a couple of thugs shade his decision? He didn't get hurt much, and besides, they could move to the suburbs of Philly to avoid that type of crime.

"It is for the best that we do this. It is affordable, and we need to think about how much money we have so that we can retire. It is too expensive here in the Northeast, and you wouldn't want us to be in financial trouble," Henry offered in their defense.

Grace didn't say a word. She was trying hard to hide her devastation at the news.

"You know what's funny?" said Aunt Amanda. "We need to be married to purchase the house. It is a rule of living in this retirement community."

Grace felt her strength returning. She could hear her mother saying— *be careful, don't put your eggs in one basket.* So, with a fake smile, Grace said, "It's okay, Henry. We will write, and I can come visit. It will be part of my traveling life. But 'Uncle Henry' I will never get used to."

They were set to move a month after her graduation. When Grace arrived home that night, she cried into her pillow. That day, Vince didn't say a word when Henry and Aunt Amanda revealed their plans. But on the way home in the car, he did have one thing to say and that was, "How do you like your trusted mentor now?"

The day that Henry and Aunt Amanda were going to the airport, they stopped by the house on Sydenham Street. Henry took out a large book from his attaché case. It was the book on the Grand

Hotels he had promised to give her. Henry looked troubled as he handed it to her. Again, Grace held back her tears. She knew that Henry wasn't leaving only because he was attacked by some street thugs. It had to be that the loss of her mother was too difficult for him and he needed a new horizon in his life. But why did he need to go so far?

She kissed Aunt Amanda and Henry goodbye and watched them leave in the taxi. Vince had offered to drive them to the airport, but Henry declined the offer. She watched the cab pull out of the dead-end street and turn the corner.

Grace felt like she was living in a museum. The house on Sydenham Street was stuck in a time capsule. Playing music helped break the silence. She listened to Ravel's "Pavane for a Dead Princess" over and over again. She played it along with Beethoven, Chopin, and Debussy. She wanted to hear beautiful music without lyrics, yet words came to her as she listened to the Ravel piece. She jotted them down on paper—*Now that you have gone, oh my dearest, I can't linger on, oh my Princess, you are gone, and I can live no more. My beauty is sleeping gently now among the sweet and all the pure, so well loved. Children, they are still playing. Why then can't I find you to play? I know my heart is breaking. I love you so, dear, now and forever, always. My life is so cold here without you. Oh, the winter snow tells a story, and it knows I am calling your name.*

Night after night Grace endured her loneliness in the glow of candlelight and the sound of beautiful music. The only bit of life outside of her solitude was when she joined Shirley's family for dinner. It was nice to sit at a table with a family, even if it wasn't her own. It was much better than eating American cheese and tomato sandwiches at home alone. Shirley did her best to make Grace feel wanted, and Grace was grateful for the food on her plate.

Many days, Grace sat with Shirley for hours as they watched soap operas. In between the melodrama, Shirley reminisced about Kate during the commercial breaks. Grace learned that Shirley was particularly grateful for Kate's guidance in terms of her religious struggles. Shirley lived on a severely limited income since her husband had been injured in a machine accident. They had four children, two boys and two girls. The girls were Grace's buddies until the day they played with the Ouija board. Shirley couldn't imagine bringing a fifth child into the world. They were barely getting by on her husband's measly salary; he worked at a pen factory.

Shirley was afraid that if she became pregnant, she'd be in more trouble than she could possibly bear. Shirley asked Kate for advice. Kate understood Shirley's dilemma, and she guided Shirley to take natural precaution and not to have relations with her husband when she was most fertile. They called it "the rhythm method." It was the Catholic way. Sometimes, it didn't work, but that was God's will, and if Shirley did have a fifth child, then they would need to accept it and pray that God would provide. Shirley followed Kate's advice and there was no fifth child. Grace was glad the rhythm method worked, otherwise there would be no time for her.

Grace began to feel like something was growing inside her, some latent power and a big curiosity. She embraced the darkness at night. As a result, the day was ordinary, the night extraordinary. She found herself gazing into a flickering candle each night and sensed a rising power within her soul. She knew there was a way to harness things, things she could will into being, and by focusing on the candle, she could make things happen.

Grace decided to do some research. She traveled to the main library on Benjamin Franklin Parkway. She inquired at the information desk where she may find books on parapsychology. An older man approached her from a corner of the room. She wasn't sure if he worked there, but in no time, she realized he was just a visitor. He brought her to a section of the library where they found information on candle gazing and other things related to divination. He also showed her a book of incantations. He suggested that she should familiarize herself with telekinesis, astral projection, crystal gazing, clairvoyance, premonitions, prophetic dreams, and automatic handwriting. Grace found a new excitement that there was so much to learn. She made several trips to the library, and each time she looked for the old man who helped her on that first visit, but she only saw him one more time.

Grace spotted him in the main reading room crouched in a corner. She started to walk toward him. When he looked up, Grace noticed his eyes. They were like black holes. She then looked down at his feet—he was wearing ugly orthopedic shoes. It crossed her mind that there was something unnatural about the man. She couldn't understand why she hadn't noticed these features when she first met him. Again, she had to discard the idea that he had anything to do with the story of Father Brice. The devil could disguise himself. She felt a shiver run down her spine. He had been so close to her when he helped her to find those books that first day she met him. Could she have been that close to a demon?

Then, Grace remembered how once something comes into her awareness, she will start seeing those things more. If someone says something about a blue sports car, all of a sudden, she will see blue sports cars everywhere. Since her mother had told her that Father Brice said the devil had ugly feet, anytime she saw men with ugly feet, Grace suspected that these men could be the devil's disciples.

Lonely souls spent their days in places like libraries and churches. This man was probably one of them, not the devil. But what Grace didn't know was when she left the library, the man was right behind her all the way when she walked to the bus stop, while she was riding on the bus, and her walk home as well. He was directly behind her until she reached her front door, then he vanished.

Not long after spotting the man at the library, Grace started to change her appearance. She wore black eye liner in a way that extended her natural eyelid, with small points flicking out the corners of her eyes. She also wore her hair like Angelique on *Dark Shadows* and only wore black, even down to her underwear. This new identity began forming with her new sense of power. All she needed now was a friend, someone interested in similar things— someone she could trust.

It was a Sunday afternoon when the doorbell rang. Grace couldn't imagine who it could be since she never had visitors. When she opened the door, there was Diana, the girl she'd met on the steps of the Cathedral on the day of the Baccalaureate Mass. Diana handed Grace a brown paper bag.

"I brought you a meatball sandwich," she said. "My mother makes them every Sunday, and I thought you may like it."

"Wow, that was nice of you," Grace said, and she motioned for Diana to come inside the house.

"I looked for you on the C bus, but I didn't see you. I thought it may be all right to stop by and bring you something, and this was the best thing I could think of."

"Come on in. I have iced tea if you want."

"Yeah, that would be great."

Grace opened the paper bag and took out a nicely wrapped sandwich. It smelled great. This was exactly what she needed. Only Shirley knew that she didn't have much to eat at home. Grace took a plate from the cabinet and placed the sandwich on it and then cut it in half. She then took two glasses from the cabinet and poured the iced tea.

"Oh my God, this is the best meatball sandwich I've ever had," Grace said after taking a bite of the sandwich.

"I'm glad you like it. You know how people are about meatballs in South Philly."

"True. My mother couldn't believe how important gravy and meatballs were to the Italians in the neighborhood. Each family thinks they have the best. But I do have to say these are the best!"

"And my mother is Irish."

"You mean of Irish descent? My mother was of Irish descent too."

"Really? By the way, I am so sorry. I heard you lost your mom last year."

"She died a year and a half ago, a few days before Christmas. She was a great person, and I'm not saying that because she was my mother. People respected her. Now it's only me. My father is at the church hall all the time, and my mother's sister, Aunt Amanda, and her companion, Henry, recently married to move into a house in Sun City, Arizona. It's some kind of law out there. So, basically, I am on my own."

"What about friends or cousins?"

Grace shook her head. "I wasn't close to my father's side of the family, and there was only my Aunt Amanda on my mother's side. As far as friends go, I've been burned, and to tell you the truth, I was too heartbroken that I lost my mother to care about having friends. I did have my mentor, Henry until he moved to Arizona with my Aunt Amanda. Since they recently married I should refer to him as "Uncle Henry"—no, that just doesn't sound right! He's Henry to me and that's that."

"I know how you were burned by friends," said Diana. "I heard all the rumors. Those girls can be cruel. I didn't believe any of it."

"Thanks, I appreciate it."

"I have a sister and two brothers," Diana said. "My sister is a brainiac, and my two brothers are terrific athletes. Somehow, I am lost in the shuffle. I am the oldest, and I don't have anything going for me."

"Don't say that. Things can change. Life takes many turns—you may end up being the most successful of the bunch."

"I doubt it. You know, my mother had polio when she was a kid," Diana revealed. "She doesn't go out much because of it. She is deformed—her upper back curves over as a result of the disease. It's a small hump that she covers up as best as she can."

"I'm sorry. Make sure you show her how much you love her. She doesn't need to be perfect. Life without your mother is dreadful."

Diana conveniently changed the subject. "You wanna watch TV or something?"

"Okay, let's find a movie," Grace responded.

They found a classic movie to watch and adjusted the antenna before curling up on each end of the couch. Grace felt like her life was changing for the better.

Grace was ecstatic; she finally had a good friend.

A week later, Diana came by Grace's. "Here, these are for you," Diana said as she handed the wrapped present to Grace.

"Oh my God, Diana, these are great. It's the Rider deck—perfect!"

"Like *Dark Shadows*. Oh, and you know you shouldn't buy the tarot cards for yourself, don't you? Someone needs to buy them for you," Diana said with pride.

"Let's do a reading! You will be my first to have a card reading by Madame Grace."

They both giggled as they went into the kitchen. Grace opened the box of cards and removed the tiny booklet from the box. She flipped through the instructions and acquainted herself with the Celtic Cross layout. The deck had the traditional playing cards with four suits, but it had additional cards, the Major Arcana, which had significant meanings.

She chose the Page of Pentacles to represent Diana. Pages were younger than Queens, and the Page of Pentacles looked similar to Diana with her dark hair. Diana had shiny dark brown hair, almost black. Her skin was smooth, her features dainty. She had perfect white teeth and pretty rose-colored lips. Diana's grandfather was from Naples, and her mother's family came to America in the late 1800's from Ireland. Lots of kids in the neighborhood had grandparents who were from Naples, but not as many had the Irish blood running through their veins. Grace thought that maybe that's why they were destined to align together in these supernatural endeavors—the bit of the Irish.

Grace placed the Page of Pentacles card on the kitchen table, and she had the urge to place a lit candle on the table as well. She had a feeling that the element of fire would enhance the reading. Grace remembered the candlesticks that were in the dining room china closet. They had belonged to Grandmom Rosie. Grace retrieved one of the candlesticks that still held a tall, unscented candle. She placed it on the table and took the cards out of the box, reverently. Grace then asked Diana to shuffle the cards and separate the deck into two stacks using her left hand. Grace didn't read this in the book, she was following her own intuition.

Grace put the stacks together and drew a card, placing it on top of the Page of Pentacles. This card represented what was influencing a person's life in the present. The Six of Swords was drawn, which meant transition or moving on and leaving behind. Then Grace drew the next card and placed it horizontally across the Six of Swords. This card represented the challenge in a person's life that could impede the influence of the first card. This card was from the Major Arcana, Temperance, and it was upside down. Grace thought that if the card was upside down that would mean intemperance or excess.

Grace drew the third card and placed it below the two crossed cards. The Four of Wands was drawn, and this position represented the basis of what was influencing Diana at this stage of her life. Grace referred to the booklet to see what this card meant. It signified home conflicts and a lack of support. The next card to be placed was positioned to the left of the first two cards that designated the past. Here was another of the Major Arcana, the High Priestess. The card was in a reversed position. Grace checked in the book to find the meaning; it was referred to as a lost inner voice, a lack of center, and a desire for connection.

Grace was getting the impression that Diana had a lot of hidden wounds in her life that were serious enough to generate these negative cards in her reading. When the fifth card was placed above the center cards, Grace felt relief when it was a positive one. This card position illustrated the goal, or the path that should be taken to render a good outcome. She had drawn the Page of Wands, meaning a sense of exploration, freedom, and excitement.

The sixth card was placed on the right side of the center cards, and it represented the near future, which turned out to be another Major Arcana—the Fool. This card predicted that Diana would be jumping into new beginnings with a certain naiveté. The next card was placed at the bottom of a four-card stack and to the right of the layout. This seventh card revealed who Diana was becoming. The card in this position was the Page of Swords, which meant curiosity, restlessness, and mental energy.

The eighth card signified the outer environment. The card drawn here was the Devil, which meant addiction, mischief, and deception. Grace didn't like this card and felt uncomfortable that it was part of Diana's reading, but it was the outer environment that was surrounding Diana. She also told herself it wasn't as bad as if the Devil had been in the seventh position, representing who Diana was becoming.

The ninth card described hopes and fears, and she drew the Tower. There was a frightening image on this card. the Tower meant disaster, upheaval, and broken pride. The tenth and last card predicted that the outcome would be the Sun—the end result would be bright and sunny, a sense of contentment. Grace could justify all the other negative cards as long as the outcome was a good one.

When Grace placed this last card on the table, her father opened the front door. He came into the dining room and put his hat on top of the china closet before looking into the kitchen. He saw Grace and Diana enveloped in the glimmer of candlelight and the mysterious cards displayed on the table. He looked at them inquisitively but didn't acknowledge that anything was askew. Instead, he said what he routinely said every weeknight, "Six o'clock rolls around pretty early." Then he went upstairs to bed.

"So, what do you think the cards mean?" asked Diana.

"In a nutshell, I think it means that you are not appreciated at home, that you have some hidden feelings, but you are now reaching out to explore new things. Your curiosity is a good thing provided you don't get carried away. It seems that you will be influenced by outside forces that will lead you down a negative path. You will experience some form of what could be considered a disaster, but in the end, you will be happy, and your future is bright and sunny."

"When will this all happen?"

"Who knows?"

"What do you mean?"

"Let's see how the future plays out, and we will know the timeline then."

"You are so good at this, Grace. When you were reading, I could see that you had your own meaning of some of the cards, and that somehow, you understood them better than some ordinary card reader who had memorized the whole book. But there was something else that was going on while you were doing the reading. There was a scent in the air. It smelled of something familiar, but I didn't know where it was coming from, and as soon as your father opened the door, the scent disappeared. And another thing that was really freaky was that your eyes became like glass."

"You know, my mother said when I was twelve my eyes changed from blue to green overnight."

"Weird. You should have seen them tonight. They are back to normal now, well, normal for you since they are an unusual green, anyway. You do have beautiful eyes. My father said that about you when I told my parents I was hanging out with you."

"Really? I don't think people notice me that much," Grace said.

"Are you kidding? You know that people are afraid of you, right?"

"Get out of here!"

"I think it would be fun to really scare them," said Diana, enthusiastically.

"Let's just start with the cards," Grace said. "We should have a card reading business."

From that night, Grace and Diana became great partners. They were destined to be together. Grace was the seer and Diana promoted her. Diana spread the word that Grace was doing tarot readings. They came up with a price of five dollars for a general reading, and if there were any additional specific questions, they would charge another seven dollars per question. They started with the kids on the block, and some of the mothers liked having their cards read too.

One neighbor had a sick relative. Grace said the sickness would disappear and another healthy relative would die instead. That was it. When the reading manifested just as Grace predicted, the whole neighborhood believed that she could tell the future. It circulated around the neighborhood that Grace was a great card reader, and many women in the neighborhood set up reading nights in their homes. Grace limited herself to five people per night since she found out that any more than five zapped her energy, especially if they asked specific questions.

Expanding the tarot card reading business was of upmost importance, but they needed transportation. It was already July, and Vince hadn't given Grace a graduation present. Many of the girls in her class were getting their first cars. That was a stretch for Vince, and besides, she needed to learn how to drive first. Diana suggested that Grace ask her father for a new bicycle. Grace had stopped riding her old second-hand bike years ago soon after the horrible incident with Angelo in his garage. In order for Grace to get a new bike she needed to ask her father for a car. Diana would get one too, and they could both ride around the city together. Somehow, she needed to make it look like it was her father's idea to secure the deal.

Vince bought all of Grace's bikes at Gerace's Bike Shop, the most popular shop in South Philly. Her father always bought used bikes. Her first one was bright red, and she learned to ride it in one lesson without training wheels. All the kids on the block had shiny new bikes, but Grace had this used red bike that they liked best.

She was four years old when she rode her first two-wheeler, and a few years later she started to teach other kids how to ride their bikes. Kate held her breath when she watched Grace from the screen door perform tricks on her bike. Sometimes, Grace played chicken with the cars on Pollack Street, but that one her mother didn't know about. Grace's favorite thing to do was to ride toward the dead-end wall at the end of the street. Just as it seemed like she would crash into it, she put on the brakes at the very last second.

Grace waited until she found a good time to approach her father about getting a new bike. She sat in Shirley's living room for a few afternoons and watched soap operas. As she sat there, she had an eye on her front porch. Shirley was rooting for Grace to get a new bike, so she kept the front door open to see when Vince would come home from work. They knew he would be in a hurry to go to the church hall, so it would be an opportune time to corner him. Finally, one day Grace summoned the courage to approach him. Grace gingerly walked out the door to deliver her request. The only thing separating them was the concrete half-wall that designated Shirley's porch from the Marco's porch.

"Dad, Shirley and I were just talking, and we think I should get my permit to learn to drive. It doesn't mean I need my own car, but I could drive yours once in a while. It is good to know how to drive in case of emergencies.

"Where do you think you're going? Everything you need is right here. The C bus takes you anywhere you need to go. You have peanuts in your head."

"There are plenty of places I want to go that the bus doesn't take me. I have girlfriends who live at Seventh and Fitzwater, and there is no direct route there. And you know I could shop at the 9th Street market. I could buy all those fresh vegetables from the street vendors and I could go to DiBruno Brothers and Claudio's cheese shop. Even Fante's for kitchen stuff and I can go to Esposito's for pork."

"Forget a car, we can go over to Gerace's and get you a bike instead."

Her plan had worked. Vince thought it was his idea. And all that stuff about shopping on 9th Street was totally made up, she didn't even know how to cook. Grace went back into Shirley's with a big, fat smile on her face.

Grace was the proud owner of a black ten-speed Raleigh racer. It took a bit of maneuvering at the bike shop to get a new one since her father kept eyeing the used ones. Fortunately, the salesperson wanted to upgrade her father to the new Raleigh. He worked on Vince and managed to persuade him that he should go with the new bike. Grace remained silent throughout the whole transaction, because she learned a long time ago that if she showed any desire for something, her father nipped it in the bud.

Diana's parents bought a folding bike for Diana a few days later. It was the cutest thing and fast too. Grace and Diana had their means of transportation; now all they needed to do was establish their card reading business on the street corners in South Philly.

Grace had already read the cards for their neighborhood street corner at Sixteenth and Pollack; the next one was Tenth and Bigler. Neither Diana nor Grace knew any of these corner loungers. They rode up to them, and Diana asked if anyone wanted a card reading. She told them that Grace was a great card reader and she could prove it. Often it was one of the girls who complied. She always started off with something from the person's past. That's how she captivated them. After that, they believed whatever she told them about their futures. She also stopped reading if she wasn't getting anything. This made Grace more authentic in their eyes. Once she hooked the first person, then the rest followed, and Diana collected five bucks from each one who opted for a general reading. They didn't offer specific questions on their corner rounds; they saved those for indoor home readings where Grace had more time. Grace was getting better the more she read, and she knew when to stop before she became exhausted.

Since it was summertime, Diana had an idea to expand the card reading business to Atlantic City, as the vacationers would be there. Diana and Grace took the bus from the Philly Greyhound bus terminal to Atlantic City and were up and back on Saturdays. The boardwalk had many gypsies who read palms and cards. They were con artists but lots of people still went into those small establishments to get suckered. Grace was the real thing. She did the readings on the beach and moved around from blanket to blanket. Diana asked the sunbathers if they would like their cards read by a famous reader from Philly. When the beachgoers saw a young Grace in her black one-piece bathing suit with her wild hair and stunning green eyes, they seemed a bit startled. They probably expected some old, hairy gypsy woman who had a shop on the boardwalk and a mustache.

Grace wore a black ribbon around her neck with a silver pentagram pinned to it. She kept her cards in a black, fringed suede satchel. She delved into her card reading mode and knocked the readings out fast. It seemed that Grace received messages quickly that were like flashes of light in her mind. She'd blurt out the information and stunned her customers.

It was the hottest beach day that summer when an old, eccentric man appeared out of nowhere and approached Grace. He wore a black suit and dress shoes. He handed Grace a card with the name and address of an occult book shop. He said he had an opportunity that would make her famous. Before Grace could say anything, he turned and walked off the beach. Both Grace and Diana thought the man was strange, especially that he didn't have on beach attire; he looked like a quirky minister ready to give a sermon. Grace put the card in her satchel before heading over to Million Dollar pier where Grace and Diana spent some of their profits on pizza, and then they stopped by Mac Fries for crispy fries with vinegar. The two of them were thrilled with the tarot business. It gave them the opportunity to explore new places, and more importantly, to develop a great friendship. At times, Grace saw in Diana a happiness that longed to emerge. Grace felt partly responsible for Diana's new attitude. She was glad that she took the chance to have a friend after the awful treatment she'd received from the girls at school.

Diana and Grace enjoyed exploring Philadelphia on their bikes, aside from using them to travel for the tarot reading business. They loved riding on Broad Street, the main street in Philadelphia, where William Penn towered over the streets from City Hall. This was the tallest building in the city due to an old gentleman's agreement. Henry said that someday there would be much taller buildings once the city authorities approved a building that could exceed the top of William Penn's hat.

The statue was installed in 1894 and was designed by Alexander Milne Calder. Grace knew all about the statue since she chose it as a topic for one of her history papers in high school. William Penn was an English writer and a religious thinker who lived in the late seventeenth and early eighteenth centuries. Under his direction, he developed Pennsylvania. The city streets are numbered, and others are named after trees since Pennsylvania means Penn's Woods. William Penn believed in democracy and was a champion for religious freedom. He had been imprisoned in the Tower of London several times due to his faith. Penn wrote about a union of all the English colonies in what became the Unites States of America years later.

The cobblestone streets and the colonial style homes in Society Hill were Diana and Grace's favorite part of the city. They discovered courtyards, narrow alleyways, old churches, and cemeteries. They loved exploring the country's history while riding around at night. This was far better than a history class at school. They rode by Independence Hall, Congress Hall, The Liberty Bell, Carpenter's Hall, and the Presidential House. They sat outside these historical sites and visualized what it must have been like to live in those days. Sometimes, they would venture to Old City, where they viewed Philosophical Hall, Old City Hall, Christ Church Burial Ground, and Elfreth's Alley. Grace felt compelled to conjure up old souls in the burial grounds they toured. Nothing materialized, but she was sure that there were spirits who were still roaming around these parts of the city and made a note to try and find them at a later time.

Delaware Avenue was the hardest street for a smooth bike ride but Grace and Diana occasionally navigated the cobble stones and the railroad tracks so they could buy either a cherry or lemon "water ice." There were mostly old men who sold their homemade ices on the streets in Philly, but no one knew when the men would be at their locations. The only one that was certain to be there was the friendly, Italian man on Delaware Avenue. They had to arrive before sundown to guarantee they would catch him before he left. It was exciting to see his two silver barrels coming into their view as they bounced on their bikes due to the rough terrain. It was a rare occasion that Grace would opt for the cherry, she couldn't resist the bits of lemon in the lemon ice. Eventually, the "water ice" business grew and South Philly had an explosion of Italian families who opened a portion of their homes to sell the ices and then they added flavors and soft pretzels.

Riding around Philadelphia gave Grace and Diana a glimpse of what the city was like back in its colonial days and they witnessed how the city was growing as well. But for Grace, nothing beat South Philly. She could see why her father loved it. It was filled with close neighborhoods, great food, music and dance, singers that emulated Frankie Avalon and Bobby Rydell, and the actor James Darren. Grace thought it was funny that the city of Brotherly Love, had an edge, a type of humor, a sarcasm unique to its residents and South Philly had an extra layer, a toughness and that was exactly what Grace loved about it. It was tough, but it was friendly too.

One night when they rode near Edgar Allan Poe's National Historical Site on North 7th Street in the Spring Garden area of Philly, Grace convinced Diana that they needed to stay there until midnight. They parked their bikes and sat on the steps in front of what used to be one of the homes where the poet had lived. There was a raven statue on top of the black fence adjacent to the brick house.

"Do you know 'The Raven,' the poem Poe wrote?" Grace asked.

"I read it a few years ago in English class but I don't remember it," Diana responded.

"I love the whole poem, but it is the second stanza that I memorized. Do you want to hear it?"

"Yes, I would love to hear it," said Diana.

"Okay, here are the words that resonated with me, I will try my best to remember them," Grace said and then she began reciting—- *Ah, distinctly I remember it was in the bleak December; and each separate dying ember wrought its ghost upon the floor. Eagerly I wished the morrow—vainly I had sought to borrow from my books surcease of sorrow—sorrow for the lost Lenore—for the rare and radiant maiden whom the angels name Lenore—for the rare and radiant maiden whom the angels name Lenore—nameless here for evermore.*

Diana stood and said, "Oh, my God, Grace! This is just like the way you remember your mother."

"True, and she died in December," Grace added. "I too, have an 'evermore.'"

Twelve

♥

GRACE BOUGHT A CRYSTAL ball at the occult store on South Street. It was the end of that summer after graduation and soon, Diana would be going back to school and Grace would search for a job. She was not looking forward to working at some boring job. It was a possibility that if she developed more of her interest in the occult, she could avoid being ordinary in a dead-end job. The store had more books about witchcraft than the main Philadelphia Library. Grace chose a book of incantations and spells, and Diana bought another set of cards.

"Who are the cards for?" Grace asked.

"I thought I'd get them for my sister. After you read her cards and things came true, she wanted to learn how to read them on her own," Diana explained.

They walked to the front counter.

"Ah, welcome to my shop, I am glad you accepted my invitation," said the mysterious man they'd met on the beach.

"I kept your card," said Grace.

"You will notice that we have a wonderful display of all things that can interest a person with your gift. Please let me show you what we have here."

He ushered them over to a table with an array of crystal balls of numerous sizes. Grace focused on each of them until she came to one where she saw the word "swing" that appeared within the ball itself.

"I'll take this one," Grace said to the owner of the shop.

"Did you see something in the crystal?" he asked.

"How did you know that? I saw the word 'swing.'"

"You are a receiver; you are receiving messages that are linked in the eleventh dimension. It has something to do with string theory. There are devices that assist you in tapping into the parallel universe. The word flashes in your brain, and when you focus on the crystal, the word or the image will project into the ball. It is about energy and the power to harness it. I knew you had this ability, more so than just reading cards. We are in need of someone like you to lead the group so that we can develop our intuitive powers. We could accomplish great things if you join us."

"Is it a group of psychics?"

"Some are, but mostly we are wiccans, and we are in need of a High Priestess."

"I don't know much about wiccans, but I would love to learn more about them," Grace said as she moved toward the counter to pay for her crystal and her book of spells.

"Diana, give me your sister's cards. I'll pay for them out of our profits."

At that moment, when Grace reached for cash in her satchel, she noticed the old man's long, yellow fingernails. He had returned to the cash register behind the counter. A large cockroach ran across his hand and down the side of the glass counter. He didn't flinch. She felt an instant heaving in her stomach. Grace paid for her items and gathered them trying not to show her disgust. She began to move to the exit. She turned back and said to the old man, "This sounds like something I would love to do. I will get in touch soon. C'mon, Diana, we will be late."

Grace tried to remain calm as she urged Diana out of the unholy place.

"Oh my God," Grace said once outside the store. "He was the scariest man ever. Did you see his fingernails? They looked like a demon's."

"No, I didn't see them, but if you think he is bad, then we will stay away," Diana answered.

"Bad doesn't describe it," Grace said.

Grace and Diana couldn't wait to get back to Sydenham Street. They hopped on their bikes and rode down Broad Street "like bats out of hell" as Grandmom Rosie used to say.

When they returned, Vince was getting home from his job at the bank. He mentioned that one of the women on Sydenham Street said they had openings at Blue Cross and Blue Shield. It was the end of August, and Grace knew that she'd better get her act together and start looking for a job. She loathed the thought of a job search. Reading the classified ads made her feel completely useless. She took the academic track in high school. She must have been dreaming. She should have taken the secretarial course, she thought. Grace knew her father would not support the idea of her going to college, so she applied for the job.

Grace got the job. All she had to do was agree to a training program, where she would get paid to remove nineteen-year-olds from their parents' health insurance; she could buy time to find something more exciting.

The best thing about working for Blue Cross and Blue Shield was the coffee cart that made its rounds to the departments in the morning. Grace had her first cup of coffee at that office. She opted to have it with cream and sugar—what they called "regular." She ate the doughnuts each day since she skipped breakfast at home. Not wanting to work at this place made her late many mornings. It was difficult for her to get up early, especially since she spent her nights reading cards and putting spells on people.

The first spells she cast were on Angelo and Janice. She'd vowed that someday she would get back at them.

Grace and Diana sat in the kitchen with the candle flickering. Grace recited a general incantation that called upon spirits to help formulate the specific spell she would cast upon her victims.

"I am not sure what would be fitting for Angelo," Grace said.

"Let me think. After what you told me he did to you in his garage, I think maybe you should do something, like make him impotent? Diana suggested.

"No, that doesn't work for me. Too obvious. It needs to be something else, something that is unique to him."

"What does he do? What does he want?"

"Well, I know he loves food," Grace answered.

"How can you take away his food?"

"Not take it away," Grace said. "Wait—I got it! We can keep his desire for food but take away his sense of taste and smell."

"That's perfect, Grace. You think it will work?"

"If we put our wills together and conjure the spirits of the dead, we can do it. He attacked me. It would have been rape if I hadn't fought him off."

"What about Janice?" Diana asked.

"I told you that even though Angelo did a violent thing, I think what Janice did is equally terrible—to leave me there, then to spread rumors about me. And I lost the religion prize! I think I need to do something to her, something that is symbolic of gossip."

"Could we put a spell on someone who would spread rumors about her?" Diana asked.

"No, I think it needs to be something else, something that would drive her nuts. You know, I remember in those old movies when people revealed secrets or gossiped, they would say, 'they sang like a canary.' What if before Janice goes to sleep, she hears a canary singing and she can't fall asleep?"

"That's good, and what if sometimes there are lots of canaries flying around her?" said Diana, delighted at the prospect of having lots of birds flying around Janice.

"Yes, I like that too. We can try both. What we need now is something of theirs so we can burn the objects that they touched. You get out that big ashtray in the breakfront while I go search for things of Angelo's and Janice's."

Grace had a stack of books on the desk in the middle bedroom. The bedroom was supposed to be hers but that hadn't happened since she slept in the front bedroom with her mother. They used the small bedroom for storage. Grace kept her books and records in the room. She found a pressed rose that Angelo gave her. She had placed it in the *Norton Anthology of Poetry*— a gift from Henry.

Grace thought how Henry would disapprove of her involvement with the occult. In their letters, Grace never mentioned any of these practices. She only let him know she had a good friend, Diana, and that they explored the city on their bikes. Henry's letters were boring. He only described his swimming routines, the desert sun, and cacti. It was a good thing Grace was occupied with her new endeavors and that she had a new, important person in her life.

Grace removed the rose from the book. This would be perfect for Angelo's spell. Angelo gave her the flower the first time she invited him to play records on her porch. She looked around the desk and found a graduation party invitation that Janice had given her. When she returned to the kitchen, Diana had placed the ashtray in the middle of the table. Grace tore a piece of Janice's invitation and placed it in the ashtray. She lit the invite with the candle, and as it burned, she conjured up what she was going to say and uttered, "May all the spirits of the dead who are around me, and all the power I have within me, and all the power that Diana, my sister has within her, in this deed, together, we cast a spell on Janice, the slanderous one who caused me pain. We cast a spell that she will find no rest when she needs it the most. We envision the canary, the symbol of joy, the sun, and blessings but also represents someone who gossips, to sing a song as Janice drifts off to sleep. She will awaken to the song, and at times, she will see many of these singing canaries. I put this spell upon Janice until the time I see fit to remove it."

Grace then took the flower and placed it in the ashtray. "With the placement of this rose in this vessel of conjuring, abruptly eliminate the sense of taste and smell that Angelo, the evil one, possesses in order that he may not enjoy his food or drink. His desire will remain but it will not be satisfied. This spell that I have cast along with the spirits of darkness and here with my sister, Diana, will remain on him until I see fit for the spell to be removed."

After a moment, Diana asked, "How will we know if it worked?"

"The spell belongs to us; we will know because the news of it will travel to us."

They packed up the evidence of the spells and they both slept well that night.

Diana was back in school, and she wanted to find new customers for the card reading business. She ran into Annamarie in the school hall. Annamarie was a popular girl who had a click of girls that swarmed around her. She was the queen bee. But this queen bee was very boyish; she wore a pinky ring like the men in the neighborhood wore. She also had a strut when she walked. The whole group of girls that surrounded Annamarie were all boyish. They drove around in Annamarie's red Mustang, or in an Impala, that was driven by one of the other girls. They were all dark-haired girls, small in frame, and they smoked Marlboro cigarettes. They never wore dresses or skirts other than their school uniforms. Four of the girls were Geminis who were born in June. Another two were born under the sign of Gemini as well but their birthdays were at the end of May. It seemed more than a coincidence that six girls, all with dark hair, all in the same grade in the same high school, and all Geminis, were all friends.

Diana arranged a reading night at Annamarie's house. Grace read Annamarie's mother's cards without charge as part of the deal. There was sorrow in the woman's cards. Grace touched on this sadness, but she was gentle about it and instilled hope that things would work out after a time of disappointment. Grace knew the distress revolved around the woman's daughter, Annamarie.

Grace moved on to reading the girls' cards. But as she read each of their cards, she developed a dull headache and a feeling of exhaustion overwhelmed her. After the fourth reading, Grace stopped and promised to continue the readings on another night. They scheduled the next night at Annamarie's. The following night, Grace was in good form. She noticed that the readings of the night before, and the three that were left on this night, all had the same card in their layouts—the Devil, except for Annamarie's mother. Grace noticed something else that was strange about these girls; they each had the darkest, black eyes similar to the man she met at the library. Something was up with these girls. Grace couldn't put her finger on it, but she was afraid for Diana.

Diana began to spend more time with these girls and Grace joined them occasionally. Grace nicknamed the girls, "the Gemini girls." They drove around the city and sometimes they ventured to Fairmount Park, New Hope, and Doylestown. It was wonderful to explore places outside the city. Bucks County towns were quaint; they had small shops that sold arts and crafts. Grace felt a vibration in New Hope that had a supernatural presence. The town had a weird influence on Diana; she wandered away from the group. When she rejoined them, she looked slightly off-balance and had a vacant look in her eyes. It was the first time Grace sensed that something peculiar was happening to Diana.

The Gemini girls had their own unique way in how they dressed and how they spoke. Grace finally put it together that the girls were lesbians. It felt like she was hanging around with safe boys. Grace didn't want to get involved with boys sexually. She didn't go to the prom, and she had no intention of getting serious with a boy. She had plenty of time for that later, because for Grace, developing her gift of divination and exploring new places had enough to hold her interest.

Diana was different from Grace in that respect. She longed for something more. The Gemini girls liked to experiment with drugs, especially "downers." They scored these pills when they rode around in their cars; Tumenols and Quaaludes were their favorites. Grace didn't dare ingest one pill. There were other teens who liked smoking marijuana. Meth was another drug that was prevalent, but that attracted the boys more. There was a guy, a "meth head," in the neighborhood who was hanging with a group of buddies, and they rented a motel room. They trashed the room and left by dawn, only he remained. He restored everything that they had destroyed and he reconstructed all of the damage, even the TV—what a waste of time, Grace thought.

Heroin seemed to attract the older crowd. Grace saw a thirty-year-old man, sticking a needle into his arm in broad daylight at Marconi Plaza. Acid was around but that was more limited to special occasions. Grace heard of people taking bad LSD trips who could be mentally scarred for the rest of their lives. The pills seemed the least harmful, and they were cheap and easy to find.

Diana lost interest in finding new customers for their card reading business as she spent more and more time with the Gemini girls. She rode her bike less and became secretive. During this time Diana changed her hair into a shag. She used to have plain, long hair with a part in the middle; now she had bangs and her hair fell just below her chin. She looked like a boy rock star. Throughout the fall and winter, it became apparent that Diana's drug use was escalating. She began to slur and stumble. She disappeared for hours and then showed up at Grace's late at night. When they sat at the kitchen table, she often nodded off and Grace had to help her to the couch where Diana fell into a drug induced sleep. The signs were evident, especially when Diana found NyQuil in Grace's medicine cabinet and drank the whole bottle. Grace was losing a part of her friend each day. When the spring came, Grace spent more time with the Gemini girls so she could watch over Diana. It was a growing trend for teenagers to drive their cars to the Philadelphia Art Museum. There were beautiful grounds that nestled alongside the Schuylkill River. Along the river was Boathouse row. The boathouses on the side of the river were situated near the Art Museum and the old Waterworks. They were lit at night, and lots of cars parked on the street where couples steamed up the windows—a lover's lane. In the daytime, the paths along the grounds attracted runners and cyclists, but at night, the whole area transformed into a place for teenagers to hang out.

The Gemini girls parked their cars at the back of the art museum where they met more girls who had parked their motorcycles. Then a carload of other girls showed up. They were the prettiest girls Grace had ever seen. Suddenly, a convertible Mercedes coupe came speeding by and made its way to the spot where everyone was gathered. A beautiful young woman with a head of blonde curls parked her car and with her gorgeous hair bouncing in the night air, she walked over to the crowd.

She singled out Annamarie and placed a passionate kiss on her lips; Annamarie melted. Grace couldn't take her eyes off her; she had a magnetic quality. She was older than the teenagers and had a sophisticated style. She wore a beige straight-skirt with a silk blouse and a pair of classic beige pumps.

"That's Camila Whitmore," Diana said. "She's from Bryn Mawr and is a hair stylist at Bonwit Teller's in Center City. She's a famous fag hag. The gay guys adore her."

"How do you know about her?" Grace asked.

"Annamarie and the girls talk about her a lot. They met her at a club, The Mystique."

Grace studied Camila Whitmore. She didn't seem to fit with any of the groups at the Art Museum. She was too feminine to be one of the Gemini girls and she was not silly enough to be part of the carload of pretty girls. The motorcycle gang was way out of her league. She exuded confidence and wasn't part of any group. That sparked a desire in Grace to emulate Camila.

Suddenly, a petite red-haired girl approached Diana. Grace could see something ignite inside Diana when she looked at the girl.

"Light me," the girl said.

Diana took a lighter out of her jean's pocket and lit the girl's cigarette, then she lit her own. Diana held her cigarette like the Gemini girls did. They placed them between their thumbs and forefingers and cupped the cigarette like the guys in South Philly and the men in the movies. Grace didn't know that Diana had started smoking. The night was full of surprises.

"You wanna take a walk down to the boathouses?" asked the cute girl with the short, red hair.

"You wanna go, Grace?" Diana asked.

"No, it's too dark over there. I want to stay here. I'll stay with Annamarie and the others."

"Don't worry," said the red-haired girl, "I won't bite."

"It's not me I am worried about," Grace responded.

Diana went down the path with the girl toward the boathouses.

Grace lost interest in hanging out any longer since Camila had left but she had to wait for the girls who were having a good time. The mood was disrupted as soon as a group of guys circled the Geminis and started to taunt them, yelling, "Get out of here, you dykes! Go somewhere else."

"Get away from my girlfriend, you freak!" screamed one of the guys as he ran over to a Gemini girl who was flirting with one of the pretty girls. He pulled the girl by her hair and threw her into the carload of guys. He threatened the Geminis with a promise that he would mess them up if they were caught with her again. Grace distanced herself as soon as she smelled trouble. She recognized the guys as spoiled brats from Packer Park—they liked their meth and bullying people. As they drove away, Grace ran after them and yelled, "I hope you get in an accident!"

Diana finally came back to the group. She had missed the drama. There was a touch of white stuff on the corner of her mouth. The red head had it on her mouth too. Diana said goodbye to her friend, and Grace, Diana, and the girls piled into their cars to drive back to South Philly.

Grace and Diana sat in the back seat of Annamarie's Mustang and one of the other Gemini girls sat up front in the passenger seat.

As they were on their way home, Annamarie asked, "So, Diana, that's your girlfriend?"

"Yeah, June's my girlfriend," Diana answered, managing to pull the words out of her cotton mouth.

Grace sat quietly in the car. She knew something had changed in Diana. She knew about the drugs but she didn't realize that Diana liked girls. Diana was now slumped in the seat with her chin on her chest. It was heartbreaking to see Diana like this—this was a sign of real trouble. She couldn't understand why anyone wanted to be knocked out like that. She thought that drugs were supposed to make a person feel good.

"Look over there, to the right," Annamarie said. "It's an accident. Wait, it's those creeps from the art museum."

Sure enough, Grace saw that there on Broad Street were the guys who had harassed them earlier that night.

"Well, I guess that taught them; we have our own witch on our side," said Annamarie as she looked at Grace through the rearview mirror. "No need to worry about them anymore."

Grace was shocked at her own ability. She knew that anger motivated energy as she had read about it in many of the books on paranormal activities. This meant her power was increasing.

The girls stopped at Pat's Cheesesteaks. They ate the steaks in the cars. Diana's fell on the floor, and she had fried onions hanging out of her mouth. Grace lost her appetite. She picked up Diana's food from the car floor and threw it, along with her own sandwich, in the trash can that was a few yards from the parked car.

Annamarie dropped off Diana and the other Gemini girl at their homes. Grace moved up to the passenger seat. When they reached Grace's house, Annamarie and Grace sat outside for a while.

"I see that you guys are able to do pills without getting sloppy but Diana gets really wasted," Grace said.

"I know," Annamarie replied. "She can't handle it. I don't know if it's a physical thing or if there is something about Diana—something emotional, you know?"

"Maybe. And who is that June person?"

"She met her at the Mystique."

"The Mystique? That club where Camila Whitmore goes?

"Yep, it is a club that has a lot of us as members. It's a private club. There are some gay guys there, too, but they like going to the other club, Steps. Steps is more for the boys, less women in there."

"You know I never went to a club. God, another secret that Diana kept. She never told me about the club. How did she get in?"

"We all have fake ID cards. I gave her one a while ago. You know, I could get you one, too, and we could all go to Harlows. You would love it there. It's mixed—straight and gay. Harlow is the hostess, and she used to be a 'he.' She's gorgeous. I will get you an ID."

"Great."

Grace hesitated to get out of the car. She was enjoying this quiet time with Annamarie. It was then that Annamarie leaned in and kissed Grace on the lips. It was a soft, slow kiss. Grace could feel heat race through her veins. This must be the feeling the pills gave the Geminis. No wonder Diana was hooked.

"Phew. I knew you would be too hard to resist. Now, get out of here, you witch," Annamarie said.

As Grace settled into bed and covered herself with her blanket, she remembered the first kiss she had shared with the dark mysterious boy at the Claridge hotel. She hadn't kissed anyone since then and was way behind in the regular stuff of teenagers. Her path was different. She wasn't looking for an intimate relationship with a boy and certainly not with a girl. Yet Annamarie had stirred up something inside her. Grace put that in the back of her mind. She had to concern herself with what was happening to Diana.

Diana's tarot reading entered her thoughts. Grace remembered the Six of Swords, which meant transition and a sense of leaving something behind. There had also been home conflicts, loss of self-control, and then there had been the Devil—addiction, deception, and the Tower, which meant disaster. It was all coming true. Diana had changed from the sweet student council girl to a nodding-off drug addict. There was hope, though, since the last card in the deck was the Sun.

Maybe if Grace uncovered what was in Diana's past, she could figure out how to help her. The past card was the High Priestess. This card reminded Grace of the owner of the occult shop who wanted her to be a High Priestess. She knew there was no significance between the card in Diana's reading and the offer for Grace to be a High Priestess. But it led her to think about how her own life was unfolding. Henry was now rooted in his retirement community having dinner parties and swimming in his pool. Vince was watching cable and stuffing his face with steak. Aunt Amanda was taking trips with her lady friends and playing slot machines in casinos, and her mother had passed away, deceased, dead, gone. Now, her friend, Diana, was falling into a deep hole away from Grace.

Grace started to drift off into a much-needed slumber when she heard a rustling sound. It was coming from the closet. Grace remained still. She heard it again, and then a strong scent permeated the room. This was the same scent that enveloped the bedroom when she and her mother had played the telepathy game. She pulled the covers over her head. She was afraid something was going to come out of the closet. Could it be the little man she used to see in her dreams when she was a little girl? Many times, Grace dreamed of a three-foot man that wore a top hat and gloves. He looked like a magician. He had a white shirt with a bow tie. His exaggerated lips were bright red and his poker straight hair was painted black. Grace was seated in the living room chair to the right of the front door. In the dream, she felt trapped—she was frozen in place. She was compelled to look up to the top of the stairs. There he was, his burning eyes staring down at her. Grace kept trying to move. If only she could reach the front door and run out of the house. Then suddenly, the devilish creature flew down the stairs at a rapid speed and just as he reached the bottom step, Grace would wake from the dream. Was this recurring dream a sign that this man would finally reach her and take her away with him? Grace stayed hiding under the covers, frozen with fear when the sound began to diminish and the scent dissipated. She'd lost her protection now that her mother was gone: she wanted desperately to reach her. She fell asleep with her hand stretched out into the empty space.

A week had passed and Grace had her fake ID. The Gemini girls came by the house to take her to Harlow's club; Diana was nowhere to be found. One of the girls gave her the fake license as Grace hoped in the back seat of Annamarie's car. The whole time they drove to the club, Annamarie didn't look at Grace, not for one second.

Harlow's club was on Bank Street, a cobblestoned alley-like passageway that was filled with what Grace imagined had secrets and vestiges of intrigue from centuries ago. The club had a fire escape above the dark entrance and exit doors. Harlow's club glistened. It reminded Grace of a 1920s speakeasy. Harlow, the hostess who used to be Richard, brought glamour to the place. She won beauty pageants and was a model in New York. She always looked perfect. The effort Harlow took to present herself to the world must have been exhausting. Grace thought Harlow must have dreamed of looking like a breathtaking movie star as far back as when she was a young boy. Harlow's was a refuge. Here in Old City, Grace could express herself in a creative way. She had a lot in common with Harlow. They were both from South Philly, and they had both reinvented themselves.

Kate would have loved this place, thought Grace. It was festive and fun. It seemed similar to the places her mother described when she was having fun in her twenties. She and a group of her good friends had the best times at clubs in the Pocono Mountains. Kate had gay friends, but back in her day, a gay person had to hide their desire for someone of the same sex. Her mother was happiest when she reminisced about those days dancing at the clubs.

It was risky to get into the club, but as long as Grace had her ID and looked fashionable, it was clear she would have no trouble getting in. It was like a fantasyland where revelers were celebrating the grand things in life—nothing dull or boring.

Soon, she had new friends. Grace was surrounded by beautiful men who adored her. This was perfect for her—no attachments and no exchanging of body fluids. The nights were all about the music and the dancing.

Wednesday and Thursday nights were the best times to go to the club. Camila, the girl with the Mercedes, was there every Wednesday. Camila dressed beautifully, and she had a charm that was coquettish and flirty that seduced both men and women. Camila made people feel like they were lucky if she paid attention to them. And Grace was surprised to learn that as soon as she became more creative in her fashion choices, people began to treat her like they treated Camila.

Grace began dressing in eras. She frequented thrift shops and found great dresses, hats, and shoes. The days of looking like Angelique from *Dark Shadows* were over; she now was inspired by Bette Davis, Carole Lombard, and most importantly, Garbo. The gay guys loved her. She was a walking retrospective in film.

Grace had read Harlow's cards, and from then on, she had free drinks, but she only drank club soda with lime as she needed to keep a clear head. Grace had promised her mother that she wouldn't do drugs, but drinking could be bad too. She would wait until she was older to cultivate drinking fine wine and might add an occasional sophisticated cocktail or two. Grace couldn't break a promise to her mother, and besides, sometimes she rode her bicycle to the club.

The Gemini girls and Diana disappeared from Harlow's. Grace wondered if it was too upscale for them since it wasn't a good place to get loaded on "downers." Grace believed that it was also too lively for Diana's parasitic girlfriend, June. Grace, on the other hand, was mesmerized with the bright lights, the dance music, and the new crowd. She was also attracted to Lucas, who had a beautiful mane of blond hair. She had never seen anyone like him.

Lucas was a friend of Camila's. He worked as a hair stylist at Bonwit Teller's department store's salon with Camila. Many of the hip Center-City crowd worked in hair salons, and they had rich clientele. They always had cash to throw around, and they had expensive taste. This world took Grace away from the darkness, the loss, and the neglect she felt in her own home. These people were ostracized from society in a way and so was she; they didn't fit the norm.

Grace had Lucas to herself on Thursday nights as Camila was always preoccupied on Thursdays. One night, they danced to "I'll be There" and "Papa Was a Rolling Stone," two of her favorites. Then they went upstairs to the second floor of the club to talk in a quieter room. They talked feverishly about the occult as Lucas also dabbled in the paranormal. This brought them together in an exclusive way.

Grace made sure she left before the club closed because her mother told her that wherever she went, never to be the first to arrive or the last to leave. She took taxis now instead of riding her bike as she still had some cash left from card readings. She never let anyone know that she came to and from the club alone. In the middle of a dance or a conversation, Grace would announce she had to find her friends to see if they wanted to leave. It was all worth it; she was creating a persona.

Grace thought about giving the crystal ball to Lucas It was a perfect gift for him since he was interested in the mystic. One sunny day, she brought the crystal to her back porch and lifted it up to the sky. She channeled the sun's energy into the ball to protect Lucas. At that moment, she dropped it. Grace picked it up and found there was a small fracture on the glass, an imperfection. With that flaw, she opted not to give it to him.

A couple of weeks passed since the night Lucas and Grace spoke about the paranormal at Harlow's. Grace knew her crush was intensifying. She thought about Lucas more than anything or anyone else. She thought of him at night as she lay in bed. One night, when she couldn't sleep, Grace went downstairs to light a candle and gaze into the crystal ball. She sat at the kitchen table and set her focus on the ball. She waited until an image formed. Grace saw two question marks. This projection in the ball made Grace feel that something would happen the next time she went to the club. She had a feeling that someone would be wearing the same dress that she was wearing. This seemed like a silly concern, but the feeling of embarrassment was overwhelming.

The next week when Grace went to the club, she looked around to see if anyone was wearing the same dress as she was. But that wasn't what she found. Rather, she saw Camila and Lucas, both of them wearing the same tee shirts with question marks on them. Grace felt ill. She knew by looking at them that she had no chance with Lucas. If he went straight, it was obvious he would choose to be with Camila, not her. Grace didn't feel like hanging out there any longer that night and took a taxi back home earlier than her usual time.

When she arrived home, she found Diana on the front step. She was crying and slurring her words. Grace couldn't make out what she was saying. She helped Diana get up, and they both entered the house. Diana dropped to the floor, sobbing. What happened at Harlow's earlier that night took a back seat when Grace saw the distressed state of her best friend.

"June broke up with me," Diana sobbed. "She doesn't want to see me anymore."

Grace wanted to leap with joy, but she controlled herself. "What happened?" she asked.

"She told me she didn't want to do drugs anymore."

"You can't blame her, Diana. You two keep falling down wherever you go."

"I know, Grace. Maybe you could help me so June will take me back."

"I don't know anything about drugs. Can't you just stop?"

"I think you can taper off," Diana said.

"Okay, start decreasing the amount you take a little at a time. Maybe there's a spell in the incantation book that will help."

"I don't know if I can live without June," said Diana.

"Let's go into the kitchen and light a candle," Grace said, leading Diana to the kitchen.

They sat there and gazed into the candle. After a while, Grace recited, "By all the powers and all the gods and all the spirits, I call upon you to lift this oppression from my friend and my sister in the occult, Diana, so that she may be free from this addiction and return to her state of being, back to her natural way."

"My natural way? That's a joke," Diana said disdainfully. "You know my mother used to lock me in a closet? She didn't want me to be pretty. She told me over and over again that I was plain and that I would never amount to anything. No boys would like me. I wasn't allowed to wear makeup, and my hair had to be plain. She hated that she had polio and it left her deformed. I kept telling her she was beautiful, and that my father could have had any one of the pretty Italian girls in South Philly, but he chose her. She wouldn't believe me," Diana said, tears rolling down her cheeks.

"Did your father know she locked you in the closet?"

"He didn't know. She did it when he was on his police beat."

"I'm so sorry, Diana. You are safe here with me."

"Do you think June will take me back if I get straight?"

"Remember your cards; the last one was the Sun, which is contentment, so whatever it is you want, you will get it if you play your cards right."

They both laughed at the play on words and that helped alleviate the intense emotion in the room.

"I don't think you need the incantation book, Grace; you can do things on your own. I know you think we do these spells together but it is really you who has the power. I miss you."

"You will be better in no time. We can have fun together again. And maybe when you feel up to it, you can come with me to Harlow's. There, I will introduce you to other people that would be better for you. You don't need to hang around with the Gemini girls all the time."

Time had passed and Diana was on the mend. They were back to riding bikes. When Grace and Diana embarked on their bicycle journeys, the house was dark. Grace had learned a long time ago not to leave the lights on when she wasn't using them. One night, when they returned after a great bike ride, they noticed that the house was totally lit up. Every lamp was on. They couldn't figure out what was happening. Grace remembered that in the paranormal books, it was written that electricity was a big part of spirit energy.

This electrical phenomenon continued. It happened often when Grace and Diana went for bike rides. Vince didn't witness any of the electricity occurrences as it always occurred after dusk and before eleven o'clock when he was at the church hall. During this time, not only was the electricity playing havoc, but there were rustling noises coming from her mother's closet, and once when she had enough courage to look inside, there was an infestation of flies. She told her father about it, but when he investigated the area, the flies were gone. Grace needed to find the cause.

One night, Grace and Diana sat in the kitchen with a lit candle, as they were trying to figure out why the lights were going on and the significance of the flies in the closet. They considered calling on the spirits to find out if there was a message they needed to receive.

In the middle of their candle gazing, Vince came home and walked straight into the kitchen.

"Don't think I don't know what you're doing, Grace. Riding around with those boys. Puttin' out like you always do."

Grace looked at Diana, whose eyes were as wide as saucers, and they both subdued their laughter. The joke was on Vince. He had no idea that there were girls in the cars. Her father must have caught the glances between Grace and Diana because he instantly slapped Grace so hard that she fell on the floor and her mother's ring fell off her finger.

"You belong in a circus! Your mother is turning in her grave," Vince said as he looked at Grace who was crawling on the floor to search for her mother's ring.

Diana remained silent. Vince turned away and went upstairs. Grace began to cry as she kept searching the kitchen floor.

Her mother's ring was a beautiful sapphire in a silver setting. It was a gift from her friends for her thirtieth birthday. The only other ring that Kate owned was her wedding band which was buried with her in the coffin. After much searching, Grace finally found the ring under the stove. It was intact, unlike herself.

"Wow, I never saw your father act like that before," Diana said when she was able to speak.

"This isn't the first time he's attacked me."

"He hits you?"

"No, he never hit me before tonight. It's more like he hurts me with things he says. It was pretty bad one time when my mother was at one of her novenas. I was in the living room, sitting on the couch watching TV. He was reading the newspaper at the kitchen table, and it seemed he was enjoying a cup of coffee. Suddenly, he put down the newspaper. He walked into the living room and stood glaring down at me with dark narrowing eyes. 'Don't think I don't know why the boys like you. You think they want to sit on the steps and listen to records? They don't like you. They hang around because you put out. And when your mother gives them glasses of water, I know that she flirts with them too. I know what you are. You aren't fooling anybody. You're a whore.' Then he turned away before I could say anything. He went back to the kitchen and continued to read the paper. I sat there stunned."

"Yeah, that's what they call abuse," Diana said, sympathetically.

"I started to cry, but I was afraid my mother would find out what he said to me, so I wiped my tears on my sleeve and curled up on the couch. I pretended to be interested in what was playing on the TV. When my mother came home, she knew something was wrong. She could smell trouble. I tried to conceal it, but she peered into my mind. I had to tell her what he said. I left out the part of how he said she flirts with the boys. I think that would have put her over the edge. It was pretty bad, though. She stormed out of the living room as if she was leading a charge. Then she took the broom out of the cellar way and hit him with it. She hit him more than once. He didn't defend himself. I heard her say—'How dare you speak to Grace like that! There is nothing going on with those boys, but how would you know? Your mind is in the gutter. That's how you think. You have a dirty mind. You have no idea who your daughter is. I am glad I don't let your dirty hands touch me. You served your purpose.' I was petrified," continued Grace.

"I guess there was a lot of stuff going on between your mom and dad. Don't blame yourself. Sounds like he is more upset with your mom than you," Diana said.

"True, but I was so scared that she would leave. She locked herself in the bathroom. I stood outside of the bathroom door and pleaded with her not to leave. She told me not to worry, she wasn't going anywhere."

"Parents don't leave. They stay together. That's the Catholic thing to do," said Diana.

"Yeah, but eventually she did leave. She left the earth. She tried to live for me but being with my father took its toll."

The candle was still burning. Grace gazed into the candle and requested, "Please, all of you who are on the other side, and all the gods and powers of the universe, let me know if my father is rotten. Show me a sign that it is he who is rotten and not me."

The next morning when Grace entered the kitchen, she saw a note from Vince on the table. It read— *I had to go to the hospital. There is something wrong with my leg.*

Grace walked to the kitchen sink. There was a mirror above the sink, and she looked into it. She studied her face and saw the power in her eyes looking back at her. She knew she had done something to her father. She'd asked for a sign, and she received it.

She called Diana and told her about the note. They both knew she could do things, but this was beyond anything they thought she could do, and the swiftness of it was stunning.

The next day, Grace and Diana ventured to the Methodist Hospital to visit Vince.

"Yeah, I took my uniform off and my leg was completely blue," Vince said when he saw Grace and Diana enter his room. "It wasn't like that in the morning. The doctor said it looks like gangrene."

Grace and Diana stood there in silence.

"I don't know what the two of you are up to, but you better fix it," her father demanded.

The doctor entered the room. "Which one of you is his daughter?" he asked.

"I am," Grace answered.

"We hope to release him soon, but I want to look into it further. It may take a few days. His vitals are normal, and he has no fever, but that leg concerns me. I think it is best for your dad to get some rest. He is in good hands," the doctor said as he left the room.

"Sounds like you will be okay, Dad. Get some rest," Grace said, trying to be supportive.

Grace and Diana stayed as long as they could but they felt uncomfortable and there was little conversation. When they left his hospital room, and as they passed the nurse's desk, the doctor stopped them. "I have never seen anything like this," he said. "It's almost uncanny that your dad's leg became blue in a day. Usually that takes a long period of time to appear that way." Before Grace could say anything, the intercom called the doctor and he rushed off.

"Wasn't it weird that he used the word 'uncanny?'" Grace asked Diana.

"Yeah," Diana responded. "That didn't seem like a normal medical term. We better find a way to take off the spell."

They sat at the kitchen table and lit the candle as soon as they reached the house. Grace took out the incantation book. She couldn't rely on herself to undo what she had placed on her father. She'd wanted to see a sign of his rottenness and gangrene certainly fit that description. She looked through the book of spells and found a section on "how to remove a spell."

Grace and Diana repeated the incantation ten times. They decided to take off the spells that had been cast on Angelo and Janice as well. Grace knew that those spells had worked as she accidently met Steven on the C bus. Grace hesitated to speak to him since he did nothing to save her from Angelo's violent assault. She overlooked her feelings to avoid him, though, because she needed to know if her spells had worked. He told her that he was sorry about what had happened in Angelo's garage. He said he was playing along but didn't think it would go that far. Then he told her that he had stopped dating Janice as she wasn't herself. She had been put on a narcotic; she was having trouble sleeping. He then revealed that Angelo had a problem too and that he was miserable.

Grace hid her delight at the news when she heard that her spells had worked, but now she just wanted to take them off. She felt that if she continued putting spells on people that "thing" in her house would steal her away somehow.

The next day Vince came home. He showed Grace his leg. Nothing was there. The incantation worked.

Thirteen

♥

DIANA FINALLY AGREED TO go to Harlow's with Grace. She was in a good state. The Gemini girls decided to go as well since Diana was doing better, and they wanted to support her.

The Gemini girls planned to take Grace and Diana to the club. That night, Grace gazed into the crystal before the girls showed up. Diana and Grace had the crystal in the center of the table. Grace had found a stemmed metal cup that housed the crystal perfectly. She sat quietly and focused her gaze into the ball. Even though it had a small flaw, the word "winter" came to her. Suddenly, they heard a car horn beeping outside. It was the Geminis. Diana and Grace left the house and ran toward the cars when Grace suddenly stopped in her tracks.

"I'm not going!" Grace proclaimed.

"Are you crazy, Grace?" Diana asked. "You wanted to go so much. That's all you have been talking about and you convinced me to go."

"No, I can't go. I will go another time. I have to follow my instincts. I have this strong feeling not to go to the club tonight."

"But you look fabulous, get in the car!" said one of the Gemini girls. Grace noticed that Annamarie still wasn't making eye contact with her.

"You still want to go, don't you, Diana?" Annamarie asked.

"Go, Diana," Grace said. "You will be fine. You are strong enough. Don't take any pills. Remember June won't take you back if you get high. I'll go next week. I'm just getting a strong feeling that I shouldn't be there."

Diana went with them, and Grace went back into the house where she changed into her pajamas and made herself a cup of tea.

The next morning, Diana called to let Grace know that the club had been raided, and she had been taken into police headquarters. All the underage partiers were detained overnight, and their parents had to bring them home. Diana was in the most trouble since her father was on the police force. He was a decorated officer, and this incident embarrassed him. They were taken to the round house that was located on Winter Street.

Grace's crystal was working. She would have been arrested if she hadn't seen "winter" in the ball.

After that Grace took a hiatus from the club. The Gemini girls weren't going anyway, and Diana was grounded. Grace was back to being home alone again, where the weird electricity thing had subsided. Back to her books, her violin, and her memories of her mother and Henry. She had a few letters from Henry, but they were dull. She didn't think Arizona was intriguing enough for Henry, but he seemed to make the best of it. Aunt Amanda loved it out there, when traveling to casinos with her lady friends. The image of Aunt Amanda in her white cardigan sweater and house dress pulling the lever on a slot machine made Grace chuckle. Henry and Aunt Amanda were trying to get through their senior years unencumbered with too much stress and if gambling did the trick for her aunt, then so be it. Grace had her own struggles. Besides, she still harbored resentment toward Henry for leaving her.

During this quiet time, without the lights and sounds of Harlow's, and without Diana around, Grace focused on what she was going to do with her life. She had an interest in parapsychology, but that meant many years of college. She completed her training at Blue Cross, but the job was a dead-end as the better positions went to the college graduates. Something had to change.

It was over a month since Grace had any contact with Diana. She called Diana, but she couldn't get through to her. Each time Grace called, Diana's sister answered the phone. She told Grace that Diana was in no position to talk to anyone, she needed rest. Grace called one more time and that was when Diana's brother answered. He let Grace know that Diana was never allowed to associate with her again. They were trying to help Diana, who was going through a mental breakdown. Diana had told her parents that she was with Grace every time that she came home high on drugs. Grace was shocked. She was told never to call there again.

Grace felt that she was better off keeping to herself these days. She needed time to regroup and get her ducks in a row. She enjoyed the solitude. Yet that solitude was short-lived when a letter came in the mail.

Grace opened the letter that was suspiciously addressed to Melissa Swain in care of Grace Marco. The letter read—*Dear Melissa, my lovely wife, I am deeply sorry for what I did to you. I was jealous. I know now that you did not cheat on me. I should have believed you. To see you hanged for witchcraft destroyed me. I loved you more than life. Please forgive me. Always, Bartholomew.* At the bottom of the letter was the printed full name, "Bartholomew T. Harrod."

There it was—the name the Ouija board gave her when she was nine. It was spelled exactly the way her mother had corrected her; it was T. Harrod, not Tharrod.

She never told Diana about this, and she never mentioned the name Bartholomew to anyone. Grace was following her mother's order not to mention that name again.

The occult practice was losing some of its luster for Grace. It was fun to do readings and crystal gazing but now things were getting out of her control. This letter proved it. Grace had never heard of Melissa Swain.

Grace needed to contact Diana. She immediately placed a candle on the kitchen table and sat in a meditative state, gazing into it. She concentrated on Diana's face. Suddenly, Grace was interrupted by the presence of someone in the house.

Grace walked to the living room, afraid of what she may see.

It was Diana. "I sneaked out, Grace," she said.

Grace realized that Diana still had a key to the front door. "What have you done, Diana?"

"I got caught at Harlow's, that's all. My father hated that, and in front of his buddies at the precinct, he was embarrassed. That's why my parents are punishing me. They don't really care about me; they only care about their reputation."

"And what's this?" Grace showed Diana the letter. "Did you write this?"

Diana took the letter and read it. "I have no idea what this is. Besides, that isn't my handwriting."

"Well, I'll figure that out later. What is most important is why you told your parents that you were with me when you were high. It was June, Diana! How could you do this to me? I am the only one you can trust; you should know this. We are more than friends, Diana, we're soulmates. We have power together, and you destroyed it for some stupid pills and that skank, June."

"I didn't mean it, Grace. I wasn't thinking straight. I thought that if I said I was with you they wouldn't see that I was high. I thought I was good at hiding it from them. When they asked me where I was, I thought it was safe to say I was at your house."

"How dumb do you think they are? You father is a police officer! He's used to dealing with liars and drug addicts."

Diana didn't respond. She looked strange and seemed as if she fell into a trance. She walked from the living room to the kitchen. She took a large knife from the drawer and walked steadily toward Grace. She seemed possessed. Just as Diana moved closer to Grace, Diana turned and walked to the stairs. She ascended the stairs and locked herself in the bathroom. Grace took a deep breath and immediately thought to go next door and summon Shirley. She had to have a witness in case Diana did something violent. She was in enough trouble with Diana's family already, and as much as she cared for Diana, Grace knew she had to protect herself.

Grace knocked on Shirley's door and called out, "Shirley, help me. Diana is upstairs with a knife. She locked herself in the bathroom. I don't know what to do."

Shirley came out of her house immediately. She directly went upstairs and stood outside the bathroom door. Grace stayed downstairs.

"Diana, this is Grace's neighbor, Shirley. Please come out. Grace is worried about you."

Silence.

"Please let me know if you can hear me?"

No response.

"Nothing is worth this. I know it all seems terrible at the moment, but things will work out."

Grace went upstairs and joined Shirley outside the bathroom door. "Diana, it is okay. I get it, you didn't mean to get me in trouble. Come out and let's go back to the way things were. There is nothing we can't fix."

"You're only saying that," Diana responded.

"That's not true. You know how important you are to me. I needed a friend so much after my mother died, and there you were when I was lonely. Remember the meatball sandwich you brought me? You sealed your destiny in that kind gesture. You are a good person, Diana."

"You really think so, Grace?"

"Yes, I do. Don't you remember your cards? You would go through a transition. There was addiction and then deception. There would be disaster, but the last card in the reading was the Sun. That means the disaster doesn't last and you'll be happy. Now, come on. You know I am a good card reader. Make that last card come true!"

With that plea, the door opened. Shirley took the knife from Diana. Grace hugged Diana. Diana was crying. The three of them went downstairs.

"Why don't you girls come with me and I will make a fresh pot of coffee?"

Diana and Grace accepted the invitation and sat with Shirley in her house while the coffee was perking.

"I think it best if I go with you, Diana, to bring you home," Shirley said.

"You won't tell them what I did, will you?"

"No, Shirley won't say anything. Why make matters worse?" Grace said. "But I think you should tell them that it wasn't me who introduced you to drugs."

"That's what this is about?" said Shirley.

"Diana started doing drugs and hanging out with a girl named June. She told her family that she was here with me instead, and somehow, Diana thought that her family would think that was okay."

"That's such a shame. I think Grace is right. Tell them the truth, and then all of this can be put behind you."

"Will you forgive me, Grace?"

"I already did. I wasn't saying that just to get you to come out of the bathroom. I really meant it."

"After our coffee, I will take you home, but I don't think Grace should go with us," said Shirley.

"True," Grace agreed.

They finished their coffee. Shirley and Diana were leaving, and when they neared the front door, Diana turned to Grace and said, "Goodbye, Melissa."

Grace froze. She was petrified that Diana had called her by the name, Melissa.

Grace sat with Shirley for the rest of the day and they finished the pot of coffee together. The drama that ensued earlier made the fact that Grace was fired from her job a small matter. Now it bubbled up as she settled down with her neighbor following Diana's cry for attention.

"I lost my job, Shirley," Grace admitted.

"What? What happened?" Shirley asked.

"I hated that job. It was so boring. I showed up late a lot. They warned me I would lose the job if I continued to show up late, but I couldn't help it. I wasn't motivated to go. I pressed the snooze button too many times."

"That's a shame, Grace. Your father will be disappointed. He was so proud that you worked for Blue Cross."

"Yeah, I guess I can believe that. He likes places like that. He actually wanted me to work for the post office, and if not that, then he wanted me to be an x-ray technician at Saint Agnes Hospital. I swear he either wanted me to be bored to death at the post office or he was trying to kill me with radiation."

"Oh, Grace, you are too funny."

"I dread having to tell him."

"Don't say anything yet. You had a rough day. To tell you the truth, Grace, I didn't like you hanging around with Diana. She's a damaged girl. She is too attached to you. I watched you two going in and out of the house, and I could see from my kitchen window that you sat at your table with a candle lots of nights."

"We were experimenting. You know I do the cards and that I have a reputation as a witch. The whole neighborhood knows."

"I had a feeling something like this would happen. Your mother was afraid to leave you. That was why she never did anything about her cancer. She thought that if they opened her up the cancer would spread. I tried to make her go to the doctor right after you were born, but she was determined not to disturb what was growing inside her. She wanted to make sure that she lived long enough to be with you and protect you."

"I wish she was here, Shirley. My father is so mean."

"Your father was angry for a long time. He may have mistreated your mom, but there was no way she would leave him. She didn't want to upset you. She wanted you to have a stable home as long as she could hold out. It didn't surprise me that you started to read the cards and get involved with all that other stuff. Your mother knew that you had a unique gift."

"Shirley, it was fun reading the cards and testing new ways of making things happen, but I am too scared of it now. There are so many things happening in the house. I hear noises. Something is in there. There's something else too."

"I am here, Grace. You can tell me anything," said Shirley.

"My father came home one night when Diana and I were in the kitchen doing our thing with the candle. Out of the blue, he shouted at me that he knew what I was doing riding around with boys. He said that Mommy was turning in her grave. And then he slapped me so hard that her ring flew off my finger."

"Grace, I am so sorry. I know how much that must have hurt."

"It wasn't the first time. Well, I mean it wasn't the first time he said an awful thing. This was the first time he hit me."

"What else did he say?"

"When I was thirteen, he called me a whore. He said he knew why the boys came around, he said it was because I put out."

"I remember when you and the boys played records. There was nothing going on. You were outside the house the whole time. You know he always had a suspicious mind. It drove your mother crazy."

"Mommy hit him with a broom when she fished it out of me. I tried to keep it from her but you know how perceptive she was. She came home from her Tuesday night novena and as soon as she saw me sitting silently on the couch, she saw that something was the matter with me."

"Oh, I can imagine. Those wise eyes must have been peering right through you."

"I didn't say anything. She took a few seconds to wait for me to say something. I tried hard not to cry, but I started to, and that's when I told her what he said. And within seconds she was in the kitchen hitting him with the broom. Then she stormed out of the kitchen, went upstairs, and locked herself in the bathroom. I went upstairs and pleaded with her outside the bathroom door not to leave. She said she wouldn't leave and not to worry, she wasn't going anywhere. She said it wasn't my fault."

"Don't blame yourself. There are things between your parents that you will never understand."

Grace considered telling Shirley what she did to her father's leg, but hesitated.

"Without going into too much detail," Shirley said, "your mom had a tough time with your father. Besides, he was jealous of Henry being around. He was jealous of everyone that your mom came in contact with. The beer man, the bread man, the milk man."

"That's funny. The milk man too?"

Shirley got up from her comfy chair to get another pack of unfiltered Camel cigarettes. When she came back to her chair, she had a fresh Camel and a loose piece of tobacco on her bottom lip. Grace couldn't take her eyes away from that speck on Shirley's mouth.

"If you feel scared, my door is always open," offered Shirley. "Now, what are you going to do about a job?"

It was a perfect night with a soft breeze blowing when Grace decided to take a long bike ride. It was approaching midnight and the streets were empty, allowing her to go any way she liked; zigzagging, swirling, and speeding, all things she could not do when there was traffic. As she moved through the open air, Grace asked the sky above, "Where are you, Mommy? Can you hear me? I am the receiver, remember? Please find me. I miss you so."

There was no answer out there in the night. Grace continued to ride in a different direction, and she found herself back on Broad Street where there was some traffic. She stopped at a red light. While she waited for the light to turn green, a newspaper caught her eye. It was on the ground by her foot. It was opened to a classified page, and someone had circled an item in red. She picked up the paper. She saw a notice for ushers at Walnut Street Theater. The Walnut Street Theater was the oldest theater in the country. Many a performance premiered there before they hit the Broadway stage. She ripped out the page and stuffed it into her jeans pocket. The next day Grace called the contact number and made an appointment for an interview. She was hired immediately.

Vince disliked Grace's new job. In his eyes, it was a step down from Blue Cross. For Grace, this was a great job. She wore a long skirt and a ruffled blouse, and she chose a pair of ankle boots that were reminiscent of the style of the late nineteenth century. The hours were great. She didn't need to report to work until evening, except for matinee days—Wednesdays and Saturdays.

Grace loved entering through the stage door. She had never seen a live stage production. *Molière's Tartuffe* was her first. She was following in her father's footsteps, as Vince had been an usher at the Academy of Music. That is where he learned the opera arias. It was a great opportunity for anyone who wanted to study the performing arts to get an usher job. It was also a way to get paid to watch performances over and over again while standing by the exit doors.

Within a few months, Grace figured out that she could sit in the glass VIP room after the audience was seated. There were six ushers per performance, four on the main floor of the orchestra level and two in the balcony. The six ushers became friends, and they alternated between who remained at their posts and who could sit in the VIP booth.

In no time, Grace was promoted to the "candy girl." She had a key to the candy closet. Those candy bars were the same size as the ones they had at the movies. It was tempting to take some of the bars home but her mother hadn't raised a thief.

The theater had many secret passageways, and there was a tunnel that had been closed off for years. The ushers liked to hang out in the tunnel whenever the manager, Gregory, wasn't around. Eventually, they stayed a little longer after their shifts. Each usher left by the stage door exit, signed out and said goodnight to the stage door man. Then, one at a time, they made their way around the block, and Grace opened the entrance door to let them inside. She was the last one to leave the theater, and she left by the stage door as well. Grace walked around the block like the rest of the ushers, and they were there to let her in the entrance. They sat in the candy room until the stage doorman did his rounds, and once he returned to his post, they had the run of the theater. They explored the tunnel and played on the stage too. She tried to stop them from eating the candy but that was part of the fun. She did give in and ate the candy as well, but she made sure they each ate a conservative amount.

The ushers smoked weed in the tunnel. Grace had fun regardless of the fact that she refrained from smoking the stuff. Although Grace didn't partake in smoking, she thought she was hallucinating. When they ran through the tunnel, Grace sensed another presence lurking in the tunnel with them. It wasn't the first time she felt this presence. She knew the theater was haunted. It was a common belief that circulated among theater types. They thought all old theaters were haunted. But, for Grace, she knew this presence wasn't an old-time theater ghost who liked to play mischief. This was a dark, evil spirit that seemed all too familiar.

The tunnel still had a few dim lights hanging on the side walls. It was a passageway at one time, connecting the dressing rooms to the stage. The lights cast shadows that made the tunnel look like a sinister scene in a suspense film. Grace heard her buddies laughing as they made their way out of the tunnel. As soon as they left, a foul odor filled the tunnel. She heard someone breathing nearby. Then she heard the click of a lighter. It illuminated a small area in front of her. There before her, only a foot away, were two eyes in the darkness—blazing eyes. She couldn't see the rest of the facial features, but she knew standing in front of her was an angry, evil man.

Grace was frozen in place. She couldn't move forward and she was afraid to turn her back to run in the other direction. Her heart was beating loudly. Trapped there in the theater's tunnel, she had to think of something. Before she could even have a thought in her head, she instinctively reached inside her blouse and revealed her mother's scapular. Grace had started wearing it since she sensed that an evil force was hovering around her. As soon as the man saw her scapular, he clicked the lighter shut and extinguished the small flame; he vanished into thin air. From then on, Grace never set foot in that tunnel and she kept her mother's scapular close to her heart at all times.

Grace contemplated telling Gregory, the staff manager, about what lurks in the theater tunnel but opted to keep it to herself. What good would it do? She couldn't prove it and besides the spirit in there was attached to her, not the theater. Grace trusted Gregory. He was a good manager. He and his wife, Tammy, were hippies, and they lived in a funky apartment on Pine Street. They were in their twenties, and Gregory was a true intellectual. There wasn't a subject he couldn't discuss. Not since Henry did Grace see this in a person. Gregory was a theater aficionado. He and Tammy took a liking to her and invited her to their apartment often. Grace loved to sit and listen to Gregory talk about the theater, specifically the history of the Walnut Street Theater.

The theater opened its doors on February 2, 1809, as a circus. In 1812, it was converted to a legitimate theater with its first production, *The Rivals*, with Thomas Jefferson and the Marquis de Lafayette in attendance on opening night. Some of the stars that performed there over the years included Edwin Forrest, Edwin Booth, the Drews, the Barrymores, Gregory M. Cohan, Katherine Hepburn, Marlon Brando, Sidney Poitier, Robert Redford, Jack Lemon, and William Shatner.

Backstage continued to operate the original grid, rope, pulley, and sandbag system. The fire curtain still hung above the stage with a hand-painted reproduction of *The Liberty Bell's First Note*, originally painted by Jean Leon Gerome Ferris in 1753.

Gregory had a great library, which included plays. He gave Grace classic plays as well as modern ones to read. He liked Pinter & Ionesco. Grace preferred Ibsen, Eugene O'Neil, and Tennessee Williams.

Tammy was a musician. She played folk guitar. Grace felt peaceful around them, and they were great listeners. She liked lounging on their waterbed and watching the lava lamp as they played music and had deep conversations. Tammy introduced Grace to stir fry and hummus. Tofu was also served, but Grace didn't have a taste for that. What she did like were the grilled hamburgers mixed with Worcestershire sauce.

Pine Street was a whole other world compared to Sydenham Street and it was quite a departure from the glamourous days at Harlow's. Pine Street was filled with antique stores and hippies, or maybe they weren't really hippies but more like academics. The neighborhood was interesting but it lacked the warmth of South Philly. But this window into another world ignited a desire in Grace to further her education. She knew her biggest problem would be how to pay for college. Being around Gregory and Tammy inspired her. The domestic life of a loving couple with many talents and interests wasn't looking so dull in their rooms that were separated by colorful beads.

On many nights, Grace was able to express herself freely to Gregory and Tammy. She felt that she had no direction since her mother and Henry were gone. She appeared to be strong, but deep inside, she lacked confidence, and essentially, she felt like an orphan. Tammy was perceptive and was able to look inside Grace and see the little girl who was traveling through life's phases looking confident but who was actually lost. Tammy had been in therapy for a few years, and she thought it was the best thing she ever did. She said that it wasn't about being crazy or sick but that it was a healthy thing to do. Tammy lived by the philosophy that life could be hard to navigate, so why not find support while going through it? Grace never thought of going to a psychologist. No one in her family believed in psychiatry, and she didn't know of anyone who went to a therapist. Tammy reassured Grace that therapy only involved talking to a trained expert who listens, reflects, and helps support you to make changes. She said that therapists help "normal" people.

A few weeks after Tammy brought up the idea of therapy, Grace made an appointment with Tammy's therapist, Dr. Cohen.

Dr. Cohen's office was located in Center City on the west side of Broad Street. The entrance to the building had thick glass double doors that opened into a vestibule with an intercom. There were a couple of marble steps that led to another set of glass doors. Once buzzed in, the doors opened into a grand reception area. These old buildings had tall ceilings, ornate built-in bookcases, gorgeous hardwood floors, and huge fireplaces. There were two plush couches facing each other, positioned on an expensive oriental rug. The reception desk was mahogany. Grace surmised that Dr. Cohen's practice was expensive by the luxurious reception area. Tammy had mentioned that Dr. Cohen had a sliding scale in terms of fees. Grace hoped she would be on the lowest side of the scale.

The receptionist gave her a thick set of papers on a clipboard. Some of the questions were difficult to answer but she managed to complete them as best she could.

Dr. Cohen greeted Grace in the hallway, and they both walked to the end of the hall where Dr. Cohen had her office. The door opened into a beautiful room. The large windows were complemented with thick draperies that were pulled back on the sides by gold ropes with tassels. There was a dark green couch in front of a floor-to-ceiling bookcase. Next to the couch was a leather chair and a small table with a box of tissues. On the adjacent wall from the couch were diplomas and certifications framed with Dr. Cohen's academic and professional achievements. Her desk sat in front of the wall of accomplishments. It looked like cherry wood but Grace wasn't sure. She wanted to compliment Dr. Cohen on the décor of her office, but she didn't know if that was allowed.

"Please, make yourself comfortable," said Dr. Cohen as she led Grace to the couch. "Please sit here on the sofa. I am not a psychoanalyst. There is no need to lie down unless you choose to. I will tell you about that later."

Grace sat on the sofa as Dr. Cohen called it. In her house, it was a couch. Grandmom Rosie called it a davenport. Whatever it was called, it was lush.

"Let's get started," said Dr. Cohen. "Have you ever been in therapy?"

"No, never," Grace responded nervously.

"There's nothing to be nervous about, Grace. This is a safe place. Anything you say here is confidential. There are no right or wrong answers to questions I will ask. It is all about you. Remember to relax. Therapy is a process, and the more you engage in it the easier and the more beneficial it becomes. Before I get into the process and the business of our sessions, I want to begin with the reason you are seeking therapy. In other words, what is the issue you would like to resolve?"

Grace took her time answering this question. She had so many issues that choosing one was a difficult task. "I don't know if there is one main issue. I have many, I think," she said, trying to be honest.

"Okay then, why don't we start with a list of issues? We can work together to prioritize them until we get to the primary issue. Does that sound like something you would like to do?"

"Yes, that makes sense."

"Take your time, silence is important. There is no rush to answer quickly. This isn't school, and you are not being graded. Judgment is left at the doorstep."

Grace rummaged through the debris in her mind. Without the pressure of choosing one problem, Grace was finally able to speak. "Well, I have this hollow feeling ever since my mother died. But I think that is normal. I managed pretty well, but then there is this feeling like whenever I get close to someone, they leave."

Dr. Cohen didn't respond.

"Then there is the horrible relationship I have with my father," Grace continued.

Dr. Cohen was silent.

"Then I have no idea what I want to do with my life. I feel like nobody cares what I do. I feel lost."

Grace waited for some kind of response from Dr. Cohen but there was only silence again. This forced Grace to continue to reveal more about herself. "Then there is the psychic stuff, and I am afraid that something is going to get me."

Dr. Cohen perked up when hearing this last statement. "Psychic stuff? Could you elaborate?"

"I started reading tarot cards, having premonitions, and a lot of other things."

"How did engaging in these things make you feel?"

"I was fascinated at first. I realized I had power. I liked having power...but then it became scary."

"Scary to have power?"

"No, I was afraid that I was opening a door to something and that I would lose control."

"Interesting," Dr. Cohen said as she wrote in her notebook. "We can explore this further at another time, but for now, I want to reflect back to you the issues you mentioned and then we can go from there. I heard from you that you feel like whenever you get close to someone, they leave. Correct?"

"Yes, I did say that," Grace answered, trying to be a good student.

"Then, you mentioned that you had a horrible relationship with your father. You did use the word 'horrible,' correct?"

"Yes, that is the word I used to describe it."

"After that, you said you don't know what to do with your life. You feel lost. You feel as though nobody cares. And finally, you mentioned psychic stuff. If I am understanding you, the psychic stuff was powerful for a while but now you are afraid of it?"

"Yes, I sometimes think if I keep using these abilities, I will be in real trouble."

Dr. Cohen made several notes in her notebook. Grace sat quietly looking around the office. The silence didn't bother Grace. She liked that someone was taking an interest in her and writing comments about her.

"Before we go over what will be expected of you, what I as a therapist will adhere to, the terms of confidentiality, and the cost of our sessions, I would like to know what it is that you want to receive from our therapy sessions?"

Grace hesitated for a bit and then said, "I want to have hope that I will have nothing to fear, and that I will have the confidence to go out into the world and make a better life for myself."

"Okay, Grace, I am here to support you on your journey to become a confident, fearless young woman who has the knowledge to take action for a better life. If there is one word to describe your goal, what would that be?"

"Courage," Grace responded.

The rest of the session determined how many sessions were to be set before there came the decision to continue or terminate. The pricing was affordable. Grace was thankful. She would be able to use her Walnut Street Theater salary to pay for therapy and carfare.

Even though the therapy sessions were affordable, Grace needed to think about getting a a second job. The theater job wouldn't cover all of her expenses. No way did she want to give up the job at the theater. Grace loved it there, and she liked the staff, too, especially

Gregory. If it wasn't for Gregory, she would have never met Tammy, and she wouldn't be in therapy.

Fourteen

♥

"WHAT WOULD YOU LIKE to bring to your session today?" Dr. Cohen asked.

It had been only a week since the first session, yet Grace felt more comfortable in Dr. Cohen's presence.

"I thought about the list of issues I mentioned, and I want to narrow them down, or at least be able to choose one to work on first," Grace said confidently.

"Before we officially begin our session today, I want to commend you for being able to articulate what you want to do at this time," said Dr. Cohen. "When choosing one particular issue, it doesn't mean which one is most important. What I am asking you to do is to choose one to start with and focus on; the rest can follow at your pace. We can always shift gears too. Nothing is set in stone; therapy is fluid. You set the agenda, Grace. I can make suggestions at times, and I will ask your permission to give you direction, but in no way, will I project my values on to you. If I don't know what it is you are trying to do or trying to express, I will not force you to give the answer. Therapy is a process. It took you years to get where you are now, and to expect a shift in a couple of sessions is unrealistic. Does this make sense to you?"

"Yes, this makes total sense," Grace agreed.

"Good. Now, does anything come to mind that may help you in the present?"

"Well, the relationship with my father isn't as important to me as finding my future path. I haven't been close to him for years, and even though it would be nice to have a better relationship, it doesn't really affect my life much. My mother was the most important person in my life."

"Was important?"

"My mother died when I turned sixteen."

"Ah, yes, that was written on your intake form. Can you tell me more about your mother?" Dr. Cohen asked compassionately.

"My mother was the best person. She was fair. She believed in me. I liked how she confided in me and taught me how to think on my own and be an individual. I couldn't get away with anything. I mean, she didn't always think I was perfect, and she wouldn't lie for me or pick up for me if I did something wrong. It was different if someone wronged me, though. She was my loyal ally. She defended me in the neighborhood when people were ruining my reputation, and she defended me against my father when he said nasty things about me. That's why I don't really care about fixing anything with my father. I had my mother's belief in me, and that carries me even today, and I know it will continue to do so in the future."

"Excellent description. Thank you for sharing that with me. At this time, the issue of having a horrible relationship with your father is not your first priority?"

"Exactly. I don't want to paint a picture that my father is totally bad. He was great when I was a little kid. He didn't like that I changed into a teenager, you know, and he didn't know how to handle a girl."

"I want to tap into something before we narrow down to your primary issue. Since your mother's death, who do you have for support?"

"I don't have any siblings, but I did have Henry and my Aunt Amanda. Not so much Aunt Amanda, but Henry was very supportive of me. It made my father so jealous."

"You said Henry was supportive. Why the past tense?"

"He moved to Sun City, Arizona, with my Aunt Amanda. They're married now. That was it for my mother's side of the family."

"What about your father's side?"

"I lost contact with them. My grandparents on the Marco side never had much of a relationship with me. They preferred my cousins, who were full-blooded Italians. My mother was Irish. That didn't go over well with them. My father had three brothers and one sister. The last time I saw them was at my mother's wake. My father has dinner with his sister's family on holidays, but I never get an invite."

"I see. How does that make you feel?"

"I wouldn't want to be with them, anyway, so it doesn't bother me. I like Shirley instead. You know, sometimes you are better off with friends or neighbors rather than family. Shirley lives next door to me, and I can go to her house anytime I want. I eat dinner there often. So, I guess I can say she is my support in a way and now there are Gregory and Tammy."

"Thank you for your honesty. Let's move on. What about finding your path?" Dr. Cohen asked.

"I think that can come later too. I think the thing I need to address first is the fear I have about the psychic stuff. That is where I want to begin. I don't think I can fix anything if I have this fear hanging over me."

"All right, Grace. This is where we will focus. When did the 'psychic stuff' begin?"

"It began when my mother and I played telepathy games at night before we went to sleep. See, we were adept at knowing what we each thought, that is, about an object in the bedroom. My mother told me I was a receiver. I had this experience once when we were playing the game. I heard a voice tell me what my mother was thinking, and I felt like I was in a different time too. Then the next thing that happened was really scary. I was playing with my Ouija board that was a Christmas gift. I played it with my neighbor's kids, Shirley's two girls. I asked the question, 'Who is the devil?' It answered with a man's name. I told my mother about it, and she was upset. She told me never to mention that name again, and I had to put away the Ouija board. I never touched it again. Nothing happened for a long time until after my mother died. That's when everything started to really happen.

"Fast forward to Mr. O'Hara, my Algebra teacher. One year in high school, we had a substitute teacher who, would you believe, didn't know a thing about Algebra? Instead he taught us about other things, like lost continents. He really loved this old Fellowship, the Rosicrucian Order. There was another girl in the class that was attracted to these topics; the rest of the class could give a hoot. The two of us had dreamt of this teacher every night for most of the school year when he had been substituting. Oddly, he introduced us to his wife, Elyse. She invited us to their home and like two idiots, we went. There, an extraordinary event happened. We raised a table and Mr. O'Hara channeled the spirit of the founder of the Rosicrucians. I knew then that this wasn't a cool thing to do. After the night at his house, he was spooked by something and he ignored me and the other girl in my class."

Grace revealed to Dr. Cohen that she started a tarot card reading business with her friend, Diana. She also confessed that she divined a car accident and she put spells on Janice and Angelo. She felt guilty telling Dr. Cohen that she put a spell on her father and that he was admitted to the hospital because of it. She felt that these things were what she controlled. It was when the electricity in the house did strange things that Grace felt she was losing control and something else was taking over. She told Dr. Cohen that there were times when she and Diana came back from bike rides only to find that all the lights were on in the house, yet when they left the house earlier, the lights were off. That is when her fear grew, and she began to feel like she was losing her mind. When she received the letter signed by the name she saw on the Ouija years earlier, Grace knew she needed to seek help.

Grace left the office feeling like she had shared a part of her private story, a part of her soul in a way. She wasn't totally sure that this was a good thing to do, but she hoped it was worth it, especially to get rid of that feeling that something was out to get her.

Grace had wanted to continue with therapy until she resolved her issues, but she needed another job to pay for it. She knew that the smart thing to do was to read cards again, but she feared that this would incite the presence that was hanging around her. She started to look in the newspaper classifieds but didn't have the skills that were in demand. She still didn't want to do administrative work. If only there was something more suited for her, Grace thought.

Luckily for Grace, just at this time when she needed it the most, Gregory approached her with the news that the house manager's assistant was leaving. Gregory recommended her for the position. The job entailed answering the phones. The phones were extremely busy, particularly during performances. She would need to know everything about the performances, and learn how to dispatch the calls to the appropriate people in the theater. Grace would also need to know performance information, times, cost of tickets, and other general questions about upcoming scheduled shows. If the call pertained to purchasing tickets, she would need to send them through to the box office. Much of the work included taking messages for the theater cast, the crew, and the house manager. She would be an information booth both on the phone and in-person. The House Manager, Mr. Sullivan, agreed to interview Grace. Gregory and the staff, even the stagehands, supported her for the job. Mr. Sullivan was pressured to hire her. There was a tinge of apprehension that Mr. Sullivan was similar to that authoritarian order, the Sisters of the Blessed Sacrament who often saw Grace as a threat. At least he couldn't flunk her on self-control; but he could fire her instead. As long as the staff liked her, she was eager to accept the position. This was the perfect job that enabled her to pay for her expenses.

Grace loved her new position. It was challenging. She particularly liked that she was invited by the actors to the cast parties. The staff weren't supposed to go to these wrap parties, but Grace was often invited because she fostered good relationships with the actors. Mr. Sullivan was furious when he saw her at the parties. He never missed the chance to approach her to let her know she wasn't supposed to be there. His face became beet red when she said that a famous actor or actress insisted on her being there.

One afternoon, Grace was seated at her desk. If she turned her face to the left, she could see down a hallway, and at the end of the hallway was a glass door. There was a buzzer at her desk to let people into the front of the theater area where her office and that of the house manager's office were located. All actors and staff entered around the corner at the stage entrance. There had been a few incidences where people were buzzed into the theater who were not supposed to be there. The staff was told not to let anyone enter through that entrance. The buzzer rang, and what Grace could see were two homeless people standing at the door. She didn't buzz them in. They kept buzzing the intercom. They were dressed in ragged clothes and had tattered shopping bags with them. She kept waving them away and finally, they left.

Minutes passed when an enraged woman stormed into Grace's office. She was a famous actress who was starring in the current production at the theater. She was accompanied by her husband, also a well-known actor. They were the two who were trying to enter the theater who Grace refused to let in. This actress was known for being feisty and not someone to insult. She was scolding

Grace with her signature shrill voice when suddenly she stopped. She heard herself speaking from the adjacent room. She was being interviewed on the Mike Douglas talk show that had been recorded earlier that week. Thank goodness, she left Grace's office to watch herself on TV. Her husband on the other hand, apologized for his wife's behavior. Grace told him that she was prohibited to let anyone enter that entrance and that they had looked like bums. She had no idea who they were. He laughed so hard his wife screamed at him to shut up.

However, the incident that put Grace in the doghouse was when the Governor of Pennsylvania showed up with eleven guests for a Saturday night performance. The Governor's assistant called earlier that day and wanted to purchase twelve tickets. Grace told her that the production was sold out; there was nothing she could do. When the Governor and his entourage showed up, they had to set up folding chairs in the aisles. Mr. Sullivan blamed Grace. That was it, Grace was fired on the spot. This was something she wasn't going to accept. She decided that she would show up for work anyway.

The following Monday, Mr. Sullivan came to work and when he saw Grace seated at her desk, he was shocked. She told him that there was no reason for him to fire her, and if he tried to force her out, she would keep coming back every day, even if he called the police. He gave in and let her stay.

Grace wrote to Henry about her experiences at the theater. She let him know that she was leaning toward an acting career. She didn't want to be a celebrity or a movie star; she wanted to be a legitimate, trained theater actress. Grace could see herself acting, producing, and teaching theater as a college professor. Henry wrote back that he was proud of her. He particularly liked how she stood up for herself when the house manager fired her. He wrote that she was indeed Kate's daughter, full of gumption.

Three months had passed, and Grace progressed well in her therapy sessions. Dr. Cohen managed to help her develop new perspectives, and it was time to determine if further therapy was needed.

"How do you feel about continuing our sessions, Grace?" Dr. Cohen asked.

"I think I am beginning to scratch the surface and I want to continue," she responded.

"Let me summarize what we have explored so far. Is that okay with you?" Dr. Cohen asked.

"Yeah, that would be great."

"When you first came to my office, you were nervous and cut off in a way. That was to be expected. But once we developed a close relationship, I saw a change in you. You illustrated trust in me and in the process. We had agreed to start with addressing your fear of an unwelcomed presence in your home but we actually explored a few other issues and we didn't address the initial concern about the danger you felt. We were able to identify your feelings of abandonment. First, by your mother through no fault of her own, then Henry, who needed to survive in a better way, and then Diana, who was a troubled girl. We focused on your father's neglect, and in a way, we identified this as a type of abandonment as well. We also explored the other relationships that didn't last—Annamarie, Jennifer, Mr. O'Hara, and let's not forget, Angelo and Janice. We realized that these were peripheral, not primary relationships and in a way helped you grow. We did, however, find that not everyone leaves you. Shirley is there for you, and it doesn't look like she is going anywhere. Tammy and Gregory came into your life and have been a great source of love and support. The rest of your relationships were like the seasons, they served you for a while but none of them were lasting.

"Grace, what you have learned here with our relationship proves that you are capable of trust. Trust is the cornerstone of all relationships. I have confidence that you will have lasting relationships in your life. Once we worked through that issue, we focused on how you sought power after your mother died. You mentioned that the psychic experiences accelerated after your mother's death. After several sessions, you were able to articulate that these 'events' gave you a sense of protection and of control. Does this sound correct to you?"

"Yes, I do feel that I understand the motive that lies underneath what was happening."

"Going forward, what would you like to address?" Dr. Cohen asked.

"I still want to be able to stop the feeling that there is something dark and evil around me."

"I see," said Dr. Cohen. "Let's start with one of your psychic experiences and see what we can extract from it."

"I think I would like to bring up the electricity thing. You know how I told you about when Diana and I rode our bikes, that when we left the house the lights were off, but when we got back every light in the house—even the basement light—was on?"

Dr. Cohen nodded. "Did you feel that this was an outside influence?"

"I am not sure what you mean, Dr. Cohen?"

"What I mean is that most of your experiences are about what you control, what you will, or what you see in the future. This sounds like something you are not in control of."

"Yes, that is true. That is why I am afraid of it."

"If you could find out that this is something that has a reasonable explanation, will that help you become less afraid?"

"Definitely," Grace answered with an eagerness to discern how she could make sense of this thing that frightened her.

"How many times did this happen with the lights?"

"It happened several times. Actually, I can't remember exactly, but it was more than three times."

"And over what period of time?"

"During one summer."

"Did you take frequent bike rides?"

"Yes."

"So, you took many rides and this electric occurrence happened occasionally?"

"Yes."

"Do you think your father could have done this for some reason?"

"No. It happened during those hours when he was at the church hall. Believe me, there is no way he would do something like this. He's too cheap to keep one light on, to keep all of them on, impossible!"

"Is there anyone else who has access to your home?" Dr. Cohen asked, acting more like a detective than a therapist.

"Shirley has a key. But she wouldn't do something like that. Shirley loves me, and she promised my mother she'd watch over me."

"But she does have the key? Could anyone in Shirley's house take the key and put the lights on?"

Grace hesitated. She didn't want to go down this road. A part of her thought that this was preposterous, but then again, it could be that Shirley's girls did this to her. They hadn't been friendly toward her since they played with the Ouija years ago.

"I don't want to put false blame on my neighbors but there is a chance that Shirley's girls could be playing with me."

"Why is that?" Dr. Cohen asked.

"They were the ones that were there when we played with the Ouija. I told you about how I saw the name that I am not supposed to repeat out loud or even think of."

"What would be their reason to play this trick on you?"

"I don't know."

"Didn't you mention that Diana sent you a letter with the name in the letter? It was signed by that name from the Ouija, correct?"

"Yes."

"And you said that you never told Diana the name. You only told her about the Ouija when she saw it on a shelf in your basement?"

"Yeah, we were in the basement, and she noticed the Ouija. She wanted to ask it questions. I told her that I promised my mother that

I wouldn't play with it since the time I had asked it a question about the devil and it gave me a name. I told her how the girls next door and I didn't push the pointer."

"So, the girls next door knew the name?"

"At the time, I didn't think so. They could hardly read well. But now that I think about it, I think at least one of them could of. The older one, maybe."

"What do these two incidents—the lights and the name—have in common?"

"The girls," Grace answered, feeling the wave of a new possibility fall upon her.

"If the girls knew the name, then could they have told Diana about the name?"

"Yes, they could have told her. They did talk to her occasionally. They sat on the steps that our houses share and sometimes Diana sat with them. But what could they gain from doing these things? Or what could Diana gain from it?"

"I don't think that it would serve you, Grace, to try to find out what motivated them at this time," said Dr. Cohen. "The important thing is that you can see evidence that these things are not supernatural. And if these things are not supernatural, then you have nothing to fear."

"But what about Mr. O'Hara? That is difficult to explain," said Grace.

"Tell me more about him and together we can examine what this means."

"Well, he did put things in our heads, my friend Jennifer and me. And we did read about the Rosicrucian order and we saw a drawing of the founder. Mr. O'Hara obviously knew everything about the Rosicrucians. He probably saw the drawing of the founder and noticed he resembled the man."

"If I remember in one of our sessions, you mentioned that he channeled the spirit of, sorry, what was the name?" asked Dr. Cohen.

"I didn't say a name. It was the spirit of the Christian Father, the founder of the order," replied Grace.

"What made you think it was this spirit?"

"He spoke in German, and the founder was German."

"And Mr. O'Hara knew this, certainly."

"Yes," agreed Grace.

"Were there any other details from that night that you think may shed light on what really could have happened?

Grace thought about it and then she remembered a detail she had forgotten. "We drank tea that night, right before the event."

"Do you think there could have been something in the tea that altered your senses?" Dr. Cohen asked, continuing to probe Grace.

"That would explain a lot," replied Grace.

"You know, he could have created all of it, now that I look at it," said Grace. "Jennifer and I weren't special, we were the two suckers in the class. We fell for it. He and his wife Elyse were charlatans. I knew when he didn't share his winnings for the numbers I gave him, he wasn't to be trusted," Grace revealed.

"Numbers? What about numbers. Please elaborate, Grace."

"Jennifer and I dreamt of Mr. O'Hara every night for a period of time and finally it had stopped. But I began to dream of numbers associated with the horse races."

"The street numbers—I am familiar with the illegal betting. Go on, Grace."

"Well a few times I dreamt of the numbers and I let Mr. O'Hara know. He played them and they came out."

"Do you know of any other people who have won by playing the numbers?"

"Actually, yes. Many of the older Italian ladies in my neighborhood seem to win a lot," answered Grace.

"Would you say that it isn't supernatural that you had dreams of the winning numbers?"

"I guess not. It may be something like a statistical thing. I am sure Henry, would have a logical explanation."

"Grace, let's go back a bit. I want to ask you why you referred to yourself and that of your friend as 'suckers' and please let me know why you feel this way?"

"It should have been obvious that Mr. O'Hara was up to no good immediately when he confessed that he didn't know a lick about Algebra. He filled our heads with flattery, saying that we were empaths and special. I feel like a sucker because my mother taught me to be more discerning than that. I mean, I just should have known better."

"Let me interject, here. It would be a cold world if there was no trust. It is good to protect yourself but if you live being suspicious of everyone, then you miss out on love. It makes sense that you and your schoolmate believed Mr. O'Hara. He was in an authority position and he was very interesting. You were open and many things did happen that on the surface did not have a rational perspective.

"That is true," Grace said.

"You said you felt like a 'sucker.' Were there other times, you felt this way?"

"Absolutely not!" Grace responded.

"That was a strong answer, Grace. Are you sure, you never felt that you were taken advantage of?"

"No! Look, Dr. Cohen, I do recognize that people have moved on and even a few tried to ruin me but in every one of those situations, I had my wits about me and I took action."

"Then would you say, this was the first time you felt like someone took advantage of you?"

"Yes, oh, I know you would think that Angelo took advantage of me when he attacked me in his garage. But I fought back. I think I could see the truth in all of the other situations, but with Mr. O'Hara I was blinded by my own ego. I fell for the flattery."

"And what does this mean?" asked Dr. Cohen

"It means that I was angry at myself because I fooled myself. Mr. O'Hara didn't fool me, I fooled me," responded Grace.

"Great insight, Grace!"

"You know, there is the possibility that Mr. O'Hara is delusional and he used us to conjure up a spirit. He probably didn't think of us as suckers, he could have actually believed in us. Either way, he and his wife have a perverse way of playing with people. It's okay, I'd rather think that what you said is true; the world would be cold if we couldn't trust."

"Going forward, what will this experience teach you?" asked Dr. Cohen.

"I think I need to strike a balance between total trust and caution. I don't want to be suspicious, I want to believe in people, but not be led by them either."

"Good point, Grace. I think there is another factor to consider and that is to forgive yourself. You don't need to be perfect and at times you may feel like 'you fell for it' as you said earlier."

"Yes, my curiosity leads me in the wrong direction sometimes."

"What would your life be like without your curiosity?"

"It would be mundane," responded Grace.

"Do you think it is worth the risk to keep that curiosity of yours even if it means landing in situations that are disappointing or less than perfect?"

"Yes, definitely."

"Our time is up, Grace. Thank you for your honesty and keep being curious. See you next week."

This was the most powerful session that Grace had experienced so far. Dr. Cohen was able to connect all the events. She illustrated that these psychic phenomena were actually things that could be explained through reasoning. Dr. Cohen used a cognitive therapy approach and it worked. Grace was able to see that Diana had a lot to do with the things that were happening to her. Dr. Cohen asked questions that brought Grace to the answers she embraced, and then she was able to eliminate fear.

Grace got to thinking—first of all, the letter with the name Bartholomew T. Harrod could have been a phony. Diana could have asked Shirley's girls if they remembered anything about the

Ouija. They could have known the name as they were there when it happened. Then, they could have gone into the house and turned on all the lights. They could have sent the letter too. But Diana had said "goodbye, Melissa" when she was leaving Shirley's.

Then, Dr. Cohen explained that things like the car accident and her father's leg could have been coincidences. The boy driving the car was probably high, and the chance of him getting into an accident was inevitable. Then there was the possibility that he heard Grace yelling, "I hope you get in an accident." Dr. Cohen shared with Grace that this incident could have been a perfect example of the "power of suggestion." As far as her father's situation, Vince probably didn't let Grace know that his leg was infected for a period of time before he went to the hospital. He probably didn't want to admit that he had neglected the infection. The antibiotics that were administered to him in the hospital were probably very strong. Therefore, the hospital released Vince early since he responded quickly.

Considering the two spells cast upon Angelo and Janice, Grace thought about what Steven had said when she saw him on the bus. He'd told her that Janice was on a narcotic. It was plausible to assume that Janice was on a drug because she felt uneasy about what she'd done to Grace and probably others. Guilt can fester and make a person ill. Remembering more of her conversation with Steven, Grace also didn't know for sure that Janice actually heard a canary singing, and Steven only said that Angelo was miserable. That didn't mean Angelo was miserable because of his lost sense of taste and smell; he was doomed to be miserable anyway.

Playing a telepathy game with Kate could be explained as a heightened empathy between mother and daughter. The crystal gazing could have been a visual projection of her fear— first of the club raid, and then in terms of the question marks. Seeing the evil spirit in the theater's tunnel crossed her mind. It could have been a prank by her co-workers; they knew Grace thought the theater was haunted—they all did. And after all, why would this kind of threatening spirit have a lighter?

It was Grace who needed to accept these possibilities after Dr. Cohen prompted her to form a new perspective. Most of what had occurred in Grace's past were now sewed up in a neat package of rational evidence. Yet there were still a few things that even Dr. Cohen could not describe with applied logic. She did describe Carl Jung's theory about collective unconsciousness and universal symbolism. Dr. Cohen admitted that there is much about the brain that we do not understand and that there are things we cannot explain. Maybe the supernatural is just a vast wilderness of the natural brain to be explored.

Fifteen

T AMMY INVITED GRACE TO Community College, where she was teaching a course in music appreciation. Grace was eager to meet with Tammy and see what higher learning looked like as she had never been to a college campus. She sat in Tammy's class and loved every minute of it. Grace realized she was starved for learning. This is what Henry and her mother had wanted for her, and she couldn't wait to write Henry and tell him that she was determined to further her education.

Even though it wasn't a great university like the University of Pennsylvania or Temple University, Grace was excited to be close to academia. When Tammy's class ended, Grace and Tammy walked through the lobby area. There was an elevator nearby, and when the elevator door opened, Grace saw the most beautiful young man she had ever seen. He had dark hair and blue eyes—he had a Tyrone Power look. He had a perfectly straight nose, and elegant lips. Grace was starstruck and seemed to be in a trance when Tammy nudged her to snap out of it.

"Grace, hello! Come in, Grace," Tammy said, trying to get Grace's attention.

"You see that guy over there walking over to that group? He's the type I would marry."

"He's a great looking guy. I see him now and then. I think he has a girlfriend."

"Of course, he has a girlfriend! How could he not? I don't think he would be interested in me anyway. Straight guys think I'm a freak."

"Hey, Tammy, come here for a minute," an older man called out from the group that had gathered.

Grace's heart was beating fast. As she followed Tammy and neared the beautiful young man who was part of the group, she had to control how smitten she was with him.

As Tammy conversed with her colleague, Grace stood there quietly.

"You know who you look like? Bette Davis," said the young man.

"I don't know whether to take that as a compliment or an insult. I was going for Greta Garbo," Grace barked back at him, concealing her inner immediate crush.

"Well, it's the big eyes. I meant that golden era Hollywood look."

"I guess, thank you."

Tammy pulled her away and the brief encounter was over.

"Did you hear that he said I look like Bette Davis?" she asked Tammy.

"I wasn't listening. I was busy with the administrator who may have a permanent position for me here."

"That's terrific, Tammy. You deserve it."

"You do look like Bette Davis today, as if you stepped out of *Dark Victory*."

Grace wore a 1930s hat with the brim covering one eye, red lipstick, a vintage three-quarter-length coat with wide sleeves and no buttons, a clutch bag, long gloves, and pumps. The only thing missing were seamed stockings. She had thought about drawing a seam on her hose, but that was going too far. After all, she was going to a college not a gay club.

"Don't get distracted now," Tammy said. "You have a bright future ahead of you. The right person will come along, but first, think about your next step to getting into college."

Tammy brought Grace into the cafeteria. Grace was impressed with the students who were chatting and laughing. It looked like so much fun to go to school. She had the bug. What was she going to do about it? Tammy had college applications with her. She wanted to help Grace get started in the process. First, she had to apply. Grace had achieved honors throughout high school, so getting into a good university was a possibility. She could write an essay about how no one in her family went to college, and after her mother died, she was left with her father who wouldn't support her desire to further her education. She would add that her mother dreamed of Grace attending college and this was one of her last wishes. This essay, her good marks in high school, and her decent SAT score made it a real possibility for this dream to happen. The obstacle was overcoming how she was going to pay for it.

Grace considered bringing this issue into her last therapy session. The session focused on Grace's new dream of attending college. They had discussed her attending college in former sessions, but now she was determined to make it a reality. Dr. Cohen was thrilled with her decision.

"Grace, you have achieved your goal here in therapy. You faced your fears, you eliminated doubt, and you are making a purposeful decision to go back to school. I have total trust that you will find a way to pay for your tuition. Put that enterprising thinking cap on."

"Working with you, Dr. Cohen, made this possible. I know you will say that I did it all by myself, but it was your questions and your listening that brought the answers out of me. I am in a new place."

"Very well said. You will make a fine student. What will be your major?"

"I am thinking theater. Temple University has a great theater department. Working at the Walnut Street theater and seeing those plays really gave me the desire to follow this path."

"Excellent. I will support you in whatever path you take. It has been a privilege to work with you, Grace. You have made great progress."

The session ended. Grace walked out of the office through reception and outside to the street with tears in her eyes. Dr. Cohen was wonderful. She was able to make her see that there was nothing to fear. All that nonsense of a dangerous presence and supernatural powers were put to rest.

Grace was accepted to Temple University. Receiving the letter of acceptance was the most thrilling experience of her life. How she wished her mother could be there to celebrate this day. She couldn't wait to write to Henry but she had to postpone the news until she secured her place at the university. She cycled to Pine Street and raised a glass of bubbly with Tammy and Gregory. They were proud of her. Next thing she had to do was go to the bank and apply for a loan, but the difficult thing was to get Vince to sign it. If only Henry was her father; he would sign it in a heartbeat. Actually, if Henry had paid for her college education like he wanted to, she would already be considering graduate school. However, Grace knew she had to work with what cards were dealt to her, and she had to stop wishing for a supportive father.

"What do you want to go to college for?" Vince said. Again, there it was, his disdain for whatever Grace desired.

"I want to study the theater. I learned a lot about performing by watching the plays at my job. I want to know everything about it."

"That's a waste. All college is a waste for girls. You will be wasting space until you get married."

"Well, then, I will meet a good husband at college."

"And what will you do with this college thing?"

"I will be an actress."

"An actress? You will end up in porno movies if you're lucky."

"Porno movies? How can you say that? Mommy was right. You do have a dirty mind. You don't know me at all. "

"You have peanuts in your head."

"Well then, I take after you. You were the entertainer."

"Get a steady job. An x-ray technician at St. Agnes hospital would be good, or work at a government job, like the post office."

"Again, with the radiation and the post office. How many times do I have to tell you, I am not cut out for these types of jobs. Look, Dad, you wanted to be an entertainer, but it didn't happen. Mommy said that the Depression came along, and you never got over it because you had to help with the family. I don't want that to happen to me. I want to follow my dreams and if it doesn't work out, at least I will have a college education. I can do better things with that. I could teach acting in school, or I could run a theater company. I don't need to be a movie star."

"I don't know who feeds you this crap. Did Henry put this into your head?"

"Nobody did. I've had this interest all on my own, and I think I have the talent."

"Lots of people have talent."

"Oh, forget it. I will find my way to go to school," she said, determined to prove him wrong.

Grace brought the loan papers to the bank unsigned. The loan officer was a woman in her fifties. She had a kind face. Grace told the woman that her father refused to sign the papers. She continued to tell her that going to college was a dream of hers and that she had an interview at Fidelity Bank as they hired college students. She would be able to pay for each college semester in three payments per semester. The university had a plan where she could pay one-third up front while the other two payments were deferred. She further explained that her salary could pay for most of her college tuition. She would only need to borrow a third of the cost.

Grace asked the woman if she could get a friend to sign the papers. The woman pondered a bit and then told Grace to take a walk outside and come back with her father's signature. Then she winked at Grace. Grace took a walk and found herself in the lobby of a hotel around the corner from the bank. She sat in a lovely Wingback chair, took out the papers, and forged her father's signature. She brought the application back to the bank and, without a word, the woman placed the application in her inbox. Grace thought that sometimes it is a stranger that provides.

The college campus was vast. Grace loved every inch of it. She loved the buildings that looked like castles, but she loved the food trucks the best, especially the pizza truck. Two sisters operated the pizza truck. The pizza was a thin crust with good sauce and a decent mozzarella. Occasionally, the sisters told her that they recently sold a slice to her brother. What brother? She had no brother, she was an only child she told them.

In the theater and communications building, there was a great stage and a wonderful television studio. Grace couldn't wait to start playing roles. She had psychology as one of her electives and a sociology class as well. She was in her element. However, Grace discovered that the undergraduate theater majors did not have permission to audition for any plays that the theater department produced. Instead, the undergraduates could only earn one credit per semester to dismantle the stage sets. That would mean that for four years, Grace would haul wood and remove props with no hope of performing on stage. Grace changed her major to Communications in her second semester since she felt that the theater department exploited her and the rest of the undergrads. In her new communications curriculum, she could act in videos and learn how to direct them as well. She could take essential theater classes as electives without having to strike sets.

Grace soon became the darling of the graduate video productions. While the graduate students were honing their directing abilities with dreams of working in TV, Grace was realizing the specific technique of acting for the camera lens. Memorizing lines and following direction were the basic parts of acting. To perform well, Grace learned the video technique to work within a small frame—no big movements or grand gestures. The actors had to adapt to expressing emotion with the slightest tilt of the head or the raising of an eyebrow. The acting was intimate and captured the inner life of the character. The "over the shoulder" camera shot had actors on top of each other and if the production had more than one camera, the actors needed to know which camera was assigned to them. Multiple cameras meant multiple takes. The director could stop the action and shoot the same portion of a scene repeatedly and they could also shoot the work out of order. This meant that Grace was not able to act a role from beginning to end within a logical progression. The only productions that allowed the actors to perform in the sequence of the way the work was written were the ones that shot the scenes with only one camera. At least this felt like an actor was telling a story in contrast to playing snippets of a jumbled story and just when an actor reached a pivotal moment, the crew broke for lunch. Anytime the production stopped, when it resumed, the dreaded words on the set were "let's take it from where we left off." How to reach the same state of emotion required a unique ability and Grace was willing to harness a technique that could keep her in the flow. It was a good decision to leave the theater department for Grace as she had the opportunity to hone her craft for the camera and at the same time learn acting techniques in her elective theater classes.

The theater classes allowed Grace to break free from the feeling like she was acting in a snow globe. Here, in the theater department, actors learned how to project emotion and to move about the stage. Their whole manner of gesture was broad. Grace felt like she was in an open field when she worked the stage. An actor had to reach the back of the house yet possess the inner life of the character. Both acting for the camera and acting for the stage had one thing in common—being in touch with the character. American actors adopted the "Stanislavski Method." This was based on actually feeling the way the character would be feeling. British actors kept the classic style of acting where portrayal of a role hinged on outer, physical ability and established techniques without the necessity of feeling the exact emotion that was inherent in the role. They appeared as if they were in touch with the character during a performance, yet they could actually be thinking of a pint of beer. The theater classes taught the Method technique where actors practiced "sense memory." Students took the stage and in front of their peers expressed their emotions based on a past event in their lives. They revealed the most private events that would evoke powerful emotions. Grace thought that people who needed therapy could take a theater class and save themselves money by not paying a psychologist for years of counseling. Once the actors learned to call up a memory, they could choose which memory aligned with a segment of the scene and as the character developed, so did the actor. This was exhausting for a theater production, but for the camera, it was perfect. Grace used sense memory to bring her back exactly where she left off after a break in a video production. She could produce real tears, stop, hit the vending machine, and then resume crying when the camera light turned back on. Grace excelled in theater class among her peers and camera acting, but both lacked a live general audience.

Grace had the bug to do a live performance. One of her college classmates advised her to try out for Plays and Players, a community theater on the famous Delancey Street, known for Philadelphia's old money. She auditioned and became a Plays and Players member. Grace did short walk-ons, but it wasn't until she played Eliza Doolittle in a workshop production of *Pygmalion* that she received accolades for her performance.

It was an experiment where a director cast two actresses. One played the poor cockney flower girl, and the other played the sophisticated fair lady. Grace played the role of the flower girl. She was a natural for this role, and the members recognized her talent. Vince confessed that he attended the performance but he didn't see her. If her own father couldn't tell she was on stage, that was enough evidence for Grace to continue on this acting path.

She wrote to Henry that she had played the role of Eliza on a real stage and in front of an audience who thoroughly enjoyed her performance. In a previous letter, she had shared the news of her entrance into Temple University and thanked him for introducing her to the delights of learning. She wrote that she would often think of him as she navigated the academic world. Grace knew that Henry would appreciate what was happening in her life. She wanted to write that she wished he was here with her, but she didn't go that far since she was still unable to let go of her disappointment that he moved away.

All was in place. Grace had school in the mornings and early afternoons, and after school, she reported to her new job at Fidelity Bank, in the main branch on Broad Street. It was sad to say goodbye to the theater job, but the bank job fit her schedule. The bank job was mindless, perfect for a student. Grace sat at one of four stations with a partner. All the workers were college students. The shift started at four o'clock and lasted until nine o'clock. There were two students per station. The eight of them formed a comradery and had a lot of laughs while doing the repetitious functions of the job.

For five hours, the students filed cancelled checks into a system of metal boxes that were nestled on a rotary machine. They wore a rubber finger tip on their index fingers. Speed was important. All of the students needed to move their hands quickly, fanning the checks into the boxes with their left hands while moving the dividers in the boxes with their right hands. The checks went into a customer's numbered account.

After work, Grace did her homework. This often kept her up late. Some nights, Vince checked to see if Grace was asleep and if he didn't see her studying, he'd see if she was asleep in bed. He told her that she did funny things with her hands when she was sleeping. Grace knew that she was filing checks in mid-air.

Grace was in her second year at Temple University when she saw him. There, walking toward her, was the young man she saw at Community College. She felt butterflies in her stomach when he passed her, and mustered up enough confidence to say hello to him. He smiled back at her.

"Bette?" he said, teasing her.

She laughed but couldn't utter a word. At least she looked totally different than the day she first met him. This time, she wore jeans, a white shirt, Frye boots, and a leather jacket. No hat this time. Her hair was long and super curly that day—she had set her hair with paper clips. She knew the sun was shining on her golden highlights. As she walked towards Broad Street and the moment had passed, she heard a choir practicing in one of the campus buildings. Words came to her as she passed the building—*Traveling again, alone from one place to another, the solemn face looked down. There came the old building, there was the choir, chanting Alleluia—a distant Alleluia. Their souls were still trying, voices flowing to the face that looked down. With each note, there was a slight resurrection of the wrinkled brow—the music did it so. There still could be an Alleluia.*

Certainly, these halls of learning would lift Grace's spirit, but now that her object of affection was on campus, who knows how far she could soar?

Sixteen

L IFE WAS TAKING ON a new trajectory. Grace was in school and she found a new job that fit her schedule. Those Harlow days and fleeting friends were vanishing in the background—part of her past. Then one night as Grace finished her shift at the bank and was waiting for the C bus on Broad Street, she heard someone calling her name and turned to see who it was.

"Grace, where have you been? I haven't seen you at Harlow's for a long time," said Lucas, her former crush.

"True. I stopped going because I am in college now, and I work across the street at Fidelity Bank," Grace said. "I don't have time to go to clubs."

"Good for you. I always knew you were just passing through." He laughed.

"How is everyone? And Camila?" asked Grace.

"I don't see her much anymore. She is hooked up with Roger now. You know that number who works at the Artemis counter at Wanamaker's?"

"Yeah, Roger; I've seen him there. He's gorgeous. Camila must have a thing for trying to convert gay men."

"True, but she needn't bother." Lucas laughed.

Grace knew what she'd felt for Lucas was a one-time attraction. The fact that he was gay was incidental.

"You know, Grace, I am glad I ran into you. Something happened a while ago, and I've been meaning to find you. I wanted to let you know about something, something paranormal, but I didn't have your phone number. I looked for Diana, but she never returned to the club either. I heard she's in rehab."

"Actually, I don't know if she is. We lost touch," Grace replied, feeling ashamed in a way. She should at least know what became of Diana.

"Well, I was invited to this mansion in upstate New York. It was a gathering of people from all over the world. The estate belonged to a well-known clairvoyant. He was originally an engineer from Germany and moved to the States thirty years ago. Some people think he's a former Nazi. It's only rumors. He was a rune master in those days aside from building things. Oh look, here's your bus."

"That's okay, I'll let this one go. There will be another one."

Lucas nodded and continued, "At the estate, I saw a huge swing that hung over a pool of water. This guy, this estate owner, had engineered it to mechanically move on a pulley contraption. Anyway, when you sat on the swing, you were supposed to be able to see your past lives as you swung back and forth. And the longer you stayed on it, the more lives you could see."

"That's fascinating. I never heard of anything like this in any of the books I read on this kind of stuff."

"This one woman swung back and forth on the swing for about five minutes and when she came off it, I swear she was catatonic. She needed to be revived, and when she came out of her trance, she said she only saw a dark place. I opted not to go on it. It was tempting, but the look in her eyes—a vacant look like she lost her soul—scared me. The reason why I wanted to find you was the clairvoyant told me that there was a young woman around me that has a shiny object, probably a crystal ball. He told me this young woman intended to give it to me, but she dropped it as she held it up to the sun. It has a tiny flaw in it. He then went on to say that this young woman has real power, yet it is unharnessed and he wanted me to bring her to him. I thought of you, Grace. You are the only person around me who fits that description."

"Wow, that's intense. I hate to disappoint you, Lucas, but that isn't me. I gave all that stuff up when I decided to go back to school."

"Mmm, really, who could it be then?" Lucas pondered.

"Look, here's another bus, Lucas. It was fabulous running into you. Be good, be safe, and behave!" She laughed, kissed him on the cheek, and boarded the bus.

As Grace rode home on the C bus, she felt a chill go down her spine. She was struck by the swing. That was the word she saw in the crystal when she visited the occult shop. There was no way she would let Lucas know it was her— she was the one who had dropped the crystal on the back porch. Between this clairvoyant, Mr. O'Hara, and the old wiccan at the occult shop, Grace thought that it was strange that there were people out there that wanted her to join their groups. Dr. Cohen would have said that Grace was attracting these people to herself because she was projecting this desire to belong to a family— thus, the group. And then Diana may have mentioned the crystal ball to Lucas at the club. It was true that Grace did have a tinge of interest when he mentioned the rune master. She'd bought runes when she was deeply involved in all forms of divination. The runes were ancient Germanic alphabet letters. They were used for fortune-telling, and the Swastika was one of the symbols. Grace began to understand the runes and thought that she could do readings with them, but she took a hiatus from these types of divination to focus on her college studies. She did consult I-Ching, but she didn't see that as divination. Confucius used the I-Ching for advice, so Grace embraced the notion that if the I-Ching was good enough for Confucius, then it was good enough for her.

Deep in thought, Grace almost missed her bus stop. She rushed to the front door of the bus and jumped onto the pavement just in time. When she returned home, she hit the books to study for one of her final exams. Grace sat at the table in the dining room.

Vince wasn't home yet. She was writing notes in her notebook when her pen began to move fast. It was spelling something. She thought about automatic writing, where one could sit with a blank piece of paper and hold a pen without any intention of writing anything with meaning. If she relaxed enough and let the pen move her hand across the page, a message would be revealed. This was similar to what the Ouija board could do, but instead of having printed letters, the blank page served as a place where a message could form without any preconceived ideas.

Grace decided that she didn't want to see the message. She crumbled the page and threw it in the wastebasket in the kitchen.

When she returned to the dining room, her textbook was open to a different page from where she had left off. Immediately, Grace did her own intervention. Dr. Cohen warned her that old habits come back when we were under stress. Grace knew she was nervous about the exam; running into Lucas and stirring up that mystic stuff didn't help. By identifying the cause of her stress, she was able to mitigate her fear.

She was too distracted to study. It was getting late but there was a chance that Shirley was still awake. She closed her books and went next door.

"Shirley, are you there?" Grace asked as she gently knocked on her neighbor's door.

"Come on in, the door's open," Shirley replied.

Grace was happy that the rest of Shirley's family had retired for the night. She would have Shirley to herself.

"I was having trouble studying. I have a final exam tomorrow," Grace said.

"Don't worry, what you know now for the test is all you will ever know. It's better to get rest," Shirley replied.

"You're right. Mommy used to say it wasn't worth it to cram."

"I can make you a cup of tea and I have Tastykakes Butterscotch Krimpets if you want?" Shirley offered in her kind way.

"That would be nice, you know how much I love Tastykakes but the tea will be enough, thank you, Shirley."

Shirley walked to the kitchen where she put a kettle of water on the stove. When she returned, she looked at Grace who was seated on the couch. Shirley noticed that Grace had a faraway look in her eyes.

"I was thinking of Diana. It feels strange that I don't know what is going on with her," Grace said.

"They put her away. I thought you knew," said Shirley as she sat in her favorite chair.

"No, I didn't know," Grace responded.

"I went to the corner store a while back," said Shirley.

"Wait, you went out to the store? I can't believe it," said Grace, amazed at the thought of Shirley leaving her house, something she rarely did.

"Yes, I managed to make it out one day. I was out of cigarettes."

"Aah, that makes sense."

"That day, I saw Diana's sister. I asked her how Diana was, and she said that she was sent to a rehabilitation facility to detox."

"I hope she gets better." Grace said wholeheartedly.

"Don't even think about having a friendship with her again, Grace, she is a bad seed."

Grace sat in silence. She still felt like she had something heavy weighing on her. Shirley must have noticed because she asked, "Is there something wrong? You look upset, Grace."

"Yeah, there is something wrong, sort of. Remember when I told you that my father hit me that one night? I left out something. I lit a candle, and I asked the spirits to show me that he was rotten. He developed gangrene immediately. I was so frightened when he ended up in the hospital that I had to find a spell to remove what I had done."

"Oh, Grace, you are not responsible for that. Don't blame yourself. Maybe it was something else that caused it."

"True. I discussed these things with my counselor. She helped me see it in a realistic way. She pointed out that my father may have been hiding his leg infection, and that after they treated it, he was released from the hospital just like any other patient. She also said it probably had nothing to do with me."

The tea kettle whistled.

"Let me get your tea," Shirley said as she stood up from her recliner. She came back with the cup, steam rising and handed it to Grace, then she sat back down.

"I know I probably didn't cause it," Grace continued, "but I still feel guilty about wishing harm on my dad."

"I have something to tell you, Grace. There were things between your parents that only I knew. Your mom confided in me like I did in her. I don't think she would mind if I told you now. See, your mother had lost any warm feelings she had for your father a while before you were born. She couldn't stand his touch for one second. He mistreated her, never took her out anywhere, and forced himself on her. Now, you know we wives have our wifely duty even if we don't feel like being, you know, what's the word?"

"Amorous?" asked Grace.

"Yep, that's it," Shirley responded with some embarrassment.

"I get it. It's okay, you can tell me," Grace said sensing that this topic was uncomfortable for Shirley.

"Your mom married to have children. She wasn't in love with your dad, and he knew it. After your mom had another miscarriage, her second one, she gave up on having children. Your dad began to sleep in the back room."

"I thought he moved in there once I was born."

"No, he moved in there earlier than that. I don't remember exactly when. Your mom made it clear that there would be no more physical relations between them. She couldn't go through with a chance of a third miscarriage. She thought it was God's will. But your dad didn't listen to her, and he came into the front bedroom and forced himself on her. I know times are changing, but it is still okay for a man to demand his pleasure from his wife. Nine months later, there you were. So, you see the bad thing turned into a good thing. You were your mother's precious gift."

"But I was conceived out of force, like some cruel accident."

"Don't think of it that way, Grace. Your dad didn't really hurt your mom. He did what men do. And it only happened that one time. Once you were born, he never forced himself on her again. Your mom was protective of you, though, more than usual. She even had you baptized twice. Once by the priest at the church, and then she took you over to the convent and the nuns blessed you."

"The convent? Why would she do that?"

"I don't know, it's a mystery to me."

A week later, Grace had another final exam coming up. It was an exam for her lecture class that all communications majors were required to take. The textbook was boring. At least the professor was interesting. He predicted that the movie business would change. There would be large complexes of smaller screening theaters with multiple films playing at once. Consumers also could choose films on their televisions from a library housed through a wireless network. He shared with his students that they were in the information age, where all information would be stored on a tiny computer chip. Telephones would be portable. But he warned the class that for all these modern conveniences there was a price to pay—the loss of privacy and individual freedom.

Grace wished the textbook contained the professor's information about the future, but no such luck. The book included past inventions and communication laws. She struggled reading through it. One night, as she tried her best to study this dribble, she noticed a faint, familiar scent.

Grace left the dining room and, as she walked through the living room, the scent became stronger. She was compelled to walk up the stairs and, reaching the top of the stairs, she turned toward the front bedroom. As she walked slowly past the bathroom and neared the doorway of the front bedroom, she was startled at the sight of a man lying on her mother's bed. She could only see the pair of his shiny black shoes pointed upward to the ceiling.

She couldn't move forward or backward and heard a small voice in her ear. A woman's voice. "Don't be afraid, Gracie." Grace knew it was Grandmom Rosie. The sound of her tender voice gave Grace the courage to move into the bedroom. The man looked as if he was lying in a coffin. He was dressed in a black suit, and his pale hands were crossed over his chest. The scent in the room was overwhelming. Suddenly, his eyes opened wide. He looked straight into Grace's eyes. Grace knew this day would come. She had to face this creature. All things merged into this final encounter.

The man sat up on the bed and put his feet on the floor. Was this the evil one? Did he come for his payment—her soul?

Grace summoned enough courage to speak. "Are you Bartholomew?" Grace asked.

The man laughed. "If I was, why would you hear Grandmom Rosie's voice? Do you think she would send you in here to face the devil?"

He did have a point. But the devil plays tricks. Then, Grace noticed his great head of black hair. One curl fell upon his forehead, and that one curl was pure white. He was a handsome man of about fifty. She checked his shoes again and they were normal—no ugly, unnatural devil's feet.

"Grace, don't be afraid. I am here to protect you. It is true that there is a dark force around you. I am holding him at bay. Ignore him. He hates that. Sit down next to me and concentrate on me," the man said.

Suddenly, there was a burst of a familiar fragrance permeating the room.

"What is that scent?" Grace asked.

"It's frankincense."

"That's it. It smells like church."

"Yes, the place you have rejected."

"I know I gave up on the church."

"Grace, you must return," he demanded. "If not, you will fall into a dark, perverse world for eternity. A world without God."

Grace stood in silence, and in this momentary time of recognition, she was able to see that the man was wearing a priest's collar. A warm feeling flowed with her. "You are Father Brice, aren't you?"

"Yes, I am. I have been around you, watching, but I couldn't get through."

"I knew there was something or someone around me aside from the evil spirit."

"Come sit by me here where your mother used to sleep," said Father.

Grace sat on her mother's bed as Father began to explain to her the significance of the question she'd asked all those years ago.

"Once you asked the question 'who is the devil?' you opened a channel to the demon, Bartholomew. He was the entity I initially saw on the church steps and later tried to exorcise. He was also the man you saw at your family's funeral parlor on New Year's Day. His presence was in the tunnel at the theater too. But he influenced others near you as well, including Diana. He took over the old man you met in the library. Angelo and Janice were also taken over by him.

"What about the Gemini girls? Were they influenced by the demon?" asked Grace.

"No. This group is under another influence. They are an affinity of spirits from centuries ago who have had many transformations. They are bound together until the Day of Judgment." "What binds them, Father?"

"A few centuries ago, a group of women formed a witch's coven. They were devoted to Satan and since then they continue on earth as a unique, homogenous group. Each time they incarnate in a different form. They could all be born under the same Zodiac sign at times, they could all have the same sexual preference at times, they could be the same age or have the same physical attributes—it continues as they are possessed by one of the seven facets of the devil. One day they will have the choice to break away from the group each as an individual spirit, ready to accept God or not. When people stray from God, they are open to darkness. You are no exception, Grace, but the difference is that your mother had a strong benevolent spirit and she still possesses that spirit in the afterlife. She prayed for you every day of her short life, and she made sure you had an extra blessing from the sisters when they prayed over you on their altar in the convent. After her passing, she requested an emissary to guard over you. This is why I am here. I am her emissary.

"It saddened me to see how you sought revenge on Angelo and Janice. In this world, it is the common thing to do; however, Jesus showed us not to seek revenge on our enemies. Vengeance does not satisfy. If you are evil, you will love it and want more revenge, but if you are good, vengeance leaves you with remorse. What do you gain by punishing others? A dark soul? A hardened heart? Let God be the judge of their actions in the courts of heaven. Rage against the principalities, not the flesh. Fight the evil, not the person. You need to turn away from that power to cast spells and predict the future. This is idolatry!

"When I was on earth, I did many exorcisms. The last one I performed failed. The possessed innocent—the young woman—died, and I died soon after. I should not have told your mother about it. Somehow, by knowing the demon's earthly name, your mother was in danger. The demon, Bartholomew, was trying to possess Kate but her faith was too strong. He couldn't get through, but he was able to latch on to you, but not entirely."

"Was Bartholomew ever a real person?"

"No, that was a story that the demon placed in Diana's mind. The demon uses his earthly name, Bartholomew, when he possesses his human subjects. Diana was an instrument for him to communicate with you, much like the Ouija board. She has no recollection of writing that letter."

"What about Melissa Swain? Was that me who lived long ago?"

"No. That was part of a fabricated story. Bartholomew is a formation of the archdemon, Satan. He has had this name for centuries and he possessed the young girl in Saint Stephen's parish where I attempted the exorcism. The girl's name was Melissa Swain. This archdemon prowls about the earth as a unique identity, but only as a symbol of a human form. He travels around time to steal souls."

"Then my therapist was wrong," Grace said.

"Not entirely. She helped you see how to forgive yourself if someone takes advantage of you. Your algebra teacher was a charlatan but when he played with channeling in your presence he stepped into a dangerous world and experienced a real fright. Bartholomew came through. I was very happy that you prayed to the Blessed Mother."

"But then you stayed away from God, and the demon was able to get closer to you and play havoc."

"What about the tarot readings and all the other things I was doing?"

"The devil loves to give you power. Yes, you did have a special ability from God, but you abused it. The devil loves to seduce those who are close to God, and he tempts you with extraordinary talents and skills. He loves to turn you away from the Creator. If you continued dabbling in the occult, you would have lost your soul to him. It would all seem great until he asks for his repayment. It usually takes twenty years."

"I thought this was all a hoax, a clever prank Diana played on me along with the girls who live next door. I went to therapy, and my therapist helped me to understand that much of what was happening was coincidental."

"Yes, therapists can help. God gave his children the ability to reason. Your therapist followed a line of reasoning and often this is the essential path for recovery. But God created the ability to believe and this may seem the opposite of logic. Finding the balance of the two is the way. It is best to use logic to do God's will. Many make their God, a God of logic and reject faith, and others rely on faith alone without using logic. It is as basic as the sun and the moon, day and night—everything contains its opposite. It will be a great day when Science and Spirituality unite. God gives his children talents and insights in order for them to help individuals, but in your case, it was truly something outside the realm of psychology."

"What about Diana? Will she be okay?" asked Grace.

"If she wants to be. It is her choice. All of us have a choice, Grace. God created us with free will."

"But her cards ended with the Sun. It meant she would find contentment."

"The possibility of contentment. The course of a life is determined by the myriad of choices a person makes. What you saw in the cards was a probability if Diana stayed on the course she chose. But again, God gives us free will to change our path. That is why it is a sin to read the cards—you are interfering with a person's God-given gift of free will."

"Where is my mother? Why has she never contacted me?"

"After she died, like others, she was in a room. She was there for a few days, but to you on earth, some years had passed. She had a short purifying process where she sat with God's helpers. They are like counselors but with much more loving, spiritual wisdom. Your mother completed her sessions, and she is on her spiritual continuum now."

"I miss her very much, Father."

"I know you do, but it is better not to pray for her to help you; that would make it difficult for her to move on. What you must do is pray for her to have beautiful peace in her journey of everlasting life with Christ in heaven."

"What about Grandmom Rosie? Why was she able to reach me just now?"

"Grandmom Rosie is further along on the continuum than your mother. She was able to come to you tonight with the permission of the angels. Your mother is almost at this level. She needed to resolve her feelings toward your father. She took the hurt with her when she died, and she had to learn to forgive."

"There's something I don't understand. Why the Ouija board? Why did my mother buy it for me?"

"Your mother knew that she would die early and leave you here. She knew that from when you were born."

"I remember that she told me that my heart-shaped red birthmark was where an angel kissed me. It's still on my right thigh. I often touch it to remember how sweet it was for her to tell me that," Grace said as she felt tears forming.

"Yes, your grandmother and your mother knew how to make the simplest things memorable. You will always have their love. Your mother was afraid that the demon I tried to exorcise could harm you. Many years after I died, it was just before you were born, I was permitted to come to her in a dream. I warned her about Bartholomew. I knew that this demon was a disciple of Satan, the archdemon of anger. I couldn't exorcise this demon when I was on earth. Anger is the most powerful of all the aspects of the devil. Your mother thought that somehow after she died, she could send you messages through the Ouija board so she could protect you. When you asked 'who is the devil?' she realized that wasn't a good idea and made sure you didn't use it again."

"If my mother couldn't come back to protect me, then I am glad it is you who broke through. She told me so much about you."

"Yes, we had many wonderful talks in the house on Victoria Street. She had a gift and so do you, but these gifts are to be used for good, not for revenge."

"I didn't think what I was doing was bad, Father."

"On the surface it doesn't seem bad, but God doesn't want you to know the future, unless it is his will. He does choose prophets at times. They are divine prophets with gifts able to reveal God's message. What you were doing is predicting the future and divining your will on the events that have nothing to do with God. This is not what God intended. When your mother passed, you were an open vessel. The darkness came in. The devil gives you power so you can perform the extraordinary. It is hard to resist. Grace, you must accept the ordinary and use your gift of receiving only to spread the word of God and guide others to make better choices. This will infuriate the evil one, and he will go on his way."

Father Brice leaned over to the other side of Kate's bed. He retrieved an object that had been placed on the floor. It was an old satchel with a rope handle.

"I have something here that I want to share with you," Father said as he guided her out of the bedroom. They walked down the stairs.

"Should I light a candle in the kitchen?" asked Grace.

"No, I want you to come with me outside of the house. I think it is best if we are out in the open air. There's a park nearby," said Father Brice. "We will go there."

"Yes, it's Marconi Plaza," said Grace. "You know, Marconi, the inventor of the radio."

Grace thought if any of her neighbors saw her with Father Brice what would they think? What was she doing walking around the neighborhood with a priest who was carrying a weird satchel? Fortunately, there wasn't anyone outside on her block and the few people they passed on the way, didn't act like anything was out of the ordinary. They walked a few blocks to the park off Broad Street. It had rained that day and the grounds were soggy. That had worked in their favor since no one was in the park that night. They sat on a bench where Father opened his satchel. He removed a lantern that had a candle inside. With a long wooden match, he lit the candle inside the lantern. He then placed the lantern on a patch of earth and removed from the satchel what looked like an ancient urn and an old clay cup. He placed them both on the ground.

"What you are about to do will help you heal from the disease, sometimes referred to as the infliction of the oracular slave girl," said Father Brice. "In the book of Acts Sixteen, Verses Sixteen through Eighteen, Paul and Silas had arrived in Philippi, a leading district of Macedonia, where they encountered a slave girl. She possessed an oracular spirit and was able to make large amounts of money for her owners by fortune-telling. She began to follow Paul and Silas, shouting that these men were slaves to God. Paul commanded in the name of Jesus Christ that the spirit come out of her and it came out of her at that moment."

Father lifted the urn from the ground and held it with great reverence as he said his next words. "You need to drink from this. It will seep into your body, mind, and spirit. Thank you for this gift, Lord, which you made a long time ago. Please help me protect this child of yours, Lord, and help me to rid the demon, Bartholomew, from this place and from this child. Lord, I pray that this will release me from the binds of guilt and failure that I was unable to rid the demon of that precious, young girl in my parish. Lord, you are all-loving, and you are the victor over the evil one when you died for our sins on the cross. Glory to God in the highest. Amen."

Father then said to Grace, "You must build up your immune system on four planes. First, the physical, by drinking this liquid that is within this vessel. It will permeate your cells with a healing property. Then, you must give up mental thoughts of the evil presence that surrounds you. By eliminating these thoughts, you will eliminate fear that exists on the emotional plane. As you allow the Holy Spirit to enter your being, you will be spiritually immune to the evil one."

Father took the cup and poured the dark red liquid from the urn. "Drink of this slowly, Grace. Savor the richness of the ancient grapes."

Grace brought the cup to her lips. She breathed in the bouquet of wine. She tasted a bit of it and as it flowed through her, she thought of the Eucharist—the blood of Christ that heals the world's sinners.

"This is the wine of Cana," said Father Brice.

"The one at the wedding feast?" Grace asked with amazement. "The one Jesus made from water?"

"Yes. After my death, I worked with God's counselors to help many souls who were on the precipice of their higher spiritual level. I was given a chance to resolve something from my own life. I asked to finish my failed exorcism and was guided by angels. They brought me to the wedding. I witnessed the Savior's first miracle. He couldn't refuse his mother's plea. I saw Mary, and I was humbled. I saw Jesus and his disciples, who were invited to the wedding. I saw Mary telling Jesus that they ran short of wine. There were six stone water jars there for the Jewish ceremonial washings, each holding twenty to thirty gallons. Jesus told them to fill the jars with water. They filled them and followed Jesus's instruction to give some of it to the headwaiter. The water had become wine and the headwaiter noticed that the wine was superior. He couldn't understand why this wine wasn't served at first since the best wine was served early and then the inferior wine was served later. Jesus did this as the beginning of his signs at Cana in Galilee and so his disciples began to believe in him. Jesus gave me this urn and this cup. I felt pure love in his presence. His miracle lives on. I am doing the work of a disciple in a world where time and space are one. Take another sip of this sacred wine and repeat after me, 'Blessed are you, Lord God of all creation.'"

"Blessed are you, Lord God of all creation," Grace repeated.

At that moment, a ghastly odor surrounded them. Grace remembered the disgusting smell that was in the tunnel at the theater; this was indeed the same.

"Grace, do you smell that?"

"Yes, Father, I know this awful odor."

"It is sulfur; a sign that evil is near."

"Sip again and repeat after me, 'For through your goodness, we have received the wine we offer you.'"

"For through your goodness, we have received the wine we offer you," Grace continued.

"Drink again and repeat, 'Fruit of the vine and work of human hands, it will become our spiritual drink.'"

"Fruit of the vine and work of human hands, it will become our spiritual drink."

A ripple in the air formed. It looked like a wave where an image was swaying within the twisting, swirling mist. And then there he was—Bartholomew T. Harrod. He wore a gentleman's long waistcoat with a ruffled white shirt. He was looking straight at Father Brice as he laughed at him.

Father rose from the bench, placing the wine vessel on the ground. He turned to Grace and said, "This demon is part of Satan. He appears to be a man, but he is only in the form of a man. He is something else, something unholy. Grace, I failed on earth to do a proper exorcism. Here in this place, I will rid this evil that surrounds you. I will finish what I started many years ago when I failed Melissa, and I will recite the original prayer to Saint Michael."

Father walked away from Grace and toward Bartholomew. He stood directly in front of this evil being. He retrieved a paper from his pocket and read these words— *O glorious Archangel St. Michael, Prince of the heavenly host, defend us in battle and in the struggle, which is ours against the principalities and powers, against the rulers of this world of darkness, against spirits of evil in high places. Come to the aid of men, whom God created immortal, made in his own image and likeness, and redeemed at a great price from the tyranny of the devil. Fight this day the battle of the Lord, together with the holy angels, as already thou hast fought the leader of the proud angels, Lucifer, and his apostate host, who were powerless to resist thee, nor was there a place for them any longer in Heaven. That cruel, that ancient serpent, who is called the devil or Satan, who seduces the whole world, was cast into the abyss with all his angels.*

Bartholomew had stopped laughing and his beautiful face started to age.

Father continued—*Behold this primeval enemy and slayer of man has taken courage. Transformed into an angel of light, he wanders about with all the multitude of wicked spirits, invading the earth in order to blot out the name of God and of his Christ; to seize upon, slay and cast into eternal perdition souls destined for the crown of eternal glory. This wicked dragon pours out, as a most impure flood, the venom of his malice on men of depraved mind and corrupt heart, the spirit of lying, of impiety, of blasphemy, and the persistent breath of impurity, and of every vice and iniquity.*

The image of the man before them was melting away. There were flies beginning to gather around the vanishing form. Grace looked down and she saw the demon's ugly feet—they were diseased. There were crawling things moving within them, and a thick substance oozed out of them and into the ground.

Father continued—*Most crafty enemies have filled and inebriated with gall and bitterness the Church, the spouse of the Immaculate Lamb, and have laid impious hands on her most sacred possessions. In the Holy Place itself, where has been set up the See of the most blessed, Peter and the Chair of Truth, for the light of the world. They have raised the throne of their abominable impiety, with the iniquitous design that when the Pastor has been struck, the sheep may be scattered. Arise then, O invincible prince, bring help against the attacks of the most spirits to the people of God, and give them the victory. They venerate thee as protector and patron; in thee, holy Church glories as her defense against the malicious powers of the world and of hell. To thee has God entrusted the souls of man to be established in heavenly beatitude. Oh, pray to the God of peace that He may put Satan under our feet, so far conquered that he may no longer be able to hold men in captivity and harm the Church. Offer our prayers in the sight of the Most High so that they may quickly conciliate the mercies of the Lord;*

and beating down the dragon, the ancient serpent, who I, the devil, and Satan, do thou again make him captive in the abyss that he may no longer seduce the nations. Amen.

"Father, you did it! Look, he's gone," exclaimed Grace.

Father Brice was victorious. The flies were gone, and any remnant of Bartholomew vanished. The rippled air straightened itself, and the smell of sulfur dissipated.

Through his battle that night in the park, Father faced his own failure, and he rid Grace of the demon who was lusting to possess her soul.

"Father, does this mean you have finished what you were meant to do?"

"Yes, Grace, I can move on like your mother has. But there are still some things I need you to do. I want you to gather up all your paraphernalia of anything unholy; that means your tarot cards, the crystal ball, any books of divination including the *I-Ching*, the runes, and the pentagram you wore on the black velvet ribbon. You must throw that Ouija board away. Discard the whole lot of these worthless objects. Then, I want you to receive the sacraments, pray, and read scripture. This is the way. This is what your mother wants for you. Did she not say to you that it is all true?"

"Yes, she did, but I ignored it. I was doing fine without all that religious stuff."

"You thought you were doing fine. God always loves you, and he has sent his son, Jesus, to forgive you of your sins. Stay on this path and you will have a good life. If you find it difficult to forgive others, then pray to God to forgive them. Hate the sin, not the sinner. When you are confused about your thoughts or actions, ask yourself if this thought or deed would please or would it offend God? Then you will know the right thing to do. Remember you have been invited to God's house. We all are invited but few of us accept his invitation.

"There is a parable in the Bible where Luke describes the great feast. It appears in Chapter Fourteen, Verses Fifteen through Twenty-Four. The story is about a man who gave a dinner and invited many. He sent his servant to invite his guests. But, one by one, they all made excuses not to attend. One said that he had purchased land and had to examine it and another said that he had purchased yokes of oxen and had to inspect them and yet another had the excuse that he had just married. Then the man sent his servant to invite the poor and the crippled, the blind and the lame. But the dinner was not full and he sent his servant out to the highways to make people come into his home so that it would be full. The parable tells the story of God's invitation, told by Jesus, as an example for all of us to answer his father's invitation so that we may dine with him in the Kingdom of God. God is inviting you to his dinner, will you accept, Grace? And if so, how will you prepare? Let me put it this way, when you are invited to someone's home, what do you do to prepare?"

"I bring something, I try to look my best, and I tell myself to be on my good behavior," Grace answered.

"Then what is it you need to do to accept God's invitation? Are you to make sure you take care of your body and soul? Will you grow in love to bring that gift to God's house? And will you continually repent your sins? This way, when you enter God's house, you will join with all the other guests who are pure in spirit. On this fallen earth, your temptation will be to use your power, so you must be humble instead. The Bible states that the humble will be exalted and the exalted will be humbled.

"You will face many trials that will be difficult. Life is supposed to be difficult. God will give you the strength to do the right thing. Believe in Him and let the Holy Spirit guide you. Don't put your trust in leaders. Many of them are deceptive and have an agenda. The world will become more and more secular, and tyranny will be disguised as the common good. Each century has its markers of the spiritual battle that exist between God and the devil. The twentieth century has many markers of this continuous battle on earth. World Wars, dictatorships, and communism are just a part of it. Your time has lessons for you, Grace, just as it does for your generation and those future generations coming after you. Do not give into the Jezebel spirit, the one that rids the earth of many innocent ones in their mother's wombs. Pray to Mary, the Mother of God who is the first Tabernacle—she held the Savior in her womb. There was a major shift the day President Kennedy died. It was the beginning of a breakdown of Godliness. Put your trust in God. Live up to your namesake. Your mother named you Grace as a reminder to stay with God and receive a blessing. She can move on now knowing that you are safe."

Father Brice's solid body was disappearing in front of Grace's eyes. The jug, the satchel and the cup had already faded away. Grace wanted him to stay there longer. She had so many questions for him. "Father, will Jesus come again? Will there be a second coming?"

"I can't tell you when, but yes, Jesus returns to earth again. You see, everyone deserves a second chance. I had my second chance, and now you have yours."

Father smiled at Grace the way she knew he smiled at her mother. She could see why he was an important person in her mother's life. His smile was intoxicating. Grace looked down at the lantern; it illuminated the space and gave her a feeling that she could move on without fear. When she looked up, Father was gone. She was left in the park. Kate would have been amused that this exorcism took place in the park named after the man who invented the radio; she did have that belief that human beings have an antenna in their heads. Grace felt a warmth emanating from her heart. The lantern was still there. She picked it up, extinguished the candle, and carried it home with a new revival in her soul. When she reached home, she saw her father unlocking the front door.

"Hi, Dad," Grace said.

Vince looked at her strangely, not because she was carrying a lantern, but he saw a different Grace. It looked as if she had a soft glow about her. They went into the house together. Something had changed about the house. The holy scent of frankincense no longer filed the space and the smell of sulfur was gone. Vince put his hat on top of the china closet, hung his jacket in the cellar hall closet, and turned to her and said, "Six o'clock rolls around pretty early."

Seventeen

♥

G RACE WAS CAST AS the lead, Jill Tanner, in *Butterflies are Free*. Plays and Players served Grace well. Vince planned to attend her opening night. Grace was beginning to see her father in a new light. When she drank the sacred wine all her stiffness went away. The seed of the ancient grapes grew inside her. Her power was love. Jesus was within. And she knew He was the true power.

Grace returned to what she was born into, the Christian life. She discarded amulets, books, tarot cards and her crystal. As soon as she relinquished her connection to the dark powers, she possessed a new discernment. She knew right from wrong immediately. Confusion was cast aside. Old hurts and resentment faded away. She understood that Henry and Aunt Amanda needed to find a new way of living. She still loved Henry, but she realized she needed to stop holding him up to an impossible standard. Grace promised herself she would continue to write to him, and she hoped someday to visit him in his desert oasis. She also found it in her heart to nurture a fondness for Aunt Amanda. It was better to be with Christ.

It truly was a miracle that Grace escaped the devil. The darkness that had held her became light. She was changed. Yet she knew that her life would still have its temptations, its obstacles, and its losses. But she understood that resorting to false beliefs, no matter how enticing they were, could never bring her the joy of living simply in the presence of God. She was grateful that her mother was able to send Father Brice to save her from the clutches of the master deceiver. But what about others who may not have anyone who prays for them or teaches them to follow God's will? She would try her best to share the truth with those who would appear on her path in the coming days of her time on earth.

Grace witnessed her father's transformation when she accepted the blessing. She had to soften her heart first, then he was able to face something he had buried within himself for a long time. One night when she returned from her play rehearsal, she saw her father sitting in the kitchen and she sensed that he was waiting for her to come home.

"Come in here, Grace, I want to talk to you," her father said in a stern tone.

She promptly walked into the kitchen.

"I don't know how to say this," he began. "I am not good with stuff like this. But I have to say that I am proud of you. I see how you are studying hard, and now you will have a lead in your first play. I know your mother would be extremely proud. You know I never knew how to treat your mother properly. Whatever I did, it was wrong. So, I gave up. I loved her more than anything in the world, but she didn't love me back. It wasn't her fault; I told her I had enough love for both of us. After the second miscarriage, she didn't want to be near me. I can't describe the hurt I felt. I slept alone in the back bedroom and I missed having her next to me. It was a spring night years ago and for some reason we were getting along again. I thought that your mother was finally getting over the loss of our two babies. I tried to rekindle our— you know what I mean. It seemed fine but your mother suddenly stopped during the middle—oh, my God, this is so hard."

"Dad, you don't have to say anything more."

"But I have to. I didn't respect your mother's wishes and I took advantage of her. When she became pregnant, I thought it would erase that part of the night when you were conceived. But your birth did the opposite. She was totally devoted to you and I faded into the background."

"Not to me, Dad, you were never in the background when I was growing up."

"I only knew how to be when you were little," Vince continued. "As soon as you grew older, I couldn't handle it. You and your mother were like glue. I lost my place. I was so angry. I said things to hurt you both. Neither of you needed me."

"All I care about is that we have each other from now on," Grace said. She could see that this conversation was uncomfortable for her father.

"Oh, and if you could get cable TV, that would be perfect."

Vince laughed. The brief exchange ended but it gave Grace hope that their relationship would improve.

It was time for Grace to leave for the theater. It was opening night. She gave him that "Hollywood kiss" like she had as a child, but she kissed him on the cheek and didn't slap him as hard.

When Grace arrived at the theater, she went over her lines with the woman who was playing the mother of the male lead. They sipped tea with lots of lemon. This was a good thing to do to ensure their throats remained moist. They did vocal exercises and stretched their limbs. Acting encompasses all of a person's being. Grace learned this in her studies. She had relied on using sense memory to empathize with the characters she portrayed. However, none of this would matter, if she couldn't illustrate the essence of the role by using her physical body.

Grace learned to loosen her body before she adopted a posture that suited the role she was playing. She also learned that talking to the back of the house meant using her diaphragm. Anytime she was called on to do a scene in acting class she did breathing exercises. This night she incorporated all she had learned so far. Her favorite theater professor and many of her classmates promised to be there. Tammy and Gregory were attending and most importantly, her father. The pressure was building as time passed. Her fellow actress was nervous, too, and she only had one scene—Grace was in the whole play.

There was a portable record player backstage that the theater used as a prop with a stack of albums in the dusty corner by the dressing room. Grace sat at the dressing table and started to apply her makeup as the other actress put on one of the albums. Beautiful tones circled the room. She recognized the music.

"That's Ravel; I know it," Grace said.

"I love Ravel. I brought the album here to calm my nerves," revealed the cast member.

"It's "Pavane for a Dead Princess." I was obsessed with this piece. I played it many times after my mother died and I wrote lyrics to it."

"Really? What are they?"

Grace tried to remember the words. "It was something about children—*Now that you have gone, oh my dearest, I can't linger on, oh my princess, you are gone, and I can live no more.*

"Then there were more lines and I remember writing—*Children they are still playing. Why then can't I find you to play?*

"Interesting," said the actress. "Ravel never had children but he was known to love them. Your lyrics reflect that. You know there is a misconception about the piece."

"Really?"

"When I was studying music in college, there was a class where we delved into the history of the 19th Century composers. Many students thought that the Pavane was a funeral lament to a dead child. But our professor said that the piece was written with a 16th Century dance, a pavane, in mind—danced by a little princess as painted by Velazquez."

"Fascinating. All I know is when I wrote those words, they flowed through me and I fit the piece with my own story," commented Grace.

It was fifteen minutes to curtain. Grace felt her stomach hit the floor. All the relaxation exercises, the breathing, the limbering, it all went out the window. She was a mess. Her nerves were firing, and she felt flushed. No amount of therapy or lemons could help her in this moment. Grace shut her eyes and said a prayer. She asked God to give her strength. Even though this was only opening night jitters, there was something about being on stage with all eyes upon her that made her feel exposed. Grace told herself she had fought the devil; getting through the play should be a cinch.

It was time for her to stand behind the door that was center stage. Once she knocked on the door and the young actor opened it, she would face the audience. Once she entered the stage, the warm lights welcomed her to the play. The fear fell away immediately; she was home. The stage was a safe place. It was a controlled world. She fit. Grace became Jill Tanner, and the show was on.

The opening performance of the play was a hit. When the performance was over, the actors hugged each other backstage. They were jumping with glee. The director was happy. Grace felt like she had satisfied a part of something she had desired for a long time. At one point when she was on stage, she glanced into the audience. The house was packed, but there was an empty seat in the front row. She hoped that her mother was in that space. Grace wanted to believe that, but if Father Brice did his job, she knew that it was selfish to hold her mother to this earth. Kate was moving on her own spiritual path. Grace had to face life on earth with courage, the courage that her mother instilled in her, and the courage that God provides to everyone who loves him. For too long, she had forgotten that Jesus was by her side and that the Holy Spirit would guide her. This was the beginning of a new path. Henry's rational world had its merit, it loved creation, but it didn't stack up to the spiritual world, the one that loved the Creator.

"You were terrific," Vince said as he came backstage. He handed her a Whitman's Sampler box of chocolates.

Grace withheld her laughter. She didn't want her father to see that the box had significance. It was such a point of contention in her parents' relationship.

"Thanks, Dad, this is perfect. I love Whitman's," Grace said, whether she liked it or not.

At that moment Tammy and Gregory appeared.

"Dad, these are my good friends from the Walnut Street Theater."

"Great to meet you," said Tammy.

"Yes, good to meet you," said Gregory. "You have a delightful daughter and talented too."

"She sure is a good one. She was born with talent and a real comedian," said Vince proudly.

"I told them of your days in Vaudeville, Dad. So, they know I inherited it from you!"

A bit embarrassed, Vince responded, "Well, I'll let you to your friends. It was nice meeting you both," and he rushed to leave the backstage area.

"We want to celebrate your opening night," said Tammy.

"We thought we should do something different. Let's go to a night club and dance. We also thought to have a party at our place, but we didn't know how many people were coming to opening night and if there would be enough room," said Gregory. "There are about ten Temple students out there. I guess we could invite them."

"That's a good idea, let's see if they want to go." Grace responded.

Her college buddies and her favorite professor were waiting for her to come out from backstage. She was very happy to see their smiling faces. She was especially happy to see one of the students she befriended in the Communications department. She was a petite girl, younger than Grace, who was studying to be an actress as well. Grace was a bit cautious to become friends with anyone after her track record with past friendships, but she had a good feeling about this person. She had a premonition recently that she would meet a young woman who would become a life-long friend; Grace felt it was this girl. She was grateful to have Tammy, Gregory, Shirley, and Dr. Cohen who each had helped her with trusting others, but she longed for a friend who had the same interest in the acting world. It was time for Grace to accept new people in her life and let the hurt of those in the past reside in a closed corner of her heart.

Standing nearby was Vince who was watching Grace with her group of admirers. When Grace spotted him, she immediately ran to him and gave him a hug. "Oh, good, you're still here. Thanks for coming, Dad. It means a lot to me," said Grace.

"Sure, Grace, now go have fun with your fans."

Grace returned to the group and looked back at her father. She watched Vince pass by the rows of seats toward the exit door. She watched him go through the door and watched the door slowly close. That chapter came to an end, the one of hurt and misunderstanding. She had found love for him again.

Grace changed into her civilian clothes and joined her party of friends and acquaintances to embark on a night of celebration.

Naturally, Tammy and Gregory picked a straight club for the festivities. Grace only knew Harlow's. What a difference between the two. The music and the dancing in Harlow's were much better and it was pure spectacle. But she was content to be out with her colleagues celebrating the success of the play.

Grace was having a good time on this memorable night, but how memorable would it be now that across the dance floor stood the young man she had seen on campus?

"Tammy, look over there—he's here! Look, look! He's by the bar with that blond guy."

"Amazing—you found him! Aren't you happy you came here tonight?" asked Tammy, excited for Grace.

"I am going to walk by him and, if he stops me, I will talk to him; but if he doesn't, I will keep walking by."

Grace moved to the other side of the dance floor. She neared him. Her eyes were fixed in front of her. She didn't want him to see that she had recognized him. He reached out his hand, touched her arm and stopped her.

Grace had played it cool at the club. The young man had asked for her phone number but she declined. She told him she was rarely home. Between school, work, and homework, he wouldn't have success in getting in touch with her. She had to play hard to get; he was too good-looking and other girls certainly fawned all over him. He let her know that he worked at his uncle's movie theater in Center City; Grace made a mental note to casually stop by there.

Grace waited a week before she happened to pass the theater and there he was seated in the window of the box office. He was surprised to see her.

They had lunch together at the deli next to the theater. She wasn't embarrassed to eat her whole BLT sandwich in front of him. They talked about the classic black and white movies. They shared the books they loved as well. His favorite was "The Little Prince" and hers was "Little Anne of Canada."

He was nothing like she thought he would be. He wasn't conceited at all and he didn't have a girlfriend either. He told her his last date was with a beautiful girl that was the daughter of his mother's friend. He took her out for dinner recently and when she ordered a drink, she swept her hair with her fingers and shook her head from side to side and dramatically said, "Chablis," as if she was in an alluring commercial. That was it for him. He knew he wouldn't go out with her again. He didn't like veneer, he liked the real thing.

From that day forward, they were together. Soon, he was taking acting classes. Grace loved acting so much that she brought out his secret desire to become an actor. He had that special aura that few actors had. Many were handsome but only a handful had that extra charisma. He liked going to the movie theaters alone and it was there that the films gave him his view of the world. No way was he a stage actor, he was strictly made for the camera. The thought of them acting together filled Grace with joy.

Grace's birthday had arrived and she was acting in a thesis production at Temple's video studio. She was playing the role of Hedda Gabler. She understood Ibsen and found it a joy to play this character. She also loved playing, Anna Christie, and Lizzie in Jean-Paul Sartre's *The Respectful Prostitute*. The shoot took much longer than expected and she was late for her birthday celebration with her new love. When she arrived home, there on the kitchen table instead of a candle and a crystal ball was a birthday cake and gifts waiting for her to open. Her young man had arrived earlier and with Vince's permission, set up the table. When she saw what he had put together for her, the thrill of acting earlier did not compare to this touching gesture. There was a white blazer and a skirt to match, hot rollers, and a charming music box. The little music box played Mozart's "Serenade Minuet." Grace took this as a sign that this was her soulmate; she had dreamed of this music box in the past. The gifts were perfect—something practical, something to wear, and something that touched her heart. He had her favorite cake from the Melrose Diner and he lit the candles. Grace blew out the candles and wished that they would go through life together no matter what, even if they weren't going to be famous actors. Not since her mother, did Grace feel this kind of true love.

Eighteen

♥

A SUBTLE BREEZE TOUCHED Grace's cheek. It was an overcast day. When she leaned to the left she could see the ocean through the misty air. Grace looked into the distance. She saw the Claridge Hotel.

She was back in Atlantic City, and it came as no surprise that she and her perfect object of affection declared their love for each other. It had to happen there in the city, where a kaleidoscope of exquisite memories lived. She could see as far back as a baby, where she could sense that Henry was admiring her little hands as he pushed her stroller on the boardwalk. She could see her mother and Aunt Amanda with the boardwalk guards on their high heels. And there was Grandmom Rosie with her pearls and black shawl. Vince was there in his short sleeve shirt and his Timex watch. This was a happy picture in Grace's mind, just like her image of the other families on the boardwalk.

Then Grace remembered the solarium at the Claridge where she had her first kiss. Years later, she had hilarious fun with her gay friends on New York Avenue, where they frequented Dirty Edna's nightclub. The drag show with *Ruby Red Lips* was a glorious outrage.

Now, she was here with her college friends and her soon-to-be husband. They had rented a house for the summer. It was a bit south of the Claridge Hotel, but she could see the hotel from the rooftop where she sat. It had only been a year since she celebrated her first lead role and fell in love that opening night. Ever since he touched her arm as she passed him in the club, they were inseparable.

It was fitting that their friends had left to go back home. She and her love had the Atlantic City rental to themselves. They sat on the rooftop.

"Your eyes are so green today."

"Your eyes are so blue today," Grace said. They were quiet for a minute as they gazed into each other's eyes until she asked him, "Where do they go? Do we ever see them again?"

"You will see your mother again, Grace." He leaned in and embraced his bride-to-be. They sat there holding each other in silence, and then he went inside to take a nap.

Grace remained on the rooftop. She was hypnotized by the summer breeze and the memory of a time when Kate, Aunt Amanda, and Henry were happy in the Claridge Hotel Solarium. She turned to see the hotel in the present time—it was calling her back. Something stirred in her at this moment, and she could hear these words silently forming within her—

Summer, so warm and glowing, takes a holiday, and it is a dark day. I sit upon this sunroof, although there is no sun. The breeze touches my body, hair blowing out of place. I, a shaken figure on the high spot, alone. The salt air surrounds me, and if I squint my eyes, I can see the sand, the sea, and the horizon. The water is gray and dull. The moment comes, I grab it. I turn and see the Claridge Hotel. I am thirteen and death is hinting at my world. She says, 'Why don't you go and buy a molasses taffy?' And so, I will. I leave her up there in the room on the twelfth floor and walk independently up the street, nearing the beach and the boardwalk of people. Over and over, I hear a voice within myself to look up, as if I could catch this moment etched on her face. She will not always be here. I must look at her in a still time and take a universal picture of my love, my mother, at the window. She is a portrait of a pure queen, a regal statue glaring down at me.

I boyishly whistle. She jolts with laughter. So far away, yet I can hear her distinctive laugh. The slowness of the second ceases, and my feet begin to resume their routine. I have my taffy and return to her up there. But the mystic is with us now, a sad and shared secret. No one says it, but death is near for my queen. Oh, bitter life, please don't take the one that is mine. The one. Here again on the rooftop, the breeze touches my body, hair blowing out of place. I, a shaken figure on the high spot, alone. The salt air surrounds me. And if I squint my eyes, I can see the sand, the sea, and the horizon. But I am not alone. It's gone now, that world with her, and I must not be dead all my life, still alive. I didn't know until this moment when I see you as you are—my friend, brother, lover, husband. I ask you, "Where do they go? Do we ever see them again?" You hold me and it all goes away. I feel you, life. Welcome back. The silent vow is made here on the sunroof without a sun. The sky lets us shine. We kiss forever. Look at me, God, I'm living and must give again.

Author's Note

♥

T HE MAIN CHARACTER, GRACE is based on myself and most of the events are based on true experiences and others are imagined. The family members are real. I changed the names of the characters, except for public figures. The character of Diana, is an amalgamation of two real individuals. The therapist is a fictional character who is based on my graduate study in Counseling Psychology and my work as a certified coach. Father Brice is based on my mother's friend, a priest who did perform exorcisms, however, I never met him and the ritual in the park is purely fictional.

The names of locations are real. It was a pleasure to remember the sixties and the seventies growing up in South Philadelphia. Center City, Society Hill, and Olde City also have a place in my heart. Anyone who lived through the sixties and seventies in Philadelphia can appreciate the backdrop of familiar locations, and the distinctive culture, that is the City of Brotherly Love.

The lyrics of Ravel's "Pavane for a Dead Princess," the portion of the poem, "A Distant Alleluia" and the last passage—a poem that was originally titled "Sunroof," were written by me in my youth.

References to the Bible are not direct quotations with the exception of the Deuteronomy verse, quoted from the King James Bible which is in the public domain.

The original Saint Michael prayer was composed by Pope Leo XIII in 1884. There are shortened versions but for this novel, I felt it most appropriate to keep the long version.

Many of the characters in this novel are deceased. I have lived with their memory most of my life. By writing this story, I brought them closer to my heart and I hope to yours as well.

DiMonte Publishing will be publishing Christian themed works, both fiction and non-fiction. Receiving Grace is the first of the Christian themed novels.

For more information, contact: info@dimontepublishing.com